# CRIMSON

## Book 3, Exilon 5 Series

## About the Author

Eliza Green tried her hand at fashion designing, massage, painting, and even ghost hunting, before finding her love of writing. She often wonders if her desire to change the ending of a particular glittery vampire story steered her in that direction (it did). After earning her degree in marketing, Eliza went on to work in everything but marketing, but swears she uses it in everyday life, or so she tells her bank manager.

Born and raised in Dublin, Ireland, she lives there with her sci-fi loving, evil genius best friend. When not working on her next amazing science fiction adventure, you can find her reading, indulging in new food at an amazing restaurant or simply singing along to something with a half decent beat.

*Becoming Human, Altered Reality* and *Crimson Dawn* make up the Exilon 5 series so far. *Derailed Conscience* is her interesting foray into psychological thrillers with a sci-fi twist.

*Feeder*, brand new young adult sci-fi, coming soon November 2016. Preorder the e-book at www.elizagreenbooks.com

**www.elizagreenbooks.com**

# Crimson Dawn
## Eliza Green

Eliza Green

Copyright © 2014 Eliza Green

The moral right of the author has been asserted in accordance with the Copyright, Designs and Patents Act 1988.
All rights reserved. No part of this publication may be reproduced, stored in a retrieval system, or transmitted, in any form or by any means, without the prior written permission of the author, nor be otherwise circulated in any form of binding or cover other than that in which it is published and without a similar condition being imposed on the subsequent purchaser.
All characters in this publication are fictitious and any resemblance to real persons, living or dead, is purely coincidental.

ISBN-13: 978-1501015946

ISBN-10: 150101594X

Cover Designed by Andrew Brown
www.designforwriters.com

Content Editor: Averill Buchanan
Proofreader: Mary McCauley

Crimson Dawn

To JG and JH

Eliza Green

# 1

*October 2163, Exilon 5*

Stephen pushed open the metal hatch that covered one of the many tunnel entrances leading out to the stony wasteland beyond New London. The hatch was well camouflaged—dirty and covered with tiny rock fragments—to make it look like part of the landscape, and the entrance was hidden behind large rocks that were strewn around. The soundproofing ability of the omicron rock in the tunnel from which they had emerged gave them the advantage, preventing the military on the surface from hearing them arrive and from tracking them.

Crouching low behind a large rock, Stephen watched the military in the distance; not far away from him to his left was his intended target. The wolf had caught the scent of the meat Stephen had left as a lure behind a tall cluster of rocks, out of sight of the military, and was wandering away from the biodome towards it.

Stephen's foot accidentally scuffed some loose rubble. The wolf looked up sharply and Stephen could smell its fear. But it stayed where it was, clearly willing to take a chance and snatch the meat before it had to flee. Serena emerged from the tunnel and moved closer to Stephen's side, her eyes narrowing. He could hear her low growls as her hunting instincts kicked in.

He stood up and risked a look over the top of the rock to check the position of the military in the dark expanse. Ever since Anton had returned with the bomb that exploded underground in the Indigenes' tunnels, the military had increased their patrols in the area. With Stephen's advanced vision, he could see their silhouettes as they stood casually leaning against their vehicles; their aura colours confirmed their relaxed attitude.

'They don't know we're here,' he whispered to Serena. 'We have time.'

Serena looked at him, then at the military. 'Can you hear what they're thinking? I can't make out anything they're saying.'

Stephen's eyes snapped back to the wolf which was dangerously close to reaching the bait. It sniffed nervously at the edge of the rocks, its head flitting from left to right as it looked around on occasion. It was not fully grown. If it had been more mature, it would have retreated by now; the fully grown biodome animals were smart enough to recognise a trap when they smelled it.

The military suddenly caught Stephen's attention. 'We'll have to make this quick,' he said. 'They're thinking about making a move.'

'How do you know that?' Serena asked.

'I can hear them. They've spotted the wolf.'

Serena shook her head. 'All I hear from them is a collective rumbling. Nothing they say is clear to me. How is it that you have no problems?'

Stephen smiled at her, but deep down he was puzzled by her inability to hear as well as he did. All Indigenes had that ability, didn't they? He switched his attention back to the wolf again. They needed to capture it, for Pierre's sake.

The wolf was distracted now, tugging at the piece of meat that was staked firmly into the ground. Stephen suddenly bolted out from behind the rock, and before the wolf even had time to turn its head, he was standing in front of it, his eyes fixed on the blood that dripped from the animal's sharp incisors. Stephen's mouth watered. Its hackles raised, the wolf turned towards him. Behind Stephen, an out-of-breath Serena caught up with him. He could hear how erratic her thoughts were, as if her mind was being pulled in different directions.

'Are you okay?' he asked, his eyes not leaving the cagey wolf.

'I'm fine. Why do you ask?' She had adopted the stance that all Indigenes did when they hunted— one leg pitched in front of the other as if taking a huge stride, head straining forward, back low, arms poised to snatch.

The young wolf growled.

'Are you worried about something?' he asked her, adopting the same pose, crouching low until his fingertips almost touched the ground.

She shook her head and closed her eyes. He was just straightening up and about to speak again when he felt the displacement of air as the wolf lunged unexpectedly at Serena.

The force of the animal knocked her to the ground. Stephen heard a high-pitched scream. He watched the animal stand over her, pinning her in place, its sharp teeth clamped on the fleshy part of her shoulder and snarling through a mouthful of Indigene flesh.

'Come on, you're stronger than it,' Stephen urged Serena. 'You can take it.'

She screamed again. 'Get it off me!'

He waited a few seconds but could watch no longer. The muscles in his arms strained as he lifted the wolf up by the scruff and snapped its neck. Only then did its teeth unclamp from Serena's shoulder and she fell back to the ground. The glistening teeth marks on her shoulder instantly began to heal.

He dropped the limp animal's body as Serena scrambled to her feet. 'I can't believe that just happened,' she said, smiling now. She wiped the dirt from her dark hunting clothes.

'Come on. We have to go!' he said, throwing the dead wolf over his shoulder.

Serena looked around her anxiously. 'How far away are they?'

'Not far. They're getting into their vehicles.'

Stephen took off, running as fast as he could with Serena close on his heels.

'Can you make it with that thing on your shoulder?' she asked, panting.

'I think so. It's heavier than I thought,' Stephen said. His legs strained with the extra weight. 'Run up ahead and open the entrance. I'm not going to have time to stop.'

Serena raced towards the unremarkable cluster of rocks and the hidden entrance as if there had been a beacon flashing outside. She pulled open the metal hatch and stood back.

Stephen didn't slow down. When he was within range he threw the wolf neatly through the hatch, vaulted over the top of the largest rock and propelled himself feet first through the opening, landing face to face with the dead wolf's open eyes and snarling jaws. Serena jumped in behind him and pulled the hatch closed, securing it with metal bars on the inside.

'That was close,' she said, releasing a short, relieved puff of air.

'What was that back there?' Stephen asked.

Serena frowned. 'I don't know what you mean.'

'The scream. It came from you.'

'No, it didn't.'

'When the wolf lunged at you, you screamed.'

'I must have been surprised,' she said nonchalantly.

They arrived at the entrance to their district, a stone door constructed from the impervious omega rock. Genetic scanners located high above the door verified them as Indigenes and the door slid back into the rock face.

'You have everything under control here?' Serena asked once the door had closed behind them and she had removed her air filtration device.

Stephen nodded, doing the same.

'Then I'll talk to you later.'

He watched her move along the tunnel with poise and grace, then vanish from sight at the first bend. He hauled the dead animal through the cold, low-lit tunnel ahead of him. With the wolf perched on his shoulder and so tantalisingly close, he could smell its blood. He licked his lips. But it wouldn't stay fresh for long. He needed to find Gabriel, the visiting elder from District Eight, and he needed to find him fast, before he tore the animal apart and ate it himself.

He could sense Gabriel in one of the tunnels leading towards the core of District Three and found him in a section that ran straight for almost half a mile. Gabriel's wife, Margaux, was close by and was clearly distracted, although Stephen had noticed that she seemed to look like that all the time, unable to stand still, her eyes wild. Gabriel was arguing with some hot-headed Indigene who was asking about Pierre. A short distance away, three other Indigenes were waiting for their friend to finish his rant.

'He's not well,' Gabriel explained. 'He needs time to come to terms with Elise's death. Have some patience.'

'You're not the elder here, and your wife needs to keep her nose out of my thoughts,' the hot-head said, pressing two fingers against his temple. 'She burrows in like a small, dark creature. I can feel her poking around inside my head. It gives me the creeps.'

Stephen noticed Margaux studying the Indigene intently, and the three others who were waiting suddenly shook their heads as if they were trying to dislodge something. The beginnings of a smile tugged at Margaux's lips forcing Gabriel to instinctively place a hand on her arm.

She dropped her intense gaze. 'Fine,' she said.

'You know full well I was invited here,' Gabriel continued. 'Until Pierre is well enough to govern this district again, you'll have to speak to him through me. Is that clear?'

'You may have been invited but you're not welcome here.' The hot-head closed the conversation by turning and walking away. The three waiting Indigenes fell into line behind him.

Gabriel rubbed his eyes with his thumb and forefinger. He had been dealing with similar confrontations since his arrival. Only three weeks had passed since Elise, Pierre's wife, had been killed by the bomb that Anton brought with him. Following the ceremony to mark her death, Pierre had sought refuge in the soundproofed Council Chambers and had refused to come out. The energy in the district was raw and confused; there was a great deal of whispered uncertainty about what had happened and what was to come.

Several other districts had been asked to help bring order to District Three. But when they found out about their human past and Anton's return to Exilon 5 with a bomb, not to mention Elise's death, they were reluctant. Alain and Beatrice from District One, Emile and Marie from District Seven, and Gabriel and Margaux from District Eight all volunteered, but in the end only Gabriel and Margaux showed up. Gabriel was apologetic when he arrived with a message from the other districts: they had voted against helping; they couldn't forgive District Three for putting them all in danger. Democracy in District Three was under threat and Gabriel was stuck in the middle of it, getting grief mostly from the younger males. Somehow, he needed to work out how to unite the district, which was falling apart without Pierre.

Stephen placed the wolf gently on the ground in front of the elder.

'I see you managed to get one?' Gabriel said.

'Wasn't easy. The military are watching.'

Gabriel folded his broad arms. He was three inches taller than Stephen and of a sturdier build. At the age of one hundred and seven, Gabriel was thirteen years younger than Pierre, and it was hoped that his more youthful energy and stamina would help calm the unrest in the district until Pierre felt able to resume his duties as elder.

Margaux clucked her tongue. 'Pierre doesn't need that,' she said looking at the dead wolf. 'He needs something else.'

'What does she mean?' Stephen frowned.

Gabriel half smiled. 'Don't pay what she says too much attention. I love my wife, but she can be a little eccentric. The Indigenes here are wary of her and the Evolvers stay away completely. They're well used to her in our district, but here, they haven't taken to her at all.'

Stephen gestured to the dead animal. 'Can you bring some to Pierre?'

Gabriel hoisted the animal onto his shoulder and winked at him. 'I'll pick the choicest cuts. And if he doesn't eat it, I'll ram it down his scrawny throat. That'll teach him to leave me with all this shit to deal with.'

Stephen smiled. He confessed to liking Gabriel's lively way with words; he found it refreshing and it comforted him somehow. He had always thought Gabriel was less like the other Indigenes. He hadn't understood it at the time, but now it was all too clear: Gabriel sounded exactly like the humans.

'Just one other thing,' Stephen said.

Gabriel turned around.

Stephen could feel Margaux trying to probe his thoughts, just like Elise used to do. 'It's about Serena,' he said.

'The female from District Eight?'

Stephen nodded. 'I need you to meet her.'

Gabriel half smiled. 'I've tried but she is always doing something. Maybe when things are a little calmer around here.'

Stephen touched him on the arm. 'No, you need to meet her soon.'

Gabriel frowned. 'What's the rush?'

'I don't think Serena is who she says she is.'

# 2

Stephen arrived in the cavernous core of District Three, the same place to which Anton had returned just a few weeks before. At the heart of the district, the core was where all the tunnels converged. It was a large open space carved out of the rock with vaulted ceilings that supported the weight of the earth above it. Over time, modifications had been necessary as new human buildings built on the surface came close to collapsing in on the large open spaces and tunnels of the district below. They had been forced to create the strong metal alloy baronium when the steel struts holding up the vaulted ceilings and tunnels were no longer able bear the weight of the city resting above it.

A low light filtered through tiny vertical conduits in the ceiling, where solar power was collected from the surface and directed to storage units in one of the laboratories. The air was cool and dry. Indigenes were gathered in loose groups, their ghostly shadows cast on the walls and ceiling of the core as they discussed the main thing on everyone's mind. The district, the very existence of the Indigene race, was in a state of crisis. Pierre, their elder, had abandoned them when they needed him most, and although Gabriel was doing his best to restore order, the Indigenes had lost faith in the leadership, undermining the democratic system they had built their lives upon.

Walking through the core felt strange to Stephen. Everything looked normal, but the atmosphere was unusual, almost hostile. There were subtle signs that made his skin prickle—the defensive stances of some Indigenes, or the unsmiling glances as he passed. One wall had several deep alcoves carved out of it. The alcoves were sometimes used as overflow areas when the teaching bays were full. Today, the alcoves were empty, except for one.

Stephen felt a vision strain to materialise inside his head. It stopped him cold. It was as if someone were sticking a hot poker in his brain and moving it around. This was becoming a regular thing, and he'd hoped with time that he might have learned how to manage the visions, but they were always just out of reach. He stuck his hand to the side of his head until the sharp pain eventually passed. He walked on to the alcove where Serena was. She was studying some drawings on the wall.

'I still can't get over this,' she said without turning around. 'How did I know how to explain your visions to you?' She sounded genuinely confused as she gestured to the drawings she'd scrawled for him over two weeks ago.

For the past few weeks, they had been working together on a strategy to deal with Stephen's new ability—to predict the future through visions. Through her drawings, Serena showed Stephen how his visions worked so he could gain control of them.

She was staring up at the image of a swirling black ball that she had drawn with charcoal. It represented the vision moving towards him, she had explained. Sweeps of yellow limonite burst out from the black ball, representing his mind opening up to the mass and breaking it apart to reveal the vision. She had drawn a second ball of black, more dense than the first, to show Stephen how the vision looked when he tried to fight it. Then she had made the ball bigger, illustrating how it would grow in size and eventually push against his skull, causing him pain.

As Stephen stood beside Serena, he had to try hard not to keep glancing in her direction. He was fascinated by her and magnetically drawn to her, yet he didn't know who she was or where she really came from. Something wasn't quite right. She had arrived in District Three only a few weeks before, around the same time that Anton had returned. She said she was from District Eight, but she seemed different from the other Indigenes. For one, she hadn't yet mastered the art of telepathy. Nor was she aware of his intrusions into her mind, and made no effort to block her private thoughts. If she was an Indigene, Serena seemed to be really bad at it.

The last time he had tuned into her mind was two days ago. He had seen several strange images, images that looked as though they belonged to someone else. He had seen an apartment like Laura O'Halloran's, which he'd been in not that long ago. There was a picture of a woman and a small child on the mantelpiece. In a separate image, a woman was examining her reflection in a shiny lab instrument—he could clearly see the lab in the background—but the female was not Serena: she was a human with blonde hair and blue eyes. Yet there was something oddly familiar about her that reminded him of Serena. Had Serena been some kind of scientist in District Eight? None of it made sense to him. This was why he needed Gabriel to meet her, now. Maybe he could shed some light on it all.

As they stood there side by side in front of her drawings, his head suddenly tingled as she tried to probe his mind. But her efforts were as effective as those of an Evolver; it was easy to hide his thoughts from her.

'What's wrong?' she asked.

'What do you mean?'

'I mean you've been acting strangely for the last couple of days.' She turned round and looked at him, making his stomach flip pleasantly. 'Tell me what's on your mind,' she said calmly.

Stephen felt an almost overwhelming desire to tell her about the images he saw in her head. It took every ounce of strength to say something else. 'It's just my visions,' he blurted out. 'I still can't control them. The pain I feel before they vanish is as bad as ever.'

He knew he had feelings for Serena and that his attraction was more than chemistry. It was as if she was controlling his actions, not unlike the way his visions were controlling his mind. Only this time, it was his heart that ached, not his head. It was a pleasurable ache—an exciting one, even—that coursed through his entire body and made him feel as if anything was possible.

Serena gave him a quick smile, then a vacant look replaced the intensity in her eyes of a few moments before. She left the alcove and walked gracefully through the core towards one of the tunnel exits. Stephen followed her, noticing the attention the other males paid her. He had to repress the desire to punch them as he caught glimpses of what they were thinking when she passed by.

She reached the tunnel leading to the Southern Quadrant and Stephen quickened his pace to keep up with her. Her bare feet barely touched the rough and tilted floor of the tunnel. Her slim, graceful body glided along effortlessly as if she hadn't a care in the world. But she did. He could feel it. He could see it in her face. Where had she come from, he wondered for the umpteenth time. He had wanted to ask her for a few weeks now, but was afraid that she would disappear as quickly as she had appeared.

His pace had slowed enough for her to notice. She waited for him and linked his arm.

'Are you coming or not?' She gently pulled him along.

'Where are we going?'

'Wait and see,' she teased.

But as soon as they moved on, she unlinked her arm and began walking a little faster again. He made an effort to catch up with her and allowed his arm to dangle close to hers until their hands grazed. She didn't pull away when he interlocked his fingers with hers, then squeezed his hand in response.

'Where did you come from?' he suddenly asked her, despite his best intentions not to. A shot of adrenaline coursed through his body as he anticipated the worst responses he could dream up in his head.

'From District Eight,' she replied frowning. 'You know that.'

Yes, she had told him. He tried to smile but it felt forced. 'Okay, so why are you here with me?'

'What do you mean?'

'I mean, there are a hundred males queuing up to speak to you, but you choose to spend your time with me.'

Serena laughed gently. 'I feel at ease with you. I don't feel the same with the other males. I can sense what they want from me and it scares me.'

'What makes you so sure I don't want the same thing?'

Serena smiled, but it was tinged with sadness. 'I'm not. To tell you the truth, I'm feeling confused. There are things I seem to know and things I don't know. Honestly, I'm struggling to figure out what's real.'

'What are you confused about?' Stephen thought about the images he'd seen in her head.

'You aren't complicated, and I like that. It's what I need right now,' was all she said.

Still holding his hand, she stared at him and a sudden feeling came over him. He felt an overwhelming pressure to drop the subject. So he did. 'When do you think I'll gain control of this?' he said, tapping the side of his head.

'Soon. You shouldn't try rushing it.'

They walked on together and it wasn't long before the omicron rock that formed the tunnel walls began to vibrate. Stephen clutched the other side of his head with his free hand.

'This might or might not work,' Serena said quietly.

Stephen grimaced from the discomfort of the vibration affecting his head. 'What are you talking about?'

She didn't answer him as they walked a little further along the tunnel that led them into the small open area where the Southern Quadrant tranquillity cave was located. She turned to him. 'I get a feeling about this place, as if everything I think and feel is enhanced.'

Stephen nodded. 'The gamma rock here has amplifying properties. It's why they built the caves out of it. It's where the Nexus is most effective.'

Serena grabbed both his hands. 'The pain in your head is just your envisioning ability becoming stronger. The gamma rock may help you to latch on to your visions—let them through. You already know that the more you fight them, the more they hurt you.'

'Makes sense when you say it, but in practice ...' he said, squeezing his eyes shut as the ache sharpened and jabbed inside his head.

He hadn't had many full-blown visions recently, only partials that he had managed to deflect on his own. But the vision that was trying to get through now was stronger than the rest and he was unable to ignore it. He could feel it growing into the tight black ball that Serena had depicted. He closed his eyes and concentrated on the vision that tried to seep through. The hard black casing surrounding it started to break apart, little by little, sending ripples through his skull and brain. The sharp pain forced him to keep his eyes closed a little while longer. When he finally opened them, the vision began to manifest on its own, without any effort from him.

In the vision, the Indigenes' faces were blurry but the scene was clear. They were hunting at night, circling their prey while the military watched from a distance. This was nothing new, but he tried to figure out if it was an event that had happened or was about to happen. As he concentrated on the scene, some other force tried to break the connection. He became agitated. Serena tightened her grip on his hand but the force was too strong for him and the vision disappeared.

'Why can't I control it yet?' he growled. He was breathing heavily.

'The ability's still too new,' Serena said. 'Your brain is only learning how to handle it. We'll work on some techniques that may help trick your brain into not fighting it.'

'If this is a part of me, I should have figured it out by now.'

'Give it time. You're still trying to rush it.' She released his hands. 'What did you learn?'

'Nothing we don't already know—that the military are watching us above ground.'

Serena cupped his face in her hands; they were cool and soft. 'Concentrate. Tell me how far you can see into the future,' she said.

Up close like that, Stephen was able to study her eyes flecked with the yellow pigmentation that all Indigenes had. But hers were different to his yellow flecks on a grey iris. They were predominately blue and they were beautiful. 'What did you say you did for work in your district?' he asked, his body quivering due to her closeness.

Serena's gaze lingered on him for a moment. 'Have you tried using the Nexus to stabilise your envisioning ability?'

Stephen frowned at the idea. He had been reluctant to use it since the last time, just before the ability had emerged. The Nexus had caused him agonising pain then. 'I don't think I can go back there, Serena, not since ... you know.'

She smiled gently. 'Well, you didn't have me then. Besides, I've never seen the Nexus in action before. I'm curious to see how it works for you.'

Stephen stared at her. 'Did you not use it in District Eight?'

She shook her head slowly. 'I heard about it from others here, about how it works, but I can't recall ever having used it.'

He watched the colours of her aura closely;

they were mostly greens and blues. He didn't want to consider Serena a threat like Anton had been—at least not unless he had some concrete evidence. 'Okay, I'll try it on one condition,' he said.

'What?'

'That you connect in too.'

Serena put her hands up defensively. 'No, no! I wouldn't know what to do.'

'That's not a problem. I'll show you.'

Reluctantly, Serena followed him inside the tranquillity cave. Carved into the rock floor were several individual units wide enough to hold several Indigenes and about ten feet deep, where the gamma rock's power was at its most concentrated. That day the Southern Quadrant tranquillity cave was quiet so it was easy for them to find a couple of free units beside each other.

Stephen pointed inside Serena's unit. 'You can use the stone steps to get in and out, or you can jump straight in.'

Serena eyes widened at the sight of the ten-foot drop. She looked at him. 'How do you do it?'

He smiled at her and dropped straight into his unit, landing skilfully on all fours. He turned and looked up at Serena who was peering anxiously over the edge.

'See? It's easy,' he said. 'Try it.'

Serena disappeared from view and he listened carefully. He could hear the sound of her feet tapping on the stone steps.

A few seconds later she called out, 'What now?'

'Just close your eyes and relax. The Nexus will find you.'

Stephen sat cross-legged on the rough stone

floor and closed his eyes. He inhaled quickly and released his breath, nervous about using the Nexus again, but after a few deep breaths he relaxed. He wasn't sure how using it might help, but the pain and frustration of not being able to manage the visions were enough of an incentive. In his mind, the wall opposite him lost its hard rock-like appearance and transformed into a shimmering golden and orange web. He saw the bright white tendrils of the Nexus reach out for him through the web. A single tendril wrapped itself around his arm a little too tightly and he resisted it. In response, the tendril's caress became gentler, encouraging his mind to open up and give in to the peace that it offered. It pulled his energy through the gold and orange web and inside the giant Nexus that was powered by the collective energy of all the Indigenes connected to it.

Stephen's energy was immediately drawn to the core of the Nexus—a large shimmering wall of energy with a luminescent ledge running along its base. He looked around him and could see the intricate webs belonging to the other units, bright luminous balls of energy showing the points where other Indigenes were being pulled in. On busier days, it resembled the night sky above Exilon 5, filled with thousands of tiny stars.

Stephen identified his own unit, which appeared brighter than the rest, and counted one space across to Serena's. He could see that she had yet to connect, but he could make out the colours of her aura; the greens and blues of earlier had changed to yellows and reds. Rapid movement in her unit caught his eye and he moved towards her for a closer look. The Nexus's tendrils were snapping at her like a dog and she was flailing her arms around to keep them away from her.

'What do I do?' she called out. Her voice sounded ethereal to him, coming from the other side of the web.

'It doesn't hurt. Just give in to it,' he said. He drifted closer, her web in front of him and the Nexus behind. He looked down briefly at the black chasm in between. 'Close your eyes,' he instructed. 'Breathe deeply. You need to be calm before entering.'

Serena did as she was told and Stephen saw her take a few deep breaths. She was frowning hard. He moved in closer still, but hesitated when he heard the snapping sounds. The tendril appeared to be whipping her arm.

'I thought you said it doesn't hurt,' she said, wincing.

It shouldn't. Stephen watched curiously as the slim tendril, no thicker than a rope, continued to attack her.

'What should I do?' Serena was trying to sound calm but he could hear the alarm in her voice.

'I ... I don't know. I've never seen it behave like this before.'

She pulled her arm back but the tendril only reached for her further. She was backed up against the far wall of the unit; there was nowhere for her to go. Suddenly, her expression changed and with it, the red of her aura turned a darker shade.

'Enough of this!' she yelled and reached out to grab the attacking tendril.

It wrapped tightly around her arm and instantly yanked her energy inside. Stephen watched as the tendril hurled her across the black chasm towards the giant wall of the Nexus. She hit it with force, then slid down and came to rest on the luminescent shelf jutting out just below it. Stephen came towards her.

In Serena's presence, the gentle ripples that the Nexus usually generated when energies connected in or out became small waves. Stephen felt her strong energy being fed back to him on a loop. His energy brightened for a second, then dulled when the other users detected the change and tried to restore order and calm. Identifying Serena as the cause of the change, tiny balls of their energy floated towards her. The Nexus quickly pulsated again and new tendrils emerged from its shimmering magnificence to form a web around her, preventing the other energies from reaching her. Trapped inside the Nexus's prison, Serena's energy shone brighter than the rest. When the other energies retreated back far enough, the tendrils loosened their hold on her.

Stephen was stunned by what he was witnessing. The Nexus was behaving as if it didn't want to share her.

'Are you sure you've never used the Nexus before?' he asked.

'Never, I swear.'

'Maybe that's the problem—it doesn't know how to react to you.'

'If I'm the same as everyone else surely it would?'

Stephen didn't know what to say to that. Just then he noticed a new energy building inside the Nexus.

'This doesn't feel right,' he said. 'I think we need to disconnect.'

'Well, I totally agree, but I can't seem to move.'

His eyes honed in on her energy and spotted the tiny web-like strands that had emerged from the

Nexus and were winding tightly around her. The longer she stayed on the luminescent ledge, the stronger the web became. He drifted closer but the tendrils mirrored his every move so he could never quite reach her. Panicking, Stephen headed back to his own unit and pulled himself free of the Nexus. Back in his own body again, he climbed out of the unit as quickly as he could and jumped into Serena's.

Her eyes were still closed; her face was paler than usual. He could see that this was not a peaceful, calming experience for her. Instead of the Nexus restoring her energy, it was draining it away.

He put his hand on her shoulder and watched her reactions closely. 'Serena! Listen to me. You need to break free from it. Follow my voice. Come on. I can't help you in there. You're going to have to break free yourself.'

Stephen resorted to shaking her, even though it was not permitted—it was considered dangerous to abruptly disconnect the mind from the Nexus. But he had to do something. He regretted having encouraged her to connect without proper guidance. He had assumed their experiences would be the same. How was he going to explain this to Pierre? The last thing anyone needed in the district was another death. No, he had to think positively. Serena was going to make it. He slapped her face.

'Come on!' he yelled.

Serena's eyes shot open and she drew in a long breath as if she was reabsorbing the energy the Nexus had stolen from her. Stephen wrapped his arms around her, unwilling to let the Nexus take her again. She was barely conscious.

With great difficulty, he slung her over his shoulder and groped around with his feet to find the stone steps in the wall of the unit. She was heavier than she looked and his legs strained with each step up. Once he was eye-level with the floor above, he carefully shifted Serena's body off his shoulder and rolled her onto the floor.

Stephen tried to follow her, but his foot slipped and with it he lost his grip. Air rushed past his face as he fell back into the unit. When his head hit the unyielding rock, everything went black.

# 3

*Earth*

In the heart of Washington D.C., Charles Deighton opened the door of his town car and got out, much to the annoyance of his driver.

'Sir, I've been instructed to take you all the way to the club,' he said, holding a gel mask to his face as the noxious air seeped into the vehicle. 'You shouldn't be walking about here on your own. It's not safe.'

Deighton made a rude noise and leaned in through the open door. 'Young man, I realise you're new but if I want to walk, I will walk. The CEO of the World Government can do whatever he likes.'

'But, Sir, I was told to drive you right to the door.'

Deighton cackled. 'My dear boy, if it makes you feel better to send a couple of the security team to follow me, then go ahead. Either way, I need to stretch my legs.'

He straightened up, closed the car door and checked the seal on his mask. A second car pulled up behind the town car and two abnormally large bodyguards carrying buzz guns got out. They kept a discreet distance and tried to be as inconspicuous as genetically altered giants in full riot gear could. Deighton shrugged; he could tolerate their presence if they stayed well out of his way. His desire to walk the dilapidated streets of 23rd Street NW was strong. He wanted the street people to see him, to be within touching distance if they dared. But mostly he wanted to walk off the tremors in his legs that got worse when he sat down for any length of time.

He looked up at the skyscrapers that enclosed the city centre, a sharp contrast to the city of old with its low-level buildings spread leisurely over a large area. As space had become limited, buildings expanded down into the ground and up into the sky, not only in Washington, but in other cities, like Dublin and Paris, too. He walked by countless boarded-up stores. Washington, the hub of industry in late twenty-first-century America, the city where the government had launched the Go Green programme, now reminded him of Victorian London. It was full of ragged-dressed boys working for the criminals that the World Government couldn't control. The only difference between Victorian London and current day Washington was that the London street urchins had been better entrepreneurs and had a better pick of rich, gullible businessmen to steal from. The boys made Deighton think of Anton and Dr Caroline Finnegan—they had also been willing to do whatever it took to stay alive.

He also thought about the board members, who all came from old money, and Peter Cantwell, one of the original board members and former Chair—his mentor and the man who'd appointed him CEO back in the day. It was the original board that had had the vision to change people into better versions of themselves. On Exilon 5, where some of the Earth's population would soon live, they planned to make room for important people, but not for those living on the streets. It was a point Deighton had been keen to make at the board meetings—that only the select few should travel to Exilon 5—but the board members were driven by their own agendas.

Deighton tried to sidestep the mounds of trash that had spilled over onto the sidewalk; it wasn't easy, especially with his unsteady legs. The stench on the streets was overpowering, even through his gel mask. Across the road was a termination clinic, formerly the George Washington University Hospital. Bags labelled with large red stickers warned him of the human waste they contained, but his failing ocular implants put paid to any reasonable attempt to identify colours. He made a mental note never to walk near that clinic again.

Trying to walk with confidence, Deighton found it hard to ignore the tremors that had spread from his hands to his arms and legs. He had felt good during the week so he hadn't bothered to get his muscle-stabilising shots at one of the private genetic manipulation clinics. He had convinced himself that the problem had gone away on its own. But as he walked on, he could feel a new twitch beginning in his arms and in one leg. The realisation that all was not right brought tears to his eyes. He wiped them away before anyone had a chance to see. He was determined to fight for the right to live in a new, genetically clean body if it was the last thing he did. He refused to end up like the street vermin he despised.

But he had no time to dwell on these things while walking. There were too many hazards to negotiate—he didn't want to fall over and break his hip yet again. The uneven paving demanded his attention, not to mention the carefully positioned street beggars, their backs up against store windows, their feet stuck out in an attempt to trip him up, or at the very least slow him down. Disgusted by the sight of so many of them, he lifted his legs high with each step, making sure his expensive, polished shoes never touched their diseased bodies. A little further on, he noticed a teenage boy who seemed dirtier than the others; he was clutching a begging bowl. The boy stared at him doe-eyed. Deighton ignored the theatrics and focused instead on the hidden excitement in the youngster's eyes.

'Do I look like a fucking chump to you?' Deighton muttered as he approached him.

In an instant, the boy sat up and knelt, holding the bowl out so that Deighton couldn't miss it. Deighton examined the dirty street urchin. If he scrubbed the boy from head to toe with a brush and carbolic soap, what would he see? His thoughts slowed him down.

The boy jumped to his feet and held his bowl out further. 'Please, sir, I'm hungry. You got any food on you, mister?' he mumbled pathetically through his gel mask.

A bit too fast on your feet for someone so hungry, Deighton thought. The entire scene made him think of novels set in Victorian London that he had read as a boy. He pulled his coat tightly around him and ran a finger along one edge of his gel mask where it clung to his face, checking the seal.

'Get a job, you degenerate runt,' he hissed. He hadn't planned to talk to any of them; he just wanted to flaunt his wealth and status.

But the boy stepped brazenly out in front of Deighton, stopping him in his tracks.

'Come on, mister. Been out 'ere all day. Got

nothin' to eat. Come on. Help me out. You got credit instead of cash? I'll take either, or both if you're willin'. I ain't fussed.'

The cheap cockney accent that the boy had suddenly acquired was a nice touch. He must have picked up on Deighton's English accent. *Paying attention. That's a good quality. If you weren't a genetic reject, I might pick you for the alteration programme.*

The boy persisted. 'There's nothin' for me. I tried everythin'. Even tried gettin' on the transfer programme, but they turned me 'way. Please mister, help out a friend.'

It didn't surprise Deighton that the boy had been rejected for transfer to Exilon 5. They were looking for the perfect genetic match and he could tell by looking at him that he was not suitable—there were irregularities in his features and his posture. The abnormalities were all fixable, but without money and the right contacts the boy didn't stand a chance. Even then, the track marks on his arm would have ruled him out instantly.

Deighton's mood turned more hostile as he suddenly became incensed by the boy's presence. 'I know your kind,' he sneered. 'Turning tricks for the men down the back alleys, pretending to enjoy it when all you're after is your next fix. You disgust me.'

'Is that what you're after, mister? I can do whatever you want.' The cockney accent melted away. The boy's eyes were pleading and desperate.

Deighton shook his head and thrust his hand in his coat pocket. The boy watched his hand to see what it might produce.

'Boy, I'm flattered. But I'm too old for you and

well out of your league,' Deighton said. He pulled out a card. 'I always carry these around for people like you. The world doesn't need your kind. But I'm not totally without a heart. I can see you need a little encouragement.'

The boy smiled eagerly and groped for the card.

Deighton held on to it for a moment longer and looked in the boy's eyes. 'Get going now, you don't want to be late. I hear they're doing a midnight special.'

The boy snatched the card and turned it over. It was a coupon for a half price deal at one of the termination clinics.

'Get off the streets, you little shit,' Deighton said through clenched teeth. 'And if I catch you out here whoring yourself to decent folk again, I'll have you arrested.'

He stepped around the boy and continued his walk towards 22nd Street NW and his ultimate destination—Les Fontaines, a private club and restaurant. Deighton smiled for a moment—the nonsense with the boy had made him forget about his tremors.

'Son of a bitch. Think you're better than me?' the boy yelled after him. 'I'll fucking show ya who you're dealing with, you crusty old shit. Come back here and fight me like a man. Fucking coward.'

Deighton's shoulders shook with laughter as he rounded the corner on I Street NW. He loved how he could always find that little trigger inside people that forced them to reveal their true colours. He stood at the corner and looked back at the boy. The boy dropped his bowl and began to follow him, anger dripping off his brow like sweat. Deighton shivered with excitement. *Here it comes.*

'Who the fuck do ya think you are?' The boy spat the words in his gel mask. Another beggar sitting nearby stood up nervously.

Deighton frowned. 'What happened to your cockney accent, dear boy? Have you no need for it anymore?' Deighton's bodyguards moved closer, but he held his hands up to tell them to stay back. He was grinning.

Just as the boy lunged towards Deighton, the beggar nearby grabbed the boy's arms and pulled him away, whispering something in his ear. Deighton took a few steps backwards.

'I don't care who he is,' the boy shouted. 'He can't get away with speaking to honest people like that.' The words were loud, but the conviction had disappeared.

'That's right, listen to your friends if you know what's good for you,' Deighton muttered quietly, his creaking laugh breaking up the words.

He nodded to the beefed-up bodyguards, who could have broken the boy's neck just by looking at him. But the weapons were out and soon, the distinctive crackle of electricity was in the air. The last thing Deighton saw as he disappeared round the corner was the boy slump to the ground like a rag doll.

But his laughter at his little encounter quickly turned to tears again as he recalled his own situation. His condition—the condition he'd managed to hide for so long—was worsening and his future was far from certain. He had worked hard to keep his medical secret under wraps and to find a solution to his problem. He hoped that he had finally found the answer in Serena.

Deighton arrived at Les Fontaines. Out of the three private clubs in the city, this was his favourite. He had life membership, whatever that meant on Earth. He walked down three steps and stopped in front of a rusted metal door with a small rectangular sliding panel in the middle. He knocked on the door: a single rap, followed by three quick successive raps. As he waited, he realised the tears had not stopped. His left hand was shaking badly, so he grabbed it and dug his fingernails into the flesh until he whimpered with pain. When he let go, he was out of breath and crying, but his hand no longer shook. When he heard a noise on the other side of the door he quickly wiped away the tears and composed himself. The panel slid to the right and a pair of bloodshot eyes appeared. The thick metal door clanged and creaked as it opened.

The bloodshot eyes belonged to a large muscular man wearing a gel mask. The doorman scanned Deighton's identity chip and unclipped the red velvet rope to let him and his bodyguards through. He called the turbo lift in the small foyer and gestured for them to enter it. The doorman had a faded tattoo on his right hand, which Deighton recognised as a tribal mark, probably inked when he was a boy. Several tribes still existed in small pockets, but they were in danger of being left behind as society moved on. Deighton wondered if, in the future, when they improved the design of human beings, there would be similar tendencies to form tribes, or would the new humans be smart enough to transcend such trivial matters.

The turbo lift opened on the seventy-seventh floor: the penthouse. He stepped into the bright restaurant and self-consciously pulled his jacket sleeve down to hide the nail indentations in his hand. His bodyguards sat down at a table close to the door.

Les Fontaines was a quirky French restaurant offering the best views of Paris. Attractive views of Washington were hard to come by, even at that height, so the owners installed high-definition visualisation screens that transformed the view into something much more pleasant. Depending on where you sat in the restaurant, you could see the Champs-Élysées, the Eiffel Tower, Notre Dame, and various other well-known places in Paris.

A waiter greeted Deighton and showed him to his usual table. The waiter handed him a gold DPad with the menu on it. The tables were made of tempered glass and the chairs covered in deep purple velvet. The floors were marbled and the waiters real. A bust of Oscar Wilde—the controversial Irish writer who spent many years living and working in Paris—was near one of the windows. A painting by Vincent Van Gogh hung on one wall. The works of dead artists, once worth a small fortune, meant little to people fighting for survival, but they still held value for the rich.

As he sat there thinking about Serena, Deighton wondered what Peter Cantwell would have thought of his most successful creation. Cantwell had once told him that he saw himself as a visionary who could protect the human race from all-out extinction and he wanted to pass that legacy on. Deighton wondered if the old man would have been proud of him now.

A waiter hovered close to his table. Deighton clicked his fingers. 'Where's François tonight?'

'Um, he's in the back. Do you want to speak to him?' The waiter sounded nervous.

Deighton hesitated for a moment. He wasn't

really in the mood for company. 'No.'

'Can I get you something to drink? Water?'

Deighton knew the wine stock off by heart. 'Get me a glass of Merlot 2122, from François's personal stock.' The wine, a little pricier than the rest, was worth it.

'And to eat?' The waited shifted from one foot to the other.

'I need more time.' Deighton sank back into the softness of the chair.

Things were going well with Serena. She had turned out to be a better version of an Indigene than he could have hoped. He knew the board members would be annoyed about his decision to send her to Exilon 5 without testing her genetic code extensively. But he already had what he needed: a sample of her DNA. Serena and Anton were to serve other purposes now: to cause mayhem among the Indigenes. He also planned to push a new alteration programme in which only the best of Earth's remaining population would be selected for change and transfer to the new planet. But before he could sell his plan to the board members, there were the Indigenes to deal with. In his mind, there was room for only one species on Exilon 5—the one that was created in Serena's image.

Deighton looked around the room. He recognised a few faces—high-level personnel from World Government, heads of security—all people he had supervised at one time or another. Now he had people to do the supervising for him.

The waiter came back with the glass of Merlot and shakily placed it on the table. A tiny drop spilled on the tabletop.

'Watch what you're doing!' Deighton roared at him. 'I'm not paying to lick the wine off the table. I'll expect to see a discount on my bill.'

The waiter flushed crimson.

'Get me some water, then you can take my order.'

The waiter hurried away.

Deighton's left hand began to shake again, so he set the DPad on the table and sat on his hand to keep it still. He studied the menu but couldn't see the words; his mind had drifted off elsewhere—to Anton and what had happened at the Galway Medical Facility. The medical team had wiped Anton's memories of his time on Earth, then implanted a tracer and recording device in his head. Deighton wanted evidence to prove to the World Government board members that the Indigenes were dangerous and should be eliminated. The device in Anton's head was monitoring his activities and would have been active when Anton brought the bomb to Exilon 5. That ought to be proof enough. But first he had to successfully download the feed.

After Dr Finnegan's unfortunate death, there had only been time to implant a tracer and recording device in one head—Anton's or Serena's—before the facilities were placed on lockdown. Deighton had chosen Anton because he was ultimately dispensable—Serena was to serve another purpose—and with Daphne Gilchrist's help, the pair had been safely transported to Exilon 5 so they could begin their carnage.

But Deighton had been unable to get a live feed from the tracking device in Anton's head. It was probably because the rock in which the Indigenes lived had soundproofing properties and masked all signals to and from it. Anton would have to leave the protection of the Indigene underground tunnels for them to access it, and Deighton wished it could be soon. He was eager to know if Anton had triggered the bomb and what the results had been. Were they busy destroying each other? How had they reacted to Anton's personality transplant?

Having to rely on the reports from the ground troops on Exilon 5 was utterly frustrating for him. They had confirmed sightings of Serena out hunting at night. She had been with other Indigenes and had clearly been accepted into their fold; she had seemed at ease as an Indigene. It excited him to hear that his protégé, the one he had falsely accused of killing Dr Finnegan, had been welcomed with open arms.

It gave him what he needed to deal with the pro-Earth board members who had invested heavily in Earth and were reluctant to move to Exilon 5 where the Indigenes threatened any business potential. He would be able to tell them how easily the Indigenes had accepted Serena—a murderer—into their community. He would tell them that full-scale Indigene retaliation was only a matter of time and that the time to take control of Exilon 5—in new bodies and with a new plan—was now. He would insist that the Indigenes should be eliminated. Then they could start over—a new race without the flaws of the old one. Without the threat of retaliation, new investments could be made with the potential for massive financial gains.

A different waiter returned with a glass of water and put it down. He didn't seem so nervous. 'Can I take your order, sir?'

Deighton looked again at the menu listing. He used a finger of his free hand to run down the length of the DPad screen, stopping on several selections. He pinched images with his fingers, pulling it out of the screen to take a closer look. He thought about asking François for a more personal rundown of the specials, but he didn't feel like company and the last thing he needed was François seeing his tremors—news travelled fast among the elite.

The options on the menu were limited, but quite rare: Vietnamese dog, genetically modified bluefin tuna, or veal, the latter sourced from one of the few meat farms still in existence. Most meat was grown in labs, but Deighton, like so many others, despised its bland flavour. Meat farms were rare and the price high—both financially and ethically. The World Government had commissioned a handful of farms to continue their trade so long as they exclusively supplied a small number of restaurants in the downtown Washington and Sydney areas, where the World Government and Earth Security Centre offices were located.

'Get me the veal,' Deighton said to the waiter who was standing calmly beside the table with his hands behind his back. The waiter nodded, took the DPad and walked away.

Deighton sat back in his seat and pulled his left hand out from under him. It was numb but the tremors had stopped—for now. He was desperate for two things—to get off Earth and to find a cure for his deteriorating medical condition. If anyone were to discover how poor his health actually was, he wouldn't stand a chance of being included in the transfer to the new planet. Either he needed to find a way to get to Exilon 5, where he stood a better chance of finding a cure without his medical condition being detected, or he needed to find the cure on Earth, a more difficult prospect, but would then make it much easier to transfer to Exilon 5. While everyone underwent preliminary genetic testing before they were allowed to transfer to Exilon 5—and his tests would show his faulty genes, cured or not—he could skip such preliminary testing because of his connections. Or, he could alter his genes and become a better version of himself.

The resistance from some board members would make it difficult for him to sell his alteration programme idea. There were the pro-Earth members who had invested money in industries on Earth and were unwilling to let go of the planet. Earth was not dying, the people were. If the population numbers on Earth were sustained, they would commit to turning around conditions to make the world habitable, and even more profitable than it currently was. But then there were the pro-Exilon 5 members who saw greater potential in investing on Exilon 5. To make their venture profitable, they needed a sizeable number of people living on the new planet. For both groups, the programme of change from human into a new race was an experiment, something to consider after they had settled on the new planet. Deighton was intent on persuading the board to both speed up the transfer process and adopt his new alteration programme. Tanya Li, Peter Cantwell's replacement as Chair, had been in the position for a full year now, and Deighton was thankful that a personal matter had distracted her from his activities behind the scenes.

Ten minutes later, the veal arrived and Deighton picked up his fork. He stabbed the bloody meat with it and his hand shuddered as the fork struck bone. The sensation reminded him of when he had killed Caroline Finnegan. He carved off a slice of meat and shoved it in his mouth. Blood dripped down his chin and he dabbed at it with the edge of his pristine white napkin, staining it pink. He picked up his wine glass and silently toasted Serena—the product of his persistence. Some of the board members would demand her return so they could test her code. Others wouldn't care; their interest was in keeping people, not Indigenes, on Earth.

Deighton took a sip of his wine and placed the glass back on the table. The waiter suddenly appeared with a bottle. He filled the glass half way. Deighton tapped the edge with his finger and the waiter continued to pour almost to the top.

'Leave the bottle,' he demanded.

The waiter complied and scurried away.

Unlike the wine from the replication machines, which contained no alcohol, François's personal stock was the real thing. Under its influence, Deighton was starting to unwind. He was keen to forget a few things, like his problem with the new Chair for one. Now that her personal distraction had passed, Tanya Li was beginning to pay attention and he was running out of good reasons to push ahead with his new alteration programme—reasons that did not draw attention to his personal agenda.

Deighton gulped down more of the wine, relishing the soothing warmth of the alcohol and the sense of confidence it brought. His fingers dug into the soft cushion of the chair and he forgot about his meal—and his tremors. The news about the tracer and recording device in Anton's head would satisfy the board members for now, but he wouldn't mention Anton's personality adjustment just yet. They wouldn't understand Deighton's reasons for turning the Indigene into a suicide bomber with a particular target in mind. The tracer and recording device gave them a viable way to get into the Indigenes' underground fortress. The World Government knew roughly where they were hiding on Exilon 5, but hadn't been able to pinpoint their exact location. New cities were being built in strategic areas to hem them in. But there was no easy way to sneak up on them.

No, tomorrow Deighton would need to convince the board members to bring the Indigenes to the surface, up to their world where they couldn't hide so easily.

# 4

*Exilon 5*

Stephen's eyes fluttered open and Serena's concerned face was the first thing he saw.

'Stephen! Are you okay?' She was cradling his head in her lap, using her sleeve to mop up the sweat on his brow.

He sat up, gingerly holding the side of his head. 'How long was I out for?'

'About ten minutes. What happened?'

'I could ask you the same question.' The throbbing pain lingered, so he closed his eyes and concentrated on it. He broke it up into bits and pushed them away to other parts of his body. His arms and torso pricked momentarily with the pain, his nerves stung for a moment and then it was gone.

Serena helped him to stand up. 'I don't know what to do. Should I get help?' she asked, frowning.

But Stephen was more concerned with what had happened to Serena in the Nexus. 'Are you all right? Why did the Nexus react to you like that?'

'I really don't know,' she said, turning away from him. 'Sometimes I feel one hundred per cent like an Indigene, but at other times I drift in and out of another life.'

'Something to do with a woman and a little girl?'

Serena's head shot round, her eyes wide. 'How do you know about them?'

'I've seen them in your mind. Who are they?' He felt braver asking her questions now— the Nexus's reaction to her gave him a good excuse.

'I don't know … What else do you want me to say?' She folded her arms and scowled.

'Well, do you remember anything else about this other life?'

She paced in a little circle in front of him, her arms still folded. 'I remember an apartment. Did I live there once? It doesn't make sense if I'm one of you.' The pitch of her voice rose as she went on. 'I'm from District Eight. I'm sure of that. But there's a part of me that thinks it's all a smokescreen.'

Stephen closed his eyes as a bout of dizziness came out of nowhere. He felt her grip his arm tightly to prevent him from falling.

'No more questions,' she said. 'You need to rest. I'm taking you back to your quarters.'

Stephen didn't argue. He wanted to talk some more about the images in her mind but the expression on her face told him to drop it. When they got to his private quarters, she left him and, grateful for the peace and quiet, he closed the door.

His quarters were small, square. He had a mattress on the floor and a timepiece propped against one wall; on another wall were scrawled his own familiar drawings, often done in the early hours of the morning—mostly equations that came to him in dreams. At night, the double moons would filter through the solar conduit in his ceiling, turning his room a calming shade of blue. During the day, he didn't care for the low light of the sun that leaked through, and often blocked it up with a small wooden plug he had fashioned for the purpose.

He sat on the mattress, his legs stretched out in front of him, his back against the wall. He was too agitated to sleep, but when a new bout of dizziness came, he lay down, closed his eyes and curled into a ball. Moments later, a knock on his door jolted him out of his rest and he shot upright. He was unable to sense who it was. Serena perhaps? Maybe she wanted to talk some more.

He opened the door. It was Arianna.

'Stephen! I was worried. I sensed your pain,' she said pushing her way inside. 'Are you all right? What did you see?'

He tried to be casual but it was difficult to hide feelings from an empath. He couldn't do it with Elise, and Arianna was rapidly becoming as skilled an empath as Elise had been. He closed the door. 'I'm okay, Ari. I hit my head in the tranquillity cave.'

She narrowed her eyes at him. 'How?'

He took a step towards her. 'I was using the Nexus with Serena. She suggested I use it to control my envisioning ability.'

'And you wind up hurt?' She seemed confused. 'In all the years we've been friends, not once have you had an accident in the Nexus. Yet you use it one time with her and it almost kills you?'

'It wasn't like that. She couldn't disconnect. I had to carry her out of her unit.'

Arianna glared at him. 'I'm worried about you, Stephen. You're putting a lot of faith in her but you've only just met her. What if she's not who she says she is?'

'Well then, who is she? What can you sense from her?'

'Nothing out of the ordinary—and that's the

problem right there.'

Stephen frowned. 'Well maybe we should give her the benefit of the doubt.'

Arianna turned towards the drawings on Stephen's wall. She traced her finger along the black line of a formula. 'I can't keep an open mind about her. She makes me feel strange. I don't trust her.'

'If it's because of our friendship, you have nothing to worry—'

Arianna waved her hand dismissively at him. 'No, no—you have it all wrong. You and I are like siblings.' She turned to look at him. 'I've spoken to other females and they feel the same way I do, while all the men lust after her. It's as if she's controlling it.'

Stephen laughed. 'That's rubbish, Ari and you know it. We all have free will. None of us can exert control over others.'

Arianna pursed her lips. 'I'm just saying, we shouldn't drop our guard when she's around. Things just don't add up about her. For instance, she says she doesn't know Anton, yet there's a rumour that she travelled from her district to see him. It doesn't make sense. Things are beginning to unravel around here. It isn't helping that Pierre has locked himself away in the Council Chambers.'

'I can't say I've heard that rumour,' Stephen said, his tone a little defensive. His heart beat a little faster as he asked. 'How is he?'

'He won't let anyone inside the Chambers. Gabriel's tried to get him to eat something—some of the wolf you killed—but he won't open the door to accept it.'

Stephen felt a pang of guilt. 'I meant Anton—how's Anton doing?'

Arianna grimaced and she looked down at the floor.

He grabbed her by both arms. 'Has something happened to him?'

'I went to see him. I went to see Anton.' Arianna defiantly met Stephen's eyes.

Stephen let go of her and took a step backwards. It was none of his business who she saw but he was angry that she went alone. His tone was sharper than he intended it to be. 'Well, what happened?'

'The malevolent personality is controlling him. I wasn't strong enough to release him,' she replied stiffly.

Stephen remembered the murderous look in Anton's eyes when they had discovered Elise's body in the makeshift medical facility just after the explosion. Stephen studied Arianna's aura; it was a yellowish-grey—she didn't know what to do.

'Then we'll have to try something else,' he said firmly.

'There was something else the invasive personality said … about Pierre.'

'Tell me.'

'I don't know where to start.'

Stephen stepped forward and placed one hand on each side of her head. He leaned forward until their foreheads were touching. 'Then show me,' he said and closed his eyes.

*Arianna headed towards the room where Anton was being held, navigating the uneven floor of the tunnel with ease. Her heart thumped unevenly in her chest. What was she doing, going to see Anton on her own and with no idea of how dangerous he really was? Pierre hadn't voiced any objections to her going to see the prisoner, even though she knew the elder hadn't really understood her request. But who else would help Anton if she didn't try? Stephen was too preoccupied with the strange female, Serena.*

'You should have told me,' Stephen said. 'I would have listened.'

'I know that now.'

*They were all still reeling from Elise's death. Those who didn't understand what had happened to Anton were quick to label him a murderer. Arianna could sense from the emotions of those around her that while most Indigenes grieved for Elise, others had been relieved at her death. It saddened her to think that the former elder had not been liked by everyone.*

*She reached a semicircular area where several private dwellings were located. She wasn't surprised to see two male Indigenes—one much older than the other—guarding the door to where Anton was being held. As her hand stroked the cool rock of the cave wall, it vibrated in reaction to her thoughts.*

*'I know. I'll be careful,' she said in response to its hidden warning.*

*The residential area was unusually quiet. The dwellings there had been evacuated so that Anton could be safely monitored around the clock and to ensure that he wasn't a danger to the others. A sudden noise from the left forced her to turn around. She saw two more Indigenes emerging from the tunnel that led from the south. They stopped and took up the position that guards usually do. To her right, a male and female closed off the north tunnel she had just come through. Arianna wondered who had given the order.*

'It was Gabriel,' Stephen said. 'He thought it

was safer if everyone used an alternative route.'

*The guards posted outside Anton's door didn't move as she approached. She stopped a foot away, trying to probe their minds and figure out what they were thinking. She struggled to get a handle on the older male's erratic emotions, but the younger male was easy to read—he was unsure of himself and a little scared.*

*She communicated with them telepathically.* 'I'm here to see the prisoner.'

*The guards looked at each other, then back at her. Arianna cleared her throat and said aloud,* 'Pierre asked me to come and speak with him.'

'He would never have asked you to do that!' Stephen said.

'I know—which is why I lied,' Arianna replied.

*The older male blinked and shook his head.* 'He would have told us.'

'Pierre is in no fit state to be telling anyone anything.' *Arianna felt anger rise to the surface.*

'Well that doesn't help you now, does it?' *the older male said cynically.* 'Things are different around here now.'

*Arianna lowered her voice in an effort to control her anger.* 'Please. I have to try. It's what Elise would have done.'

Stephen smiled sadly. 'Yes, she probably would have.'

*The younger male nudged the older guard as they engaged in a telepathic conversation.* 'Get permission from Gabriel first,' *the older male said eventually.*

'It was actually Gabriel that suggested I try,' *she said, surprising herself at how easily lying came to her.*

*The older guard shook his head. 'I'll need to hear it from him.'*

*She grabbed a fistful of her cream tunic. 'Please, you have to let me inside.' Her eyes filled with tears and she desperately blinked them back.*

*'Have Gabriel confirm it,' the older male said.*

*Arianna detected his weakening conviction and worked fast to take advantage of it. 'He doesn't have time for petty things like that. He's too busy keeping tabs on his crazy wife. Have you met her? Do you want me to waste his time dragging him all the way here, only to confirm what I've been saying?'*

*The younger male nudged the older male, who sighed reluctantly. 'Okay, but be quick.'*

Stephen shook his head. 'They shouldn't have let you in.'

'I know, but I had to try.'

*Arianna held her breath and cautiously opened the door. Her eyes darted around the small single-occupancy room. Anton was sitting on a silver metal chair—one of the human's chairs—facing the door, one leg crossed over the other. His chin was propped up on his fist, his elbow resting on his knee. He looked up slowly as she came inside and closed the door behind her. His gaze dropped back lazily to a spot on the floor and he sighed.*

*Arianna remained at a safe distance from him. His mind was open and she began to probe it. She tried to see the strong murky colours that Elise had described to her, the same ones the real Anton was supposed to be trapped behind, but on the surface the colours appeared washed out. She detected brighter colours hidden behind the washed-out ones. Then suddenly, she saw it—a small ball of light tucked in the corner behind the lacklustre colours. She pushed through the murkiness to reach the ball of light, but invisible hands fought her off and broke the mind connection. Dizziness caught hold and she tried to steady herself.*

*'It won't work, my dear,' said Anton, smiling at her. 'I don't want you poking around inside there. My thoughts are none of your business.'*

*She regained her composure and ran a hand over her smooth, hairless head. 'Why did you kill her, Anton?'*

*He shrugged. 'Why not?' Uncrossing his legs and leaning forward, he studied her closely. 'I think the question you want to ask is why did I take so long to do it?'*

*Arianna shuddered. The room was cold, but this ... entity—it certainly wasn't the real Anton— gave her the creeps. 'I don't understand,' she said. 'You loved Elise and you love Pierre. How could you have allowed this to happen?'*

*The expression on his face hardened as he stood up. 'HE loved her, and that was the point, really.' He casually stretched. 'God, I hate these chairs. No back support. And what in God's name am I wearing?' He plucked at the plain cream trousers and top.*

*'A tunic set. We wear them for modesty, Anton.'*
*'Oh, do call me by MY name, not his, my dear.'*
*'And what would that be?' Arianna asked.*
*'Benedict,' he said, smiling coldly.*
'Benedict?' Stephen said.
'Yeah, it meant nothing to me either.'
*'Okay. Benedict. I apologise,' Arianna said. The split personality was a worry and the name new. She hadn't spoken to Anton since ... that day. She wondered about him and how he was coping with*

*being trapped inside. 'Can I please speak to Anton?'*

*Benedict waved his hand dismissively. 'He's not receiving visitors at the moment. And just so you know, the politeness is nauseating: "I apologise", "please"'—he mimicked Arianna's voice—'Have we devolved into trained monkeys?'*

*Arianna quickly jumped into his mind again.*

*'I told you to get the fuck out of there!' Benedict hissed.*

*She ignored him and closed her eyes. The harder she concentrated, the easier it was to see brief glimmers of Anton, peering like a scared child around the edges of the murky greens, greys and purples. She held out her hand to him. 'Don't be afraid. I can protect you.'*

*As soon as she moved towards the ball of light, it disappeared. She thought she heard him ask, 'Where's Elise?' Anton's presence was weak but she could feel him.*

'I'm positive he saw me,' Arianna said to Stephen. 'He knew we were trying to get him out.'

*'I said, get out of my head!' Benedict roared, his face contorted with rage.*

*A strong force pushed her and the mind connection broke a second time. Arianna stumbled backwards and smacked her head against the wall. She groaned as she slid down the wall and cradled her head in her hands.*

*Benedict was shaking, furious. 'Bitch. I told you to mind your own business!'*

*There was silence for a few moments. Then Benedict stood up and came over to her. She pulled her knees up to her chest to protect herself.*

*'Here, let me see.' His voice was eerily calm now. 'I don't like it very much when people challenge*

*me.' He tugged at her hands to see the damage, but Arianna resisted. He made her skin crawl. Eventually, she gave in, if only to stop him from groping her. Still holding on to her wrists, Benedict knelt down in front of her. She noticed him wince with pain. He let go of one wrist and touched her head. 'I can see why Anton is attracted to you,' he said. 'You're strong.'*

*A shiver crept up her spine as Benedict, in Anton's body, touched the cut that was already repairing itself. His face was too close to hers and it made her feel sick to her stomach. Benedict sensed her uneasiness and climbed to his feet with great difficulty, pulling her up with him, the pain of the effort showing in his face.*

*'Are you injured?' she asked.*

*Benedict didn't answer.*

*She remembered going to Anton after Stephen had fled the core of District Three with the bomb. She had asked him telepathically if he'd lost his mind. Anton had replied with a simple nod. Her biggest regret was that she had left him alone with Elise while she helped turn one of the rooms into a medical bay. Pierre and Leon had gone after Stephen.*

*Benedict was examining her face intently. His expression had softened a little, but there was still a cruel edge to his smile—and his eyes. Benedict's mind was hard and impenetrable, like the omega rock, and she found it impossible to get beyond it to Anton. She might have to ask for Stephen's help eventually, but not until she had tried absolutely everything.*

*'Anton, are you in there? Benedict, let me speak to him,' she demanded, her voice lacking confidence.*

*'He's here. I'm here.' Benedict grinned as he*

*sang the words. 'We're both here.'*

*'Let me speak to him.'*

*'Speak away. I'm not stopping you. Ask your questions.' He kept hold of her hand.*

*'Anton, how are you feeling?'*

*'Fine, just fine. Thanks for asking.'*

*She felt Benedict's grip tighten on her hand. 'Step back. Let me speak to him,' she said firmly.*

*'Have I told you how lovely you're looking this evening? Translucent, like wet paper.' Benedict began to whistle a strange tune, then he reached out to grab her other hand, but Arianna kept it from him. He continued to grope for it.*

*'Give it to me,' he snarled.*

*She did. She had to trust that Anton would not allow Benedict to harm her.*

*He placed one of her hands on his shoulder and held the other in the air; he put his other hand on her waist and gently moved her around, making little shuffling movements with his feet. 'Have you ever danced before, my dear?' he asked, but his steps were awkward and he was clearly in pain.*

*The strange movement made her stumble at first, but she quickly picked up the rhythm. 'I can't say I have. Is this what you do where you're from?' she asked.*

*'Yes, yes. It's called a waltz. It's a bit old-fashioned, but it's been so long since I've danced with the opposite sex. But now that I have a younger man's body—' Benedict moved her slowly round the room. 'One–two–three; one–two–three ... Isn't this fun? Isn't this better than asking me a whole bunch of boring questions?'*

*'I still want to talk to Anton,' she said softly. Benedict's grip on her hand tightened. She tried to*

*get out of the hold, but he was too strong for her.*

*'In a little while,' he muttered. 'I'm enjoying this too much.' He laughed and suddenly, holding on to one of her hands, he spun her around. Arianna stumbled. 'Isn't dancing the best?' he went on. 'Lighten up, my dear. You lot are far too serious, with your boring stories and meditation and sitting in rooms with nothing to do but stare at the walls. Do you know how bored I've been sitting alone in this room? God, what I wouldn't give for something exciting to do!'*

Stephen broke the mind connection with Arianna first. He took his hands away from her head. He was furious. 'Why did Pierre not stop you?' he shouted.

'He didn't know I was going.'

'Exactly. He should have been doing his job.'

'He misses Elise. It's hard for him.'

'Ari! It's hard for all of us,' Stephen bellowed. 'Do you think I like watching this district fall apart? Gabriel's doing his best, but he's not the elder. Pierre needs to start doing his job.' He strode past her and started for the door.

'Where are you going?' Arianna was suddenly at his shoulder, her hand gripping it tightly.

He shrugged her off. 'To see Pierre. Something has to be done.'

# 5

*Earth Security Centre, Sydney, Earth*

At her workstation on Level Five, Laura O'Halloran resisted the urge to cough, but the tickle caught her by surprise. She shot a hand over her mouth and wheezed into it. The tickle came and went and the cough satisfied the urge, but it set off a chain reaction of smaller coughs that she couldn't control. She could feel the irritation in her lungs and dug her fingernails into a soft spot underneath her ribs in a futile attempt to scratch the internal tickle.

Laura, Bill and Jenny had stayed on Exilon 5 a few days after the explosion. Amidst all the chaos, it hadn't felt right to just up and leave. It was during those few days that the strange cough had first appeared. Laura had put it down to the impurities that existed naturally in Exilon 5's atmosphere. She was accustomed to the controlled purity of the oxygen gel masks on Earth and environmentally controlled spaces like her apartment in Haymarket, Sydney, and when neither Jenny nor Bill developed a similar cough, she assumed she was just adapting to the change in atmospheric conditions. But after two weeks on the passenger ship and a few days back on Earth, the cough had got worse and she began to wonder if she had an infection.

The workers in Level Five were quieter than

usual making Laura's coughing fits all the more noticeable, echoing around the room in an eerie way. Intermittent beeping filled any remaining silence. In between her coughing fits, she thought about the journey home with Jenny and Bill. No one had tried to arrest them at the docking station on Exilon 5. On the passenger ship back to Earth, they had tried to anticipate what might happen to them when they arrived home. They were bound to be punished.

'It would have been easier for the military to catch us on Exilon 5,' Bill had said.

'So why didn't they?' Laura asked.

'Probably because we're more useful to them running free than locked up somewhere. We've just been with the Indigenes. They obviously trust us. We might prove useful in leading the military to them.'

What Bill had said about their connection with the Indigenes made sense to her. They had formed an alliance with the World Government's secret race. The government was bound to try to exploit that connection at some point. But Laura desperately wanted their secrets to be brought out into the open. The stress of all this was too much.

'Do you think the government would ever consider a peaceful way of dealing with the Indigenes?' Jenny had asked.

Bill shrugged. 'It's about as likely as them bringing Charles Deighton to justice for what he's done.'

'We don't know it was him that sent the bomb with Anton,' Jenny said. 'We're only assuming it was.'

Laura had said nothing. She agreed with Bill— Deighton's behaviour was borderline psychotic and she shuddered to think that there might be similar-minded individuals on the World Government's board, eager to recruit more ruthless bastards just like him.

It turned out that they had been right about one thing: there was no one waiting for them when they arrived back on Earth. Bill and Laura had said their goodbyes to Jenny, who was pleased that she had been finally able to help Stephen. She had returned to Earth with a renewed sense of purpose, and to look for work.

'I've only ever been a pilot or a mother. It's time to try something new,' Jenny had announced. 'If the Indigenes can survive appalling treatment at the hands of humans, then I can stop complaining about a little blackballing. I'll find something else to do. I just need to figure out what.' She turned to Bill, her tone serious. 'If there's anything I can do to help in the future, promise me you'll get in touch.'

Bill had nodded in reply. 'If anything comes up, you'll be the first on my list.'

They had all promised to meet up again, but Laura had no idea when that might be.

Back in her booth on Level Five, she stared vacantly at her monitor, her thoughts drifting back to the present and the beeping silence around her. The list of documents continued to pool on her screen. Her eyes slowly focused, turning the blocks of black ink into names and numbers. She could feel another tickle in her lungs. She curled her fist to her mouth and coughed into it, then massaged the front of her neck, feeling the rawness at the back of her throat.

With greater confidence than she'd had before, she stood up and looked around the room. Of the twenty-four booths just twelve of them were occupied. The numbers had dwindled since her return. But there was one woman on whom her eyes lingered the longest—the woman from booth sixteen who had given her the micro file all those weeks ago and who had disappeared from Level Five soon after. Now here she was, back again, with no explanation for her absence. One of the other workers had mentioned something about her suffering a mental breakdown after her entire family had died in unrelated accidents. Whatever had happened, Sixteen now just sat there, glassy-eyed and compliant, the way the Earth Security Centre preferred all their workers to be. Laura had heard a different story about her family's fate, and there was nothing accidental about it.

Laura's latest cough brought up a small amount of bile and she swallowed it, but the taste lingered. It suddenly reminded her of the liquid Stephen had given her to treat her seasonal depression. She hadn't thought too hard about what his 'remedy' contained. For so long, she had wanted to feel normal and not be driven insane by the complex range of symptoms that the lack of natural light caused.

Laura remembered how eager she'd felt as she'd stood in one of District Three's laboratories watching Stephen concoct the vial of liquid at a long, metal bench. He had told her it contained microscopic nanoids and specific copies of his genetic code to swap out her own faulty genes. When he handed her the vial, she had knocked it back in one go. It had tasted revolting—like drinking metal.

Stephen hadn't been sure how long it would take to work, or, indeed, what its full effects might be.

'We've never tried this with a regular human—altering genes, fixing serotonin receptors,' he'd said. 'Nor am I sure if the effects will be temporary or permanent.'

She had asked him how it worked; the lengthy explanation that followed made her wish she hadn't.

'The liquid contains nanoids, all of which are small enough to be absorbed in the bloodstream,' he explained. 'Some nanoids will work their way up and across the blood/brain barrier to the serotonin receptors in your brain. If needed, they will deliver an extra copy of the p11 gene that fixes depression, to the nucleus accumbens. The others will examine and repair your regular genetic code by swapping out faulty genes and replacing it with copies of mine. The code fix is just an added precaution in case the nanoids are unsuccessful in fixing the faulty areas in your brain.'

He had taken one look at her face and realised he'd lost her. 'Put simply, you lack the natural ability to produce serotonin on your own, which is why you take vitamin D,' he went on. 'The nanoids can help to significantly increase the number of receptor sites that can actively receive serotonin, or if there is a blockade preventing the serotonin from reaching these receptor sites, they'll remove it. They'll work out what to do when they get there.'

She'd told him that she'd been taking larger than normal quantities of vitamin D, but they'd been ineffective lately. Stephen had explained that deficiency in humans was linked to neuropsychiatric disorders such as schizophrenia. By taking the vitamin in its purest form, she was simply maintaining the brain's equilibrium. But its effects were short term. She needed a more permanent solution.

At Stephen's insistence, she had returned to the medical facilities to rest and woke seven hours later to find him hovering over her. When he had asked her how she felt, she told him she felt no different; privately, she was disappointed, but she had accepted a long time ago that she might always suffer from Seasonal Affective Disorder. The World Government was certainly in no hurry to find a cure.

As if he had detected her disappointment, Stephen offered to give her a tour of the district, but Laura had been reluctant to take up any more of his time when he had more important things to do.

'We held Elise's funeral a few hours ago. Now I'm looking for something else to distract me,' he said kindly. 'Besides, it's part of your recovery. Please.'

She had accepted his hand and he helped her up from the bed. The coolness of his touch took her by surprise and sent a small shiver through her.

She had found out on their walk that Bill had just learned of Isla's death. Jenny was busy helping Arianna to prepare a ceremonial table to mark her passing.

On their tour of the district, Stephen had shown her the solar energy conduit that had been fashioned out of spare materials the humans had dumped in the wasteland after completing some of their cities. Stephen explained that the gamma rock in the conduits amplified the sun's natural strength, which powered the district.

Laura remembered watching him closely as he spoke, fascinated and still unaccustomed to his appearance on Exilon 5—the translucent skin and yellow-flecked eyes that seemed to look straight through her. On Earth, in her apartment, he had been wearing artificial skin and brown contact lenses and had looked almost human.

Stephen had taken the time to introduce some

of the Indigenes they encountered as they walked. It hadn't been difficult to work out how they felt about her that day; while they had been polite, she knew she wasn't welcome. Her thoughts reflected her feelings but she switched them quickly when she remembered their telepathic abilities. She brought an image of her mother's cat to the forefront.

'Don't worry. I'm keeping them out of your head,' Stephen had said, smiling. 'It's the least I can do after what you did for me—for all of us.'

What Stephen had said startled her. Could he read all her thoughts, she wondered.

'Only the ones you show me, like the image of the cat,' he replied out loud. 'You were practically forcing it on me. I'd have to really dig around inside your head for your secrets.'

They had walked for another hour along the tunnels, through the semicircular areas where the private dwellings were located and into the larger spaces where the recessed teaching alcoves were. Classes had been running and, as they stopped to watch, the young seemed openly curious about her.

'They're called Evolvers,' Stephen had explained.

She'd wanted to shake their tiny hands, but they had been reluctant to let her touch them.

As she stood there, her seasonal depression—or lack of it—entered her thoughts. Where was the panic, the anxiety? Stephen had confirmed it to her when she asked; she had been underground for a period of twenty-four hours. It was at that moment she realised she felt fine, at ease in the darkness—that the remedy he had given her was working.

Another onslaught of coughing jolted Laura right back to her booth on Level Five. She had lagged behind the others and quickly turned her attention back to the list of files on her monitor. Her throat was rough and dry and the taste of bile remained. She couldn't bear it any longer so she went to the back wall where the H2O replication terminal was. The worker in booth five casually followed her. Laura glanced at the motivational message for that day, pinned to the board on the wall. 'A quick worker is a happy worker,' it read. She wondered if it had been written just for her.

She grabbed a cone-shaped cup and filled it with replicated water, pretending not to notice the woman standing close behind her.

'Is everything okay?' Booth Five asked. 'You look ... upset.'

Laura turned to face her. She was a skinny woman, her face gaunt. She seemed tense, and looked less like a Level Five worker and more of a supervisor. Laura held up a finger and drained the cup. Then she refilled it and drank that too. Only then did she reply.

'Is it that obvious? I was just thinking about my mother.'

The woman tried to look concerned. 'How is she doing? I hear she suffered a hell of a setback.'

'Fine, fine.'

'Good. Broken backs can be really tricky to heal,' said Booth Five, folding her arms. 'It never quite fuses the way it should.'

It had been puzzling Laura that the Earth Security Centre had not queried her mother's fake second fall as much as they had the genuine first one. The injuries from the second fall had become exaggerated the more she and young Callum Preston worked it out, but they had finally settled on a fresh break of semi-healed vertebrae, which sounded more plausible. She hadn't spoken to Callum since he'd hacked the system so she could get time off to travel to Exilon 5, but she had her suspicions that Gilchrist had strong-armed the boy into divulging his involvement in the scheme and she didn't want to get him in any more trouble.

Laura started to cough again.

'You should get that checked out. Might be contagious,' said Booth Five.

'It's nothing.'

'Are you sure? Coughs aren't terribly common. Were you away recently?'

'Nowhere special,' Laura said, but she could feel herself blushing.

The woman pursed her lips, unfolded her arms and reached for a cup.

'But good suggestion,' Laura said. 'I'll talk to my mother's doctor if it doesn't improve.' She turned and walked away leaving the woman to her drink of water.

She resisted the urge to look at the woman from booth sixteen as she settled back in her seat. Sixteen had been gone for quite a while; then suddenly she was back. Her previously tidy black hair was dishevelled and she looked like she was carrying the weight of the world on her shoulders. Every now and again, a slight tremor seemed to course through her body. What had they done to her? What had really happened to her family? Laura wanted to scream at her: *Do they know about the micro file? Do they know about me? If so, why have they left me alone?* There sat Sixteen, evidence that the World Government could make any problem disappear.

For the rest of the day, Laura's need for water breaks increased, as did her need for the bathroom. But something occurred to her as she took her tenth unsanctioned break in two hours: while Booth Five kept a close eye on her, nobody actually reprimanded her.

# 6

*Earth*

In his private apartment in Nottingham, Bill Taggart sat at the glass table in his living room and checked through several internal memos he had sourced from a contact since returning from Exilon 5. He frowned at their content, realising he had been out of touch for too long.

Cradling his chin in his hand, he stared out the tinted window. He had finally removed the boxes full of Isla's things that had been stacked against it. When he had sorted through them, it turned out that there had been little he actually wanted to keep; the rest was going either to charity or to the dump.

There were only three things he kept. His eyes settled on a six-inch-tall glass obelisk sitting on his mantelpiece. Preserved inside was one of the white flowers from Isla's ceremony on Exilon 5. He gazed at it for a while, remembering his last goodbyes to her. The flower was the only thing in the room that meant anything to him. The second thing he kept, the personal letter she had written to him, was safely locked away in his suitcase. Beside it was the third thing: her military dog tags that had allowed him to decipher her coded letters.

Bill turned his attention back to the memos and rubbed his tired eyes. The memos had been circulated to staff in the Earth Security Centre and the International Task Force offices; he hadn't been able to get his hands on any from the World Government. He was scouring them for some mention of his recent unauthorised trip to Exilon 5 with Laura and Jenny. In his mind, he replayed the events in Magadan after they had visited Harvey Buchanan, when he and Laura had been attacked on their way back to the docking station. They had taken a massive risk by continuing with their trip to Exilon 5 and there wasn't a mention of it in any of the memos. Why not? Now on his fifth reading, he still couldn't find a line or a word that so much as hinted at their trip, and that bothered him.

Bill checked the time projection on the wall and decided to stop for now. He turned off his DPad, stood up and stretched, then grabbed his 'I heart Boston' mug and filled it with black coffee. He took a large gulp and shuddered as the caffeine brought back to life every wavering nerve in his body. He thought about eating something but knew it would delay him too much. He went over to the Light Box and removed the sound disruptor that was attached to it. Prising up a loose floorboard underneath the rug, he put it in a small strongbox he kept hidden there. That was also where he stored the communication stone that Stephen had given him.

The communication stone was cold now; it was no good to him while he was on Earth. Stephen had explained to him how it worked when he'd been on Exilon 5: the concentric rings on the front of the stone light up when the stone finds its match inside the tranquillity cave. The Nexus powers it and then acts as a go-between, relaying any messages the user wants to send. Bill recalled how it had glowed blue, pulsated and became very hot when he'd used it on Exilon 5.

'It's the connection and the raw energy from the Nexus that makes it heat up like that,' Stephen had explained. 'The Nexus powers the stone to do what you need it to. You were looking for a compass, so it turned it into just that.'

Bill had wanted to know if it could send verbal messages.

'Only if a user connected to the Nexus is trying to send one,' Stephen had said. 'You must be holding it at the time. The circles must be bright. You'd need to concentrate on them and tell the Nexus what you want. If there's a message, it will relay it to you.'

Bill studied the cold stone in his hand for a bit longer, then put it back in its hiding place and replaced the floorboard and the rug.

At the mirror by the front door, Bill paused. He straightened his tie and tucked his white shirt into the waistband of his trousers. He smoothed his hair and rubbed his day-old stubble. The look wasn't perfect but it would have to do. It was the least messy he had looked for quite some time. Then he grabbed his DPad and his communication device and threw them both in his bag. He slung the bag crossways over his body and left the apartment, gel mask in hand.

Half an hour later, he arrived at the ITF office in London. He stood outside for a moment and looked up at the skyscraper. It had been eighteen months since he'd last set foot inside, and since he'd seen some of his old workmates. For some reason he felt nervous, and it took him by surprise.

He passed through the force field that surrounded the building and removed his gel mask, then opened the enormous black entrance door. Just inside was a large room with a scanning station manned by autobots. He threw his bag on a conveyor belt and walked through a body scanner. On the other side, he collected his scanned bag and braced himself as he neared the white door beyond. Losing Isla had changed his world—and him—and he had lost touch with his co-workers. He had never been the easiest to work with and he was sure that many of them were glad to see the back of him. Holding his breath, he scanned his thumb on the pad beside the white door; it clicked open and he entered a wide corridor.

The corridor connecting to the open-plan ITF office looked exactly the same as he remembered it: the peeling white paint on the ceiling, the dark blue carpet that was threadbare in places. The overhead light flickered and he shielded his eyes, waiting for them to become accustomed to the artificial light. He walked towards the double doors at the end, ignoring the many offices to the right and left of the corridor. The last one on the left belonged to Simon Shaw, his supervisor at ITF. His door was ajar. Bill glanced inside but Simon wasn't there. Another corridor curving past Simon's office led to the briefing rooms. Clutching the strap of his bag tightly, he carried on to the double doors; one side opened automatically for him.

The open-plan office, with its neatly rowed workstations and information board beside the overused replication machine on the back wall, hadn't changed either. The male-dominated office smelled of sweat and testosterone. He recognised a few flustered faces, others he didn't. Bill walked in the direction of his old desk. He heard anxious voices coming from the far end of the room; one in particular grated on him, like it always had.

Halfway down the room, he changed direction and made a beeline for the information board. The roster confirmed that Simon had pencilled him in for a full week's work, his first proper shift since he'd arrived back from his official ITF trip to Exilon 5 over four months ago. Up until then, he'd received work orders through his Light Box at home. Most of the tasks were menial and designed to keep him away. He had mixed feelings about being back at work: on the one hand, he needed to know what was going on and he wanted to keep busy, but on the other hand he wanted to have nothing to do with the World Government and its subsidiary organisations now that he knew the truth about the Indigenes and what had happened to his wife.

The irritating voice rose an octave. Bill didn't need to turn around to know who was speaking. When he did, there was Dave Solan, staring at him while talking to someone a couple of desks away. Dave was a stocky man with a tight buzz cut, more used to field work than answering communication calls. But he had failed the physical exam which precluded him from military service, so instead, he had been assigned desk duties.

'Like I said, Monty, they'll let anyone work at ITF these days,' Dave said.

Bill smiled. 'Busy today I see, Dave,' he said cheerfully.

'What the hell would you know about that?' Dave grunted.

While Dave was probably irritated about Bill's practically non-existent work schedule for the last four months, his animosity towards Bill ran much deeper than that. It had begun when Bill had been tasked with assembling a team to watch the Indigenes on Exilon 5 and had deliberately overlooked ITF staff when selecting people to join him. In the end, what Bill got wasn't great; indeed, Dave might have done a better job, but he wasn't about to tell him that.

Bill wanted to announce to everyone that the lack of work wasn't his fault, but deep down, he knew it was. His curiosity and his dogged determination—the very things they'd hired him for—were most likely to blame. Bill was a risk-taker, not a rule-follower. He decided that for now he would play the game and behave himself; a full week's shift would help get him back in the fold so his colleagues would begin to trust him again and let him in on the office rumours.

Bill turned his back on Dave and punched some numbers into the replication machine, trying to shut out the office banter and friendly insults being traded behind him, and wishing that Dave's voice didn't carry so well—it was like fingernails on a blackboard to Bill. In need of a quick boost, he grabbed a clean mug from a nearby table and placed it on the tray of the replication unit. He watched the black liquid stream into the mug. He also caught the faint smell of roasted coffee beans, which the replication unit was attempting to mimic. He looked up just as Simon Shaw came through the double doors.

'I thought I heard your voice. Follow me,' Simon said, summoning him with a hooked finger.

Bill waited for the mug to fill with coffee, lifted it to his lips and took a cautious sip, then blew on it and took another sip. But Simon was waiting for him; delaying tactics weren't going to put off the inevitable chat. Mug in hand, Bill followed him through the double doors and into his office. Simon closed the door behind them, then edged around his desk and sat down.

'Take a seat,' Simon said, looking up briefly at him.

Bill sat on the chair nearest the door, letting his bag rest on his lap, and took another mouthful of coffee before he finally set the mug down on Simon's desk. Simon quickly read something on his monitor and turned to face Bill.

'I guess it's been a while,' he said.

Bill nodded.

'I'm sorry you haven't been rostered for any shifts here, but conditions have changed on Earth since your Exilon 5 mission and it was felt that you needed time to readjust to them.'

Bill smiled crookedly and folded his arms. 'Four months' readjustment?'

Simon attempted to smile back. 'When people return from Exilon 5 it takes them some time to adjust to wearing masks and to the lack of freedom. And then there's the absence of sunlight to contend with. You were away a long time. We needed to make sure you acclimatised correctly after your experience. Some detainees who were returned to Earth at the same time as you are still struggling to adapt to the conditions. They're on termination watch.'

Bill's smile cranked up to full strength. 'So let me get this straight. You thought I might be a risk to myself—that I might consider termination—so you left me alone for long periods of time without any support to give me plenty of time to think about it?'

Simon pursed his lips. 'You were being monitored the whole time.'

'And now what? No more field work—just me sitting at a desk while I answer desperate calls from the public?' Bill dismissed the idea with a wave of his hand. 'We both know that's a gross waste of my talents, Simon.'

Simon looked briefly at his monitor, then back at Bill. His expression had hardened. 'As your supervisor, I expect you to do what I ask. I don't want to hear any arguments from you. Are we clear?'

Bill could feel the anger building inside him but something made him hesitate. Simon wasn't a typical ITF supervisor—he was less abrasive than some of the others—but he had changed since Bill had been assigned to lead the investigation into the Indigenes on Exilon 5. Simon was being uncharacteristically firm and Bill suddenly found himself wondering if there were listening bugs in his office and if the World Government was watching. In a split second, Bill decided to keep up the pretence of being the hot-head they had all come to think of him as.

'Bullshit, Shaw. I'm not coming back here to be a receptionist. Give me something better to do or I walk.'

Simon leaned forward, but instead of scolding him for his outburst, he calmly said, 'I'm working on it. You need to be patient.'

Bill stood up quickly, knocking his chair over. Simon jumped to his feet. Bill jerked the door open and stormed out, leaving Simon standing speechless behind his desk.

Convinced he was still being monitored by World Government cameras, Bill burst through the double doors and into the open-plan office. He stormed over to the replication unit to get another coffee. Dave Solan followed his every move.

'So, Bill, you've finally been knocked off that pedestal of yours,' he said. Bill turned around to see him grinning. 'Not so nice when you've got to do a little work, same as the rest of us.'

Bill cocked an eyebrow. 'Oh, so is that what you do, Dave—work? Because all I see is a washed-up military hack who's no use in the field anymore.'

Dave sniggered. 'Well then, I'm in good company.'

'Except I'm not an ugly sonofabitch with no chance of getting lucky anytime soon.'

'At least I didn't kill my wife,' Dave snapped.

For a moment a profound silence descended on the office. Then Bill's fist raised and connected with Dave's jaw. Both men cried out in pain. Dave staggered backwards but recovered quickly and threw a counterpunch at Bill. Bill fell backwards and hit the ground so hard he winded himself. He lay there for a minute, shaking his head, acutely aware that Dave was towering over him. He took a gamble and stayed where he was, grabbing hold of his jaw and moving it from side to side. A sharp pain shot across his face, but he could tell nothing was broken. He examined the back of his hand where it had scraped off Dave's tooth; his knuckles were bloodied and raw. Both men were breathing heavily, eyeing each other up, waiting to see what the other would do. It was Dave who backed off first, clenching and unclenching his fist, his mates gathering round to check he was okay. Bill got to his feet.

'You've got balls, Taggart. I'll give you that,' Dave sneered, wiping his face with his hand to check for blood.

Bill turned round to see Simon Shaw standing silently at the double doors.

# 7

*Exilon 5*

Stephen stomped angrily down the steps from his quarters and took the tunnel that headed towards the Council Chambers. His head was thumping and he was still dizzy after his fall, but he hadn't had such a strong sense of purpose in weeks. Sharing Arianna's memories of her visit to Anton had been the catalyst. It had brought home to him just how much they needed Pierre back in control, and Stephen was determined to snap the elder out of his remorse and make him face up to his responsibilities to the rest of them.

Angry tears pricked Stephen's eyes. It was Pierre's job to do something about Anton and to help them find a way out of the mess they were in. It was all very well bringing in deputies, and Gabriel and Margaux were doing the best they could, but ultimately it was down to Pierre to provide leadership and show the way forward. He was useless to them as a grieving husband. There was only one thing to do, only one way to reclaim their leader.

Stephen stopped outside the Council Chambers. There was no activity in the area; everyone was avoiding Pierre. But the sound of footsteps in the tunnel behind him suggested that Arianna was not far away, having sensed what he was about to do and probably coming to try to talk him out of it.

He looked down at a plate of meat outside the large metal Chamber door. Pierre had left his food untouched. The sight of it made Stephen even more angry. He and Serena had risked their lives to catch that wolf.

Arianna caught up with him. 'Stephen. Wait!'

He turned on his heel and glared at her. 'What?'

'Let me speak to Pierre. Don't go in there feeling the way you do. You'll regret it.'

Stephen shook his head. 'I can't sit by and watch others risk their lives and this place fall apart. Pierre needs to know what's going on. He needs to face up to it, not hide away. We need him.'

'You don't know everything about my visit with Anton. Let me speak to Pierre first. I can talk him round.'

Stephen turned away from her and pulled on the cord that hung from a sealed hole in the door. He had seen it operate when the door was open; it activated a bell inside the soundproofed Chamber.

'Stephen, I really don't think this is a good idea,' Arianna pleaded. 'At least wait until you're in a calmer frame of mind.'

He pulled the cord again, this time so hard that it came off in his hand. The last of his patience vanished as he kicked the meat plate away with his foot. Just then, the door creaked open a little.

'I told Gabriel no visitors,' Pierre croaked quietly through the crack in the door. A flurry of his thoughts rushed out towards Stephen like water breaking through a dam.

*Leave me alone. Go talk to Gabriel and Margaux. That's what they're here for. They'll know what to do.*

Stephen pushed the heavy door open with one hand and strode past Pierre. 'Gabriel and Margaux don't know what to do. That's the problem,' he said.

The Council Chambers was a rectangular room with a bookshelf dividing it in half. On the floor behind the bookshelf was a well-used mattress surrounded by several items that had belonged to Elise. They were arranged in a pattern, fanning out around the mattress as if it was a shrine.

Stephen brought his eyes up to meet Pierre's. 'Why are you still in here?'

Pierre was staring at the door. 'Why is Arianna here?' he asked sounding angry. 'Tell her to leave. I don't want visitors!'

'Tell her yourself!' Stephen said, curling his fists tightly. 'She needs you. We all need you.'

Pierre turned his back on them both, sighing heavily. 'I need time, Stephen—I need to figure everything out.'

Stephen took a step towards him. 'I've done everything you've asked of me,' he said. 'I made Gabriel and Margaux feel welcome, and kept the peace where I could. We've been maintaining our ritual hunting practices to show the military on the surface that we haven't been affected by their bomb.'

Pierre waved a hand. 'Well then, keep doing all that.'

Stephen took another step towards Pierre, forcing him to turn around. 'But what happened to Arianna is a step too far.'

Pierre's eyes were wide. 'What do you mean? What happened to Arianna?'

'She went to see Anton on her own and he almost killed her.'

'No, he didn't, Stephen,' said Arianna. 'You're exaggerating.'

Pierre shook his head. 'I'm not up to leading right now. Please give me some space.' He tried to usher Stephen and Arianna out the door but Stephen refused to move.

'I'm not here to negotiate,' Stephen said. 'Things have come to a head in the district. You've been sitting in here for close to four weeks now. It's time you came out and faced reality.'

'Please leave him be,' Arianna pleaded with Stephen. 'He needs time to grieve.'

'We're all grieving,' Stephen snapped without turning round.

Pierre waved his hand dismissively again. 'Listen to her,' he said. 'You're not thinking straight. Are your visions still bothering you? Is that what this is all about?'

Stephen pulled himself up to his full height. 'I'm thinking perfectly straight. You need to listen to me.'

Pierre turned his back on him and snorted. 'Why should I listen to you? What do you know about anything? You're too young to understand what's really going on.'

The uncontrollable rage crept up on Stephen quickly. He shoved Pierre hard and sent him reeling into the bookshelf in the middle of the room. The bookshelf wobbled and several books fell off the shelves, crashing down on Pierre, now slumped on the stone floor. Stephen stood over him, panting, looking down at the crumpled body of his elder as if someone else had pushed him. Then he heard the sound of feet running away; when he looked round Arianna had vanished from the room.

Pierre rolled onto his back. Clear fluid leaked out of a neat gash on his forehead and dripped into his eyes. He glared at Stephen as he wiped it with his hand. The gash on his forehead was healing already.

'Did that get your attention?' Stephen growled. 'Wake up, Pierre, and come and have a look at what's happening in your own district. You've already created a huge mess by keeping secrets from the other elders about the human attacks. And you're no longer trusted in your own district—you withheld the truth about Anton's disappearance, only to have him return home with a bomb. Gabriel and Margaux are here to help you—not take over. So far you've ignored them.'

Pierre climbed slowly to his feet, the books on Indigene history scattered all around him. 'Gabriel and Margaux are here,' Pierre said, dusting down his white elder robe. 'So are Emile and Marie from District Seven. Between them, they have everything under control.'

Stephen shook his head. 'Emile and Marie never turned up—it seems we're not worth the trouble. And I'm not sure how useful Margaux is. She doesn't seem able to handle the pressures of this district. She keeps upsetting the younger ones, invading their thoughts, rooting around for their secrets, just like Elise used to do.'

Pierre looked unconvinced. 'The district is capable of looking after itself. Our people need time to heal. What happened weeks ago was traumatic enough without me being around to remind them that Elise is dead.'

Pierre's indifference enraged Stephen and he found himself pushing the elder again. Pierre staggered backwards, visibly shocked; he remained on his feet this time. But not for long—Stephen stepped forward and slammed his fist into Pierre's jaw. Slightly dazed, Pierre picked himself off the floor, but just as Stephen was about to apologise, he charged, shoving Stephen back awkwardly into the large Chamber door. Stunned, Stephen slid down and hit the floor with a thud.

'I think you broke something,' Stephen groaned, cradling his ribs.

'Come on! Stand up and fight me!' Pierre was panting heavily now. 'That's what you want, isn't it?'

'No, it is not,' Stephen roared. 'I want to get your attention,' he said more softly, getting to his feet.

Pierre came at him again and Stephen quickly side-stepped him. Pierre bounced off the stone wall beside the door, hurting his shoulder. He dropped to his knees coughing and gasping for air.

Voices came from outside. Gabriel appeared at the door first, followed by Arianna.

'Stop them!' she said, 'before they kill each other.'

Gabriel smiled. 'No need. I think they're done.' He held a hand out to Pierre. 'What were you in your former human life, a punching bag?'

Pierre reluctantly took his hand and he was pulled up. 'It's been a while, Gabriel.'

'Too long. You must know we're doing a crap job of keeping order out there. For some reason your district wants *you*.' Gabriel poked Pierre in the chest. 'Can't think why.'

Pierre squared up to him, smiling. 'You want to fight me too?'

Gabriel waved his hand dismissively. 'As much as I'd love to go ten rounds with your arrogant self, how about you focus that newfound energy on something more positive?'

'Like what?' Pierre straightened his elder robes.

'Arianna has something she needs to tell you,' Gabriel said.

Pierre looked at her.

'Stephen's already told him that I met with Anton,' Arianna said.

'She feels responsible for what happened to Elise,' Gabriel explained, 'as if it was somehow her fault that she couldn't sense what Anton was thinking about doing. She feels as if she let everyone down, so she went to see Anton to try to pick up from where Elise left off—to separate Anton from the imposter inside his mind. And it's not just Arianna who's taking chances,' Gabriel continued. 'Others are risking their lives to hunt up there.' He pointed to the surface. 'Without you, they're lost. They won't take orders from me, a stranger, and they won't accept Margaux.'

'You're both doing a fine job,' Pierre said.

Gabriel grimaced. 'How would you know, shut up in here? It pains me to say it but you're a good leader—a self-centred, egotistical one perhaps—but a good one, even if you kept a huge secret from the rest of us. Elise did a great job of hiding your flaws from your district, but you have the potential to be a good leader without her.'

Pierre's eyes dropped to the ground.

'Don't waste your time feeling sorry for yourself,' Gabriel said softly. 'Your wife was passionate about this district. Why not honour her memory by showing the Indigenes what you're made of and that you're willing to fight for them?'

Pierre looked up and met Stephen's eyes.

'How about you start by changing the mood in here?' Gabriel shuddered. 'You could cut the tension with a knife.'

Stephen suddenly felt sick with regret. 'I'm sorry, Pierre,' he said. 'I should never have hit you. You have a right to grieve. What happened to Arianna made me see red, but I should have controlled it better.'

Pierre looked embarrassed. He sighed deeply. 'Yes, I'm sorry too. I shouldn't have allowed my selfishness to get in the way of what's best for this district. I imagined life going on as normal—Evolvers preparing for their next class, hunters planning the next kill, you in a lab figuring out how to keep one step ahead of the humans. But if I'm being honest, I had no idea what was going on, even when Elise was alive. She was the one who dealt with the emotions. I was always better at the practical things.'

'But you could have helped,' Stephen said. 'There was plenty to do.'

Pierre looked down at the floor. 'When I had a practical problem, I spoke to Leon about it, or if I had a personal one, I talked it over with Elise. But I can't bear to look Leon in the eye now, after what happened to his son. And Elise isn't around anymore. I feel a bit lost.' He sighed again. 'Then there was the other reason I stayed in here.'

Gabriel frowned. 'Which was?'

'Because of Anton. Every single day since Elise's death, I've had to resist the urge to kill him for taking her away from me.' Pierre's voice wavered and his eyes filled with tears. He swiped at them quickly with his thumb. 'Every single day, I would squeeze that lock in my hand until I could feel something give,'—he pointed at the door's baronium locking mechanism—'then when I could take no more pain, I would walk away and slam my fist into the wall, breaking every bone in my hand. By the time the bones had healed, I didn't feel quite so angry anymore.'

'What happened wasn't Anton's fault. He wasn't in control,' Stephen said.

'I know that, but Anton—the shell of him that exists now—is the only one available to blame. I know I shouldn't take it out on him.' Pierre slowly turned to Arianna. 'You said you had something to tell me, child. What is it?'

Arianna looked shyly at the floor.

Gabriel smiled. 'No need to stand on ceremony with us, Arianna,' he said encouragingly.

'Yes, child. Tell me what you know,' Pierre said quickly.

Arianna took a deep breath. 'Anton wants to see you.'

Pierre waved his hand at her. 'I've nothing to say to him,' he said crossly.

Gabriel shot him a look. 'Does Stephen need to go another round with you or are you going to keep an open mind here?'

'Yes, yes. I get the message,' Pierre said in exasperation. 'Please continue, Arianna.'

'It's about the other personality,' she went on, 'the one that's dominating Anton's mind.'

Pierre looked at Stephen. 'Have you also spoken with him? What have your visions predicted?'

Stephen shook his head. 'My envisioning ability isn't working properly yet. Serena is helping me with that.'

Pierre looked at Gabriel. 'What about you?

Have you spoken to Anton?'

'No, it's not me he wants to talk to,' Gabriel said.

'The other personality is asking for you specifically,' Arianna explained to Pierre.

Stephen stared at her. *Why didn't you tell me?*
*You didn't give me a chance.*

'So, he just wants an audience with an elder,' Pierre stated.

'No,' Arianna corrected him. '*Benedict* says he knew you in a former life.'

A deep silence fell among them while Pierre, clearly puzzled, looked around at everyone. Suddenly, his eyes widened and he gave a little gasp. 'Could it be?' Realising everyone was staring at him, he added, 'Bring me to him. I need to see him.'

# 8

*Earth*

Deighton arrived at the World Government headquarters in Washington D.C. for his meeting with the elite board members, his bodyguards shadowing him at a discreet distance. Just outside the main entrance, his stomach did a sudden somersault and he waited for the sensation to pass before pushing through the force field. The revolving door started to move as soon as he stepped inside it, and he removed his gel mask and shoved it in his pocket.

Once in the foyer, Deighton took a left past the reception desk and headed towards the turbo lift that connected with the levels below. He stepped in and told the lift which floor he wanted. His stomach did another flip. He hadn't felt so nervous since his interview for the CEO position many years ago, although why he'd been nervous about that he wasn't sure; he'd known he was the favoured candidate for the position, and Andrew Cantwell, the son of the Chair, had been coaching him.

Peter Cantwell had interviewed him and Deighton had been careful to play it the way Andrew had instructed him: with confidence and a hint of subservience. Deighton remembered how halfway through the speech that Andrew had written for him, he'd noticed the boredom in Cantwell Senior's eyes and so had decided to inject a little more of his personality into it.

'I can tell you're a busy man so I won't waste any more of your time,' Deighton had said.

Cantwell had looked at him, expecting Deighton to leave.

'I could sit here and bullshit you that I'm right for the job, and you'd probably hire me because I seem submissive and boring, but I'd rather tell you what I can do for you,' Deighton had said.

By that time he had Cantwell's full attention.

'The situation on Earth is not improving and I've been working on a few ideas to secure the survival of the human race. But first, we need to find a suitable planet to live on. We need to invest more money in space exploration.'

'Do you think we've got money to throw around?' Cantwell had tried to sound incensed, but Deighton could tell he was intrigued. 'What do you mean "the survival of the human race"? What's wrong with the planet we're on?'

'With all due respect, you know well enough that this planet won't support us another hundred years—too many people living here. What I have to suggest needs a new planet. The idea is only experimental at this stage but with the right investment, that could change.'

By the time Deighton's interview was over, Peter Cantwell was one of his keenest supporters, and so Deighton's master plan began to be put into action.

But Cantwell Senior was gone now and Deighton's control over the board members was slipping. He wasn't sure yet if Tanya Li, the new Chair, was an ally or someone who would oppose him.

The alteration programme—changing humans into a more perfect species that could thrive on Exilon 5—was not high on anyone's list of priorities; it was something that would happen a few years in the future. But it was of the utmost importance to Deighton. He had a serious health problem that only the alteration programme could solve, and now that he had a successful prototype of the perfect species in Serena, everything he wanted seemed to be within reach.

As he travelled in the lift, a tremor shuddered down his left arm and his breathing became laboured, timely reminders of what the alteration programme meant to him. At the age of almost one hundred and twenty, the lung replacements and genetic work he'd had done were beginning to deteriorate. He needed to disguise his health problems until he could solve them because he didn't want to give those board members who were opposed to him—about half the total board—a reason to get rid of him. He needed to remain CEO of the World Government in order to see his plans through to their completion.

A droning voice broke into his thoughts. 'Third floor, please exit,' said the lift. 'Third floor, please exit ... Third floor, please exit.'

The military personnel waiting outside the open lift doors were staring silently at him. He gave himself a little shake and stepped out, removing his overcoat and draping it neatly over his arm. He cleared his throat and walked towards the security station with his chin held high. He had to endure a set of humiliating security checks, a routine procedure that he himself had been responsible for implementing, then he made his way towards the board, his stomach doing one last somersault.

When he opened the door, eleven pairs of eyes turned to look at him and silence descended. Everyone was seated at the oval table in the middle of the room. Tanya Li, Chair of the World Government, sat at the far end of the table; there was a space for Deighton in the seat next to her. Daphne Gilchrist, CEO of the Earth Security Centre, was sitting at the opposite side of the table, her fingers tapping away on its polished surface. He wondered what they had all been talking about before he came in.

He nodded to the room and hung up his overcoat. He untied his red cravat and placed it in one pocket of his coat, then took off his black gloves and slapped them in his hand before putting them in the other pocket. He turned to face the board members and glanced round at them all. Then he made his way down the room to his seat.

Tanya looked at her DPad while she waited for Deighton to get settled, then looked up and called the meeting to order. The others ignored her and continued with their private conversations until she slammed her palm down on the glossy table.

'All right, let's get going,' she said loudly. 'I have somewhere to be.'

Deighton couldn't help but admire Tanya. As well as being the Chair, she also represented the Asian countries and was not afraid to speak her mind. She was no less argumentative than the late Peter Cantwell the Third, but Deighton found her much easier to deal with.

Now that she had everyone's attention, Tanya began. 'Before I ask you to give your reports for your territories, I'd like to apologise to everyone for not being a very good Chair over the past few months. As you know, my granddaughter had been very unwell and I've been expending much of my time and energy on her. But she lost her fight recently, a small mercy in some ways, and now that I've come to terms with her death, I'd like to reassure you that you have my full attention from now on. I thank you all for picking up the slack and for your patience. Now I intend to bring myself up to speed with what's been happening. So let's get down to business. Could we go round the table, please, with your updates, beginning with Europe.'

Before anyone could speak, Deighton cleared his throat. 'I'd like to say how sorry I am to hear about your granddaughter. I hope she didn't suffer at the end.' He tried to sound sincere. Privately, he thought the world was a better place with one less junkie on the streets, but he needed to keep Tanya on side.

She blinked slowly and nodded at him. 'Thank you, Charles.' She gestured at the European board member to begin.

In the space of thirty minutes they had worked their way around the table and the globe. The situation was the same in all the colder countries: temperatures were dropping below freezing; residents were struggling to keep warm in their apartments. Those without homes were being temporarily located to the emergency shelters. Arrangements were being made to relocate the population to southern Europe where the temperatures were still bearable.

The problem was that the warmer countries were full to capacity and could not take any more immigrants. They were unable to cope; there was a shortage of housing and the most densely populated areas had huge social problems; tension was building steadily and many areas had become aggressive and hostile.

Once the final report had been read out, Tanya thanked everyone and moved on to the next item on the agenda. 'Let's start with a recap on the status of the transfer programme. So far, we have'—she touched the screen of her DPad—'four hundred million people, give or take, living on Exilon 5. I think we all agree that the original transfer target of five billion, out of a total population of twenty billion, was too ambitious. We're running out of time and money to transfer the remaining population, and we don't yet have the facilities on Exilon 5 to cope with an increase of people. We've danced around having this discussion at each meeting, but I think we need to face facts and consider alternative options. If we abandon the population on Earth, what do we leave them with?'

'Do you mean passenger ships?' one of the board members asked.

'Yes, that's one thing,' Tanya said. 'Do we leave a ship behind as a link between the two planets, or do we cut Earth off—no ships, and no factories or materials to make ships—and let them fend for themselves?'

'Well, if we transfer all the best designers and engineers to Exilon 5, there won't be anyone left on Earth who knows how to make ships,' Deighton said. He gripped his DPad so tightly the edge was biting into his hand—the thought of transferring anything less than the best genetic stock irritated him.

'Good point,' Tanya said solemnly.

'So we all agree that transfers from Earth to Exilon 5 must remain low. But if we only leave the less skilled people behind on Earth, how will industries survive?' asked another board member—

someone who had invested heavily in business on Earth. 'We need to consider the effect on investment here. How will we continue to make money?'

Tanya, resting her elbows on the table and propping her chin on her hands, said nothing for a moment. Deighton thought she looked well for a one hundred-year-old, with her sharp eyes, shoulder-length, lustrous jet-black hair and trim figure. She looked at the other members as if she was peering over a pair of glasses. Perhaps at one time she had needed them.

'I'm aware of how much money some of you have tied up here,' she said eventually. 'But we don't have the funds to hold on to this planet and invest properly in Exilon 5. Perhaps Charles can explain better why it's important we consider the new planet.' She turned to Deighton. 'Why don't you give us an update on the recent change to the transfer selection process?'

Deighton gave her a courteous smile and cleared his throat. 'Thank you, Chair. Yes, the selection process was changed recently to prioritise strong genetic types to facilitate some additional testing we were doing on their code. We've had some success in testing certain genetic traits and the blonde-haired blue-eyed combination has thrown up some interesting results when mixed with second-generation Indigene code. We also now know that second-generation Indigenes have evolved considerably from their first-generation parents. So I've also ordered a more detailed study into the Indigenes' genetic code to see how that might be of benefit to us.'

'How detailed are we going with this study?' It was Gilchrist who had asked the question.

Deighton silently cursed her. He really hoped she wasn't going to be trouble, but he could see no point in lying to the group. 'I ordered our labs to study the differences between the original and the second-generation Indigene code, and then look at our own code to see if we could utilise any of their genetic material to enhance our bodies' designs and make us more suitable for life on Exilon 5. That is why we should consider investing in Exilon 5—there are better opportunities waiting for us and the planet is largely uninhabited. But I should point out that if we are to consider putting into action a programme to genetically alter humans to become what is effectively a new species, the number of people we've set to transfer to Exilon 5 is still too high. We should reduce the target by at least half.'

He looked at the faces around the room. It was no secret that the conservative board members who resisted radical change—the ones he thought of as pro-Earth—hated him. But now he was putting them in tight spot, for they wholeheartedly supported the idea of lower transfer numbers—it would mean that there would be enough people left behind on Earth to keep their investments ticking over. At the same, he was also alienating those ostensibly on his side. The liberal board members—those pro-Exilon 5 members who favoured the move to Exilon 5—had invested in the new planet and needed the promise of high transfer numbers to make their investments worthwhile.

Deighton's eyes lingered on Gilchrist. Her face was expressionless and unreadable; only her tapping fingers gave her away. As for those he knew to be liberal, he could see them shifting uncomfortably in their seats and frowning. That was not good. He needed them on his side. Deighton realised he had been silent for too long. 'I've also had the captured Indigene—Anton—and fitted him with a tracking device,' he added quickly. 'We've sent him back to Exilon 5, where we hope he'll lead us to their underground home.'

'Let's hope the time and money spent capturing just one pays off,' a conservative member said. 'We can't allow them to break through our defences again. We need to protect ourselves here and to protect our profits. So has the tracking device yielded results?'

'No, we haven't been able to pinpoint their location,' Tanya said. 'There's some kind of magnetic field around their districts that blocks signals in and out.' She cleared her throat. 'Charles, you spoke to Anton. You were present for some of the experiments. How evolved has the second generation become? Are they a threat to us?'

'They'll always be a threat,' Deighton snapped. 'They're more evolved than we ever could have designed them to be.'

One of the liberal members frowned. 'How evolved? We haven't seen the data from the labs yet. Can we turn their presence on Exilon 5 to our advantage somehow?'

'The Galway lab will be sending the data soon. They're still coming to terms with Dr Finnegan's death.' Deighton flashed his all-teeth smile. He had convinced the staff of the Galway Medical Facility to send him all the information they had on Anton and the test subjects, including Serena. But he didn't want the board to see the raw data; nor did he want them prying into the details of the experiments. 'What we do know so far is that the testing has thrown up some promising results. Since we're running out of money and resources, the wisest thing to do now would be to narrow our focus on the genetic types that show most promise and accelerate the alteration programme for them.'

Tanya shook her head. 'You know full well that genetic targeting was meant as a long-term project. We agreed that we needed time to gather as much data on genetic selection as we could so that we'd be ready to implement the alteration programme when our move to Exilon 5 became inevitable.'

Deighton became agitated. 'Yes, I'm aware of that, Chair. But what I'm saying is we have enough data *now*. We can initiate the alteration programme sooner, not years from now.'

Everyone in the room looked confused.

'Elaborate,' Tanya said.

'Well, I can't go into detail until the data from the labs has been analysed,' Deighton said, 'but in a nutshell, the alteration programme will give us three things: better immune systems, the ability to cope with any future changes to Exilon 5's atmosphere, and the ability to think laterally. With this alteration programme, the human race will be able to evolve further than the Indigenes. What I propose is replacing all the Indigenes with a newer, better race—with an altered version of us.'

There was silence for a moment. Then one of the conservative members piped up. 'So why not also alter the people on Earth, the ones who won't be transferred? They probably need to be changed more than the people on the new planet.' His supporters nodded at this suggestion.

Deighton could feel his frustration building. 'Because even after we're gone, the people on Earth will cope as they have always done, but those travelling to Exilon 5 will need extra resources in order to thrive. Anton has demonstrated that the Indigenes can't be trusted. By altering transferees that we've handpicked, we'd be fortifying them to withstand attacks by the Indigenes ... And no, before you suggest it, we can't relocate the Indigenes to Earth—it would be unsafe for the humans still here. We have thirty years of living proof that both species can't live in harmony.'

Silence descended again. Deighton could almost hear their brains processing what he had just said. The board member for Europe shifted in his chair and the squeak of the chair leg on the hardwood floor echoed round the grey-walled meeting room. Gilchrist began tapping her nail on the table again.

Tanya turned and spoke to Deighton. 'You should know that Dr Finnegan notified me about the extra tests you asked to be carried out on a new human subject, Susan Bouchard. It seems you also held her at the facility longer than the agreed time before moving her on.'

Deighton said nothing. He smiled while trying to work out a response. How much should he tell them about Serena?

'Before you offer me an explanation,' Tanya said, holding up a finger, 'I should tell you that I know where your newest creation, Serena, is. One of Dr Finnegan's assistants called me shortly after the doctor's death. She mentioned that Serena and Anton had been transferred to the ESC before being sent to Exilon 5. She assumed I knew.'

Gilchrist stopped tapping her nail on the table.

Deighton coughed, then gave Tanya a weak smile. He wondered what else the lab assistant had told her. He could feel his hands beginning to shake again.

Tanya looked over her imaginary pair of glasses as she continued. 'We all know that the Indigenes evolve faster in life-threatening situations, so we agreed that after the study of Anton's genetic code was complete, he would be sent back to Exilon 5 with no memory of his experiences here. But the World Government did not sanction Serena's transfer. She is far too valuable to us. We need to study her.'

Deighton was relieved that Tanya hadn't mentioned Anton's personality swap, nor the bomb. He exhaled quietly.

He finally found his voice: 'Forgive me, Chair. I saw an opportunity to gather an extraordinary amount of data on the Indigenes that would help speed up the alteration programme by years, so I held on to Anton a little longer than protocol allows. Yes, Serena is valuable—she represents the next step in human development—but I decided to send her to Exilon 5 as a test to see if the Indigenes accepted her. If they do, it's further proof that they can't be trusted—Serena is a murderer and we can't trust a race that is willing to harbour criminals.'

Deighton desperately needed to conceal how important Serena was to him personally. If she had stayed on Earth, she would probably have been killed once she had been rigorously tested. He hoped the DNA sample he had taken from her would be enough to sort out his medical problem, but if not, it was of paramount importance to him that Serena remain alive so he could have her tested further.

Tanya sat back in her chair and rubbed her chin thoughtfully. 'What are everybody else's thoughts on this?' she asked. 'Daphne, I'm particularly interested to hear your opinion, seeing as you were privy to the plan to send Serena to Exilon 5.'

Daphne leaned forward in her chair and looked directly at Deighton. 'What was the real reason for sending Serena to Exilon 5, Charles?'

Deighton locked his watery eyes on her. He knew what she was doing. She was saving her own skin by implying that she'd been tricked into helping him send Serena away. He watched her silently for a moment, smiling at her. 'She is what we can become, not in the next ten or twenty years, but in a matter of weeks, months—days even. And what better environment to study her in than when she is living among the Indigenes. Serena's genetic code is the magic formula we need in order to change into better super humans and ensure our long-term survival.'

'And did the human subject agree to your tests?' Gilchrist asked.

'Yes,' Deighton lied. 'Susan Bouchard was a lab technician carrying out genetic testing for us in the lab at Toronto. She was fully aware of the work we were doing and was an advocate for the alteration programme.'

Everyone was frowning at him.

'Oh come on—who in this room wouldn't jump at the chance to live longer, healthier lives—to live on Exilon 5 in a near indestructible skin?' he said, half laughing.

'I can't help asking the same question as Daphne,' a liberal member said. 'Is there another reason you sent Serena to Exilon 5?'

Deighton stared at the man and imagined wrapping his hands around his neck, gently squeezing the life out of him.

'Charles?' Tanya prompted when Deighton didn't respond. He snapped out of his daydream.

'There most certainly is not,' he said, trying to sound offended.

Gilchrist tapped a nail on the table and cleared her throat. Everyone turned to look at her. 'Well, I have reason to believe that Susan Bouchard did not volunteer for the trials.'

Deighton squinted at her. What was she playing at? 'So?' he said out loud. 'We take people all the time. We've been doing it since we created the first hybrid. If we hadn't done it we wouldn't have got the best genetic match. What's your point?'

Gilchrist pursed her lips and clasped her hands together. 'I'm just wondering why we don't just ask people if they want to help, instead of taking them by force?'

Tanya leaned forward in her chair. 'You mean ask people if they want to be part of the alteration programme to become another species? Is it a wise move to reveal our plans to the population?'

Deighton banged his fist down on the table. 'You've been against my vision for this programme from the start, Daphne!'

'Settle down, Charles,' Tanya said calmly. 'Nobody's dismissing the idea of the alteration programme outright, but we all need a little time to think about accelerating it. I think we should put it to a vote, but not before we learn some more about Serena.' Tanya looked at everyone around the table. 'She killed Dr Finnegan, is that right? What happened that night?' she asked Deighton.

Deighton wanted them to hear his version before they read the formal report that would lack emotion and excitement. 'It was truly terrifying. It all happened so fast. I was standing beside her. The doctor had just released Serena's wrist clamps'—he shook his head, as if appalled by it all—'when suddenly Serena attacked her.' He lowered his eyes, then looked up at the board members, his eyes filled with tears.

Most of them seemed taken in by his dramatics—even Gilchrist. One of them gave a puff of disbelief.

'Did you arrange for a food basket to be sent to the doctor's family?' Tanya asked.

'She has none.' Truth be told, Deighton didn't know much about Caroline Finnegan. Even if he had, it wouldn't have occurred to him to send anything to the family.

Tanya waved her hand. 'Send it to one of the orphanages then. We should be seen to be doing something good in the doctor's name. Now, I suggest we take a vote on accelerating the alteration programme.'

But Deighton wasn't confident that he'd put his case strongly enough. 'Before we take a vote, may I explain what I propose?' He looked at Tanya.

She nodded and sighed.

'The Indigenes can't be trusted,' he began. 'By nature, they're killers. But with Serena, I have shown that with the right human host and code from a second-generation Indigene, we can produce a remarkable alpha species. Aggression in future generations need not be an issue—we can simply alter that area of the brain. What I propose is a two-stage plan of action. First, we find out where the Indigenes live on Exilon 5 and drive them out like the vermin they are. We should hold on to a few of the second-generation Indigenes, for testing purposes of course. Then we draw up a list of the strongest genetic types from the humans we've tested so far and put the alteration programme into action.'

'Have you forgotten that these "vermin", as you like to call them, were once human like us?' Tanya whispered. She sighed heavily, then spoke normally. 'How do you propose we action the first part of your suggestion—to locate the Indigenes?'

Deighton reminded them about the tracer and recording device that he'd had implanted in Anton's brain. 'Once we figure out how to penetrate the electromagnetic field that's blocking the signals we'll be able to learn so much more about their underground fortress.'

He looked around at the board members; some were nodding, others were shaking their heads. He could smell success. If he could win the board round, all he had to do was make sure that he was in good enough health to make the genetic selection.

'I'm not comfortable with putting the lives of an entire race to a vote on the strength of what I've read in a report,' Tanya said. 'I need to see for myself how dangerous they really are. We should also consider if there are investment opportunities to be had with the Indigenes. There's only one way we can determine that—we need to travel to Exilon 5 to speak to their leaders.'

Deighton's optimism fell like a flat balloon. 'But Chair, what good would come of that? We already know they're dangerous.'

'If I'm going to condemn a race to its death, I want to be damn sure they're of no further use to us. Let's have no more discussion and vote on it. All those in favour of meeting the Indigenes face to face, raise your hand.'

Seven hands shot up in the air; Gilchrist's was one of them.

'Seven to four, and I vote in favour—well, that settles it. We'll meet with the Indigenes.' Tanya switched her DPad off. 'I think we should bring Bill Taggart in on this,' she added.

'Taggart? Why?' Deighton asked, alarmed.

'Because he's the only one who got remotely close to them without them seeing him as a threat. He could prove useful in negotiations.' Tanya slapped her hand down hard on the table. 'We'll vote on the Indigenes' fate, and plans to accelerate the alteration programme after we've met the Indigenes. Meeting adjourned.'

Deighton leaned back in his chair. It wasn't how he had expected the meeting to go, but it was better than an outright dismissal. He had work to do between now and their next board meeting. For a start, he needed to change the report on Serena before the board members saw it, to make sure it mentioned her killing the doctor. He also needed to get to work on the board members themselves. He might be able to win the liberal members round—those in favour of Exilon 5—by emphasising a more advanced human race, but he was convinced the conservative pro-Earth members would always oppose any idea of change. All he needed was a majority, and he was sure Tanya Li would vote his way.

But first, he needed to deal with Gilchrist.

# 9

*Exilon 5*

'Slow down,' Stephen called after Pierre as he hurried through the tunnel to Anton's quarters. 'We need to talk about a strategy. You can't just barge in there. I've seen what he's capable of.'

Gabriel had convinced Pierre to sleep on the idea of going to see Anton, and that morning, Stephen had arrived at the Council Chambers with Gabriel and Arianna ready to talk it through with him some more. But Pierre had swept out of the Chambers past them, walking briskly ahead and refusing to listen to anyone. They all followed him, doing their best to keep up.

'There's nothing to discuss, Stephen,' Pierre said. 'Arianna, what did Anton say exactly? Tell me again what information was supposed to jog my memory.'

She ran to catch up. 'He mentioned a Benedictine University.'

Just outside the residential area the tunnel became wider. Four Indigenes stood guard across the tunnel, blocking the way to Anton's quarters beyond. Stephen was pleased to see that security had been increased since Arianna's visit.

'Let us past,' Pierre said to the guards, showing no intention of stopping.

The female halted him with her arm. 'I'm sorry. We're under strict instructions not to let anyone in here.'

'But you let me in,' Arianna reminded them.

'That was a mistake. No one else is allowed in.'

'Well, who gave you those instructions?' Pierre said angrily.

The female guard looked at Gabriel.

'Gabriel?' Pierre growled.

Gabriel shrugged. 'Once Arianna told me what had happened when she visited Anton, I ordered tighter security.'

Pierre rolled his eyes. 'Well, get rid of it now.'

Gabriel nodded to the guards and they parted to allow them all to pass through.

The residential area was circular, with two tunnels running into it, one going north and the other south. Guards stood at both tunnel entrances, enough to outnumber Anton, should he escape, and to keep others at bay. The single-occupancy living quarters were arranged on two levels around the residential area, with stone steps in the middle for access to the upper tier. To Stephen, the area looked smaller than it had done when he'd seen it through Arianna's eyes. The roof was low in comparison to his own residential area and it felt closed in to him.

'What's he doing here?' Pierre asked, pointing to a lone Indigene waiting outside Anton's door.

'I told them to let him through if he came by today,' Gabriel said.

Stephen nodded at Leon, but Leon didn't move. His eyes were blazing and firmly fixed on Pierre.

'Why are you here?' Pierre demanded of him angrily.

'I came to see my son. I heard you were

making plans to go in there. They haven't let me see him since Arianna's visit.'

'Well, you've no business being here right now,' Pierre said.

Leon half smiled. 'My only son is none of my business?'

Pierre waved his hand dismissively. 'You know what I mean.'

Gabriel stepped forward. 'Leon, this situation is difficult for everyone to take in. Tell me, how are you coping?'

Leon lowered his eyes. 'Not well. My son is not himself and I'm—' He shook his head.

'—struggling with being treated as an outcast?' Gabriel said, glancing at Pierre.

Leon looked up and nodded.

Gabriel turned to Pierre. 'Don't you think it's time you two buried the hatchet? Preferably not in each other's backs. Can't you see he needs our support? Anton does too.'

Pierre turned his head away. 'I've tried, but I can't,' he said firmly.

'Would it help if you punched him the way you did Stephen?' Gabriel asked.

Leon's eyes widened.

'No, no, no. I—I wouldn't want to do that,' Pierre said.

'Then what do you want to do?' Gabriel shouted. 'Do I have to emasculate you in front of your charges to get you to see sense?'

'Stop it. This is *my* district. You're not the elder here.'

'Well then, forgive him. It's not his fault. He didn't kill your wife.'

'Don't you think I know that? I'm not going to

punch him. It's not appropriate behaviour for an elder.'

'Screw that, Pierre!' Gabriel said through clenched teeth. 'We're on our own fighting for our very survival. What's the harm in venting now and again? You've been passive for far too long. I say it's time for a little action.'

'I told you no!' Pierre bellowed, visibly shaking.

'I know you're uncomfortable with me being in charge, so how about you reclaim your district? Start with Leon. Forgive him.'

Pierre's face darkened as he let out a wild sound. He shot past Gabriel, fist raised, and punched Leon square in the face. Leon saw it coming and had braced himself, but even so, the impact sent him reeling backwards. He hit the wall beside Anton's door, just missing the two guards that were standing there. Clear fluid oozed from a gash on his face where a jagged piece of his jawbone was protruding. The wound was already trying to heal but the displaced bone prevented it. The guards took a few steps towards Pierre but Gabriel held up his hand, signalling them to remain where they were.

Stephen and Arianna glanced at each other. Perhaps it took the death of Elise for Pierre to show his true colours.

Pierre, panting, walked over to where Leon lay on the floor and reached out his hand. 'We'll get Anton back,' was all he said as he pulled Leon to his feet. The old Pierre would have rushed to explain his outburst. But there were to be no apologies that day.

Leon touched the side of his face and winced as he gently pushed the protruding bone back into place. He held it there for a minute or so until the bone had begun to knit and the open wound had healed.

'Well, now that the fun and games are over, you need to get in there,' Gabriel said. 'Find out who this other personality is and what the hell it wants.'

Pierre nodded and went to the door.

Stephen's stomach flipped. 'No! I can't let you go in alone. It's too dangerous.'

Leon stepped forward. 'If anyone's going in it's me.'

'No.' Stephen placed his hand on Leon's chest. 'Whoever's in there right now is not Anton. It needs to be Pierre and I need to go too.'

'Why?' Leon looked annoyed.

'Because he asked for Pierre.'

'But why you?'

'Because I've already had a glimpse of the other personality—Arianna showed me—so I know what to expect. I promise I'll do everything I can to protect both Pierre and Anton.'

'I don't need a babysitter,' Pierre said.

'I'm coming in whether you like it or not,' Stephen said firmly.

Pierre shrugged.

Stephen went first, pushed the door open a crack and peered inside the room. Anton was sitting in the metal chair Stephen had seen in Arianna's visualisation. He and Pierre went inside and closed the door behind them. Gabriel, Arianna and Leon waited with the two guards outside.

Inside the room, a strong, acidic smell hit Stephen. He recognised it instantly. They inched forward, the smell of urine strengthening. Stephen could see the wet patch on the mattress, which had been shoved up into one corner. On the other side of the room, the metal chair was positioned in front of a mirror that hung on the wall. Anton was staring at his own reflection.

Anton didn't move or acknowledge their presence. Stephen could sense from his relaxed posture that it was the other personality, the one Arianna had shown him, who was sitting there.

'For so long, I've wondered what it would feel like to be one of you,' Anton said without looking up and plucking at the tight skin around his eyes. 'Now that I'm an Indigene, I'm trying to figure out what all the fuss is about.' He twisted round in the chair until he could see Pierre. 'I see now why you don't use mirrors.'

'Well, if you don't like it here, you're free to leave,' Pierre said.

'Why haven't I seen you around much? Was it because I killed your wife?'

Pierre balled up his fists. 'What are you doing here?' he said from between clenched teeth.

Anton smiled widely. 'So you *do* remember me?' He stood up slowly and turned towards Pierre, his feet apart and arms hanging loosely by his side.

It was a posture both Stephen and Pierre immediately recognised.

'I see not all of Anton is lost,' Pierre said, smiling.

'Yeah, a few annoying habits creep in now and again.' The prisoner stood up straight and folded his arms. 'And what is it with this meditation crap? It's all he thinks about.'

'You're not welcome here,' Pierre said in a low voice. 'Let me speak to Anton.'

Stephen was puzzled by the familiarity between the pair.

'Anton's not here. I'm *Benedict*. You can talk

to me—your old pal. I suppose it's safe to assume dear old wifey unlocked your memories. Otherwise, you wouldn't be here.'

'You're not the real Charles Deighton,' Pierre said calmly. 'You're just an imprint of a personality that believes he was reincarnated—or capable of possession, or some other highly illogical idea.'

Stephen called out: 'Anton, can you hear me?'

*Benedict*'s arms snapped to his side. He narrowed his eyes at Stephen. 'He's not home right now. Would you like to leave a message?' He tried to fold his arms again, but they wouldn't cooperate.

Stephen was relieved. Anton was still in there and trying to fight back. 'Hold on, Anton. We're going to get you out,' he called out.

*Benedict* struggled to fold his arms again and muttered to himself: 'Stop it! I'm talking now.' All of a sudden, his arms folded with ease and he gave Pierre and Stephen a big smile.

'So, did you like the clue I left for you?' *Benedict* asked. 'I knew you'd get the reference if you remembered enough of your past.'

'The Benedictine University in Illinois was where my human self first met Charles Deighton,' Pierre explained to Stephen.

*Benedict* took a step forward and squinted at Pierre. 'In front of me I see an elderly man with papery, translucent skin, but I also see someone else—your former self. I saw it when you made fists earlier. You can hide behind the serenity in this district, in that body, but I know the real you, the person who would screw people over to get what you wanted.'

'Where's Anton? Let me speak to him,' Pierre persisted.

'Don't worry. He's watching, as he always is. Do you remember the board meetings, Pierre?' *Benedict* said, quickly changing the subject. 'Dull. So full of sanctimonious pricks pretending to have the world's best interests at heart, but then secretly plotting behind everyone's backs to further their own cause.' He shrugged. 'I guess not much has changed.'

'Board meetings?' Pierre frowned. 'I don't remember any board meetings.'

'Sure you do.' *Benedict* smiled briefly, then paused. 'At least, I think you do.'

'Perhaps you're confusing your memories with Anton's,' Pierre suggested.

*Benedict* made a face. 'How would Anton know about board meetings, for fuck's sake?' He scowled, then pointed an unsteady finger at Pierre. 'No, I'm positive it was you.'

'He was on Earth for a long time,' Pierre went on. 'Perhaps he overheard a conversation you had with someone.'

*Benedict*'s arms snapped to his sides again. Stephen nodded at Pierre. *Keep going.*

'You're mixing your memories up with Anton's,' Pierre said. 'And look at how he controls your posture. Cognitively, we're stronger than you. You can't win ... Charles.'

*Benedict* squeezed his eyes shut and tried to gain control of his arms. Pierre and Stephen could only watch as the two personalities fought for dominance, *Benedict* smacking his hand repeatedly against his head and shouting, 'Get out of there! Stop screwing with me.'

When he seemed to have run out of energy, Pierre and Stephen lunged at him, grabbing an arm each and restraining him.

'Don't make this more difficult than it is,' Pierre said.

*Benedict* glared at him. 'You're the one who's hurt me, you piece of shit! Look what I've been forced to do—to live in someone else's mind and body just so I can get close to you. It's bullshit.'

Pierre shook his head. 'You don't exist. You're not the real Charles Deighton. You're using Anton, an innocent Indigene, to seek revenge on Deighton's behalf. You have no real control over Anton.'

Not for the first time Stephen wondered who Charles Deighton was, but he could ask about that later. He was worried that time was running out for Anton. He closed his eyes and tried to get through to him.

'What's he doing?' he heard *Benedict* say.

Stephen pushed into his friend's mind. He could see a bright spot behind the murky colours. But the murkiness was moving towards him now and growing, like it had been doing in his visions. He panicked and got out of there as quickly as he could. Opening his eyes, he saw Pierre looking at him, concerned.

'We're done here,' Pierre said and bundled Stephen out of the room.

Outside and away from *Benedict*, Stephen's head felt the same—heavy, constricted.

'Well?' Gabriel said.

Pierre ignored him. He was still holding on to Stephen. 'Are you okay?' he asked him.

Stephen tried to focus on his face, but it faded in and out. It was coming for him, he could feel it. One of his visions was on the way and he had absolutely no control over it. His head began to ache and he used his hands in vain to shield himself from its force. It felt as if he was being possessed from the inside, like Anton was.

Then it hit him and everything went dark.

# 10

*Earth*

Hundreds of people shuffled stiffly in the cold air of Nottingham city, hunched over and battling against the inclement Northern Hemisphere weather. The chill damp air of the United Kingdom was almost intolerable and it never let up.

Bill Taggart checked the time as he emerged from the bullet train station close to the small docking station in Nottingham. He had come to meet Laura, arriving from Sydney. He was out of breath by the time he reached the docking station entrance. He was out of shape and he knew it. At least he had stopped taking the Actigen, something that had given him the worst heart palpitations he'd ever experienced.

Suddenly, a flood of people emerged from the station—a sign that a spacecraft had just arrived—and collectively braced themselves as they swapped the temperature-controlled environment of the docking station for the sharp air outside. Bill craned his neck, his eyes searching among the crowd. He didn't recognise her at first with her gel mask stuck to her face and her hair spilling over her shoulders. But he recognised the heavy overcoat and her body language. He drew in a sharp breath. His eyes wandered over the rest of her, getting glimpses of a red floral dress under the coat and noticing her heavy black boots.

That made him smile. He waved once.

'What?' she said as she approached him. She looked down at her clothes for spillages or tears and ran her fingers across the parts of her face that were not covered by the gel mask like a blind person reading Braille. 'What is it, Bill?' When all she got from him was a smile, she continued. 'Ah, come on. Shit. Tell me.'

'Nothing's wrong. You look nice, that's all.'

She relaxed. 'It's my mother's dress, actually.' Bill raised his eyebrows in surprise. 'I know—I didn't think she owned anything this nice.' She held the skirt of the dress out, examining the floral pattern.

'Not sure about the boots though,' Bill said.

Laura stamped her feet on the ground. 'I couldn't decide if I should dress up or keep warm, so this outfit is a compromise. I'm happy if my feet are warm.'

'You do remember we're supposed to be on a pretend date?'

Laura folded her arms and tried to look cross, but the corners of her mouth twitched. 'I don't care. It's this or nothing. I'm not about to freeze my ass off, even for you!'

Bill smiled again and straightened his tie. He looked down at his own dishevelled appearance and suddenly wished he'd gone home and changed out of his work clothes first. He wrapped his overcoat more tightly around him.

'Do you want to go home and change first?' Laura asked as if she had just read his mind.

Bill looked down at himself once more, suddenly unsure. 'Should I?'

'Don't worry about it. You look fine,' she said with a wave of her hand. 'As you said, this is just a pretend date. Besides, I don't have much time.'

They hailed a self-drive taxi to take them to Cantaloupe, the real food restaurant in the heart of Nottingham. The journey through the congested streets was slow but it gave them time to catch up.

'I'm sorry I couldn't come to Sydney,' Bill said, 'but things are a little strange at work.'

'Yeah, that's funny. Things are a little weird for me, too,' Laura said, combing through her blonde hair with her fingers. 'By the way, the woman from booth sixteen is back.'

'Yeah I heard about that—about her family. All accidental deaths, or so they say.' Bill caught the scent of Laura's perfume. He hoped his own smell wasn't as noticeable. 'Now that they have me back working full weeks, I've noticed a few things have changed in my absence.'

'Like what?'

The taxi pulled up at the kerb and Bill scanned his thumb on the small screen that presented itself; the fare would be charged to his account. They climbed out of the taxi and Bill held the restaurant door open for her.

'Like Simon Shaw, my supervisor at ITF, for one,' he continued. 'He's different—acting really strangely.'

Once inside the restaurant they took off their gel masks.

'Hmmmm,' said Laura.

'What's wrong?'

'I feel a bit overdressed for this place,' she said.

Bill looked around at the other diners, most of them casually dressed. 'You're fine. Don't worry. You look great. Keep going right to the back.'

Laura headed off in the direction Bill pointed to

and he watched her as she tentatively removed her coat for the waitress. She slid into the seat of the private booth he had reserved for them. He sat down opposite her. For the first time, he noticed the effort she had made to look the part: she had curls in her hair, blusher on her cheeks and some gloss on her lips.

'Stop staring at me like that,' she said and slapped him on the arm. 'You're making me uncomfortable.'

'Look, we're supposed to be a couple. I can stare at you if I want,' he said half smiling. They had agreed that pretending to be in a relationship was the best way to explain to the World Government spies why they were spending so much time together.

Laura took the digital menu card from the waitress and thanked her. She smoothed down the crisp white linen tablecloth and straightened the silver cutlery.

'Gosh, it's all so old-fashioned,' she said beaming. 'I could get used to this—none of those replication machines deciding what the food should taste like. Real waiting staff and real chefs?'

Bill smiled. 'Wait until you try the food.'

'God, my mouth's watering already.' She scanned her menu, then looked up at him. 'What are you going to have?'

'What I always have—steak and chips.'

Laura pursed her lips and ran her finger down the menu again. 'I dunno. I'm not really in the mood for a hunk of beef.' She twirled a long strand of hair around her finger. 'Maybe some salmon, or oysters'—she dropped the menu and clapped her hands—'or both!'

Bill held his hands up. 'I know this is a pretend

date and I promised to treat you, but your choices are chicken or steak. That's as far as the budget will stretch. If I put this on my work tab, I'll have a string of questions to answer.'

Laura pouted, then tapped a finger on her lower lip. He couldn't take his eyes off her. And she seemed to be completely unaware that the other men in the restaurant were looking at her too, secretly glancing in her direction.

She sighed contentedly. 'Chicken it is,' she finally announced.

Ten minutes later the food arrived—Bill's steak and chips and Laura's chicken provençale with mashed potatoes and baby vegetables. Bill tucked in straight away and was eager to see what Laura's reaction would be. He tried to remember his own reaction when he'd first tasted proper food, but he had eaten too often at Cantaloupe now and the novelty of it was a far distant memory.

Laura cut a piece from the chicken covered in a thick tomato sauce and brought it up to her lips. She inhaled deeply through her nose, savouring the smell of the delicious food, and then put the piece in her mouth.

'Oh, my God! Oh my God! This is delicious,' she said through a mouthful of chicken. 'My taste buds are singing!'

She took another bite, then scooped some mashed potato on her fork. 'Mmmmmm. So creamy.'

Bill stopped eating to watch her.

She nibbled at the baby vegetables. 'They're so sweet and crisp, not like the insipid ones you get from the replicator.' A single tear was streaming down her face. She didn't seem to notice it. 'Look what I've been missing! I've been locking myself away in my job, waiting for some stupid opportunity to transfer to Exilon 5 when I could have been enjoying what's right in front of me.'

After the meal, the waitress handed them the menu cards for dessert.

Laura looked hopeful. 'Can I?'

Bill nodded. 'Aye—within reason, of course.'

Laura ordered a slice of chocolate cake and Bill ordered a coffee. He sipped the black liquid while he watched her face contort in pleasure.

'Oh … my … God! This … is … so … delicious!' She went from using a fork to using her fingers, just stopping short of shoving the entire cake into her mouth.

'Easy there, lass. You'll make yourself sick,' he warned her.

Laura made a noise—something in between a laugh and a reprimand. When she'd finished eating, she licked each finger clean and wiped them on her napkin.

'Sorry. I couldn't stop myself. I don't know what got into me,' she said, clearly bemused by her own behaviour.

'Don't worry about it. So, do you think the couple sitting in the corner of the restaurant got a good show?' He nodded to his right.

While dabbing her mouth with the napkin, Laura looked over at them. The woman was reading a menu card, and the man was looking around him as if he was bored.

'Well, they've been following us since we came back to Earth,' Bill said. 'I'd say they got a good eyeful.'

Laura coughed for a few moments. 'Some crumbs went down the wrong way,' she said, her hand on her chest. She took a sip of water.

Bill reached across the table. 'Give me your hand.'

Laura hesitated at first, then slid her hand across to him.

He caressed the back of her hand with his thumb. 'Now, tell me about the woman from booth sixteen. Has she said anything to you?'

Laura looked deeply into his eyes. 'Not a thing. She's very different now to the way she was at the beginning.' As she spoke, she grabbed her dessert fork with her free hand and waved it around, sending crumbs of chocolate cake flying off around her.

'How is she different?'

'Well, she's afraid to speak to anyone. She won't acknowledge me at all. She's a shadow of her former self.'

'But probably no different to how she was before with you. She barely spoke to you then, either.'

Laura dropped the fork noisily on to her plate. The couple in the corner looked over at them.

'Bill, there's something strange going on. Trust me,' she said.

He rubbed the top of her hand with his thumb. 'Try not to attract so much attention,' he whispered at her. 'All I'm saying is everything seems a bit too … calm—as if nothing ever happened. Booth Sixteen comes back and acts as if she never gave you the file. Not a surprise in itself but if the World Government knows about her activities, surely Gilchrist would have called you in by now. They're going to great lengths to leave you alone.'

Laura promptly pulled her hand out from under his. Her eyes narrowed. 'That's what I thought. We're getting away with too much.' She stroked her chin thoughtfully, pausing briefly to cough again. She took a couple of large gulps of water. 'Are you suggesting what I think you are?'

'Why not? We've covered everything else. It's just as I said on the flight home—we must be of some use to them.'

'But that doesn't make sense. If we're so valuable, why aren't they hassling us even more?'

Bill glanced at the couple sitting by the window. 'I don't know.'

Laura's eyes widened. 'Do you think they know about our trip to ... you know where?' she whispered.

Bill shrugged. 'There's only one man who can confirm that.'

'Who?'

'Simon Shaw.'

Laura tried to keep up with Bill's long strides as they walked back to his private apartment in Nottingham. She had offered to pay for a taxi but Bill couldn't bear the thought of another slow and arduous journey through the city. Besides, his apartment was only a couple of miles from the restaurant.

'Do you really think Simon will help?' she asked him.

Bill stopped suddenly and leaned against the wall, pulling Laura in close to him. Over her shoulder, he watched the couple that had followed them from the restaurant.

'I don't know. I've never asked him outright for help before,' he whispered in her ear. 'Simon works for Deighton, who works for those poisonous elite board members, so that makes him just like them.'

'I hate to be the one to point out the obvious, but so do you.'

Bill smiled. 'Okay, I'll give you that one.' He pushed her away gently and grabbed her hand.

'I'm not sure why they're bothering,' Laura said, nodding behind her to the couple that were following them. 'They probably already know where you live.'

'Because they're under orders to follow us, that's why. There's no proof that they know about my private apartment—I've been careful—so let's string them along anyway.'

They zigzagged their way back to Bill's apartment through the backstreets; close to his apartment they waited in the deep shadows for the couple to pass, then they walked in the opposite direction. He let go of her hand.

'You know, this reminds me of that time I followed you in Sydney, when all this started,' Laura said, a little out of breath. 'Same pace, too. You almost lost me that day. Now that you're revealing your tactics to me, I'll always be one step ahead of you.'

Back in his apartment, Bill held a finger up to Laura as he shut the door. He retrieved the sound disruptor from under the loose floorboard and connected it to the Light Box. 'Okay, we can talk now,' he said, after taking a deep breath.

Laura had picked up the glass flower ornament from his mantelpiece and was turning it round in her hand. 'This looks familiar,' she said.

Bill went over to her. 'It was from Isla's ceremony. I wanted a better reminder of her than the useless trinkets in this apartment.' He caught the scent of her hair and moved away. She had really made an effort for their pretend date and there he was in his sweaty work clothes.

'Do you want something to drink?'

'Have to make it look authentic, I guess,' Laura said shrugging. 'Water's fine. No—I'll have wine. I *mean* water.'

'Which is it to be?' Bill asked, looking at her closely.

'Actually, I'm more hungry than thirsty.' She started coughing again as she sat down on the sofa.

He left and returned with a glass of water.

She looked up at him. 'No food?'

'Where did the cough come from?' Bill asked, frowning. He sat on the arm of the sofa at the opposite end from Laura, one foot up on the seat cushion.

The mere mention of the word seemed to set her off again. Eventually, after taking a sip of water, she said, 'I've had it since we came home from Exilon 5. It's not as bad as it was. It seems to be easing off.'

'And how's the Seasonal Affective Disorder?'

'I haven't thought about it once, so I can only assume the treatment worked.' Laura coughed again.

'Any side effects from what Stephen gave you?'

She shook her head and took another sip of water. 'Not that I know of.'

Bill leaned forward, resting an arm on his raised knee. 'If that cough gets worse, you've got to tell me. We don't know anything about what Stephen used to treat you with.'

'I will,' Laura said, getting up and standing in

front of him. She playfully grabbed the back of his neck. 'So do you have any food or do I have to go hunting for it myself?'

'What are you doing?' he said, flinching away from her.

She snatched back her hand and walked off. 'Nothing. Just asking a question, that's all,' she said casually.

He eyed her curiously. First the cough, then the excessive hunger—and now the flirting. It was all out of character for her—not that he was entirely complaining.

Laura sat down again. 'Look, I don't think it's a good idea that you blurt anything out to Shaw until you know whose side he's on,' she said. 'Yes, he might have something important to tell us. Then again, he might run to Deighton as soon as you open your mouth. I think you should wait before you talk to him.'

'Maybe you're right,' he said. When Laura's expression changed he added. 'What?'

'Have you ever tried profiling him?'

'Not in any deliberate way. I mean, I notice his body language and all that, but I haven't given it much thought.'

'Well, maybe you need to study him a bit more and put some of that training of yours to good use,' she said.

He nodded. 'Aye, I might just do that.'

'When will you see him next?'

'At work tomorrow—at the briefing that they failed to invite me to … won't *he* be surprised when I show up, unannounced,' he added, smiling.

# 11

*Exilon 5*

Stephen vice gripped the sides of his head as the vision retreated into the background. He tried to keep still as he slowly regained consciousness. He was lying on the cold stone floor where he had collapsed outside Anton's door and had Pierre, Gabriel, Leon and Arianna gathered around him. He heard scuffling noises in the distance, then Serena's and Margaux's voices as they argued with the guards.

'Let them pass,' Gabriel said sharply.

Stephen closed his eyes and could hear the sound of feet running towards him. When he opened his eyes again, Serena was reaching for his hand and looking very concerned.

'Help me carry him to one of the empty living quarters,' Pierre said glancing at the guards. 'There are too many distractions here.'

Stephen felt two sets of strong arms lift and carry him to one of the unused rooms where he was placed gently on the floor.

Gabriel turned to Margaux. 'I thought I left you back at our private quarters.'

'I wanted to meet *her*,' Margaux said, nodding towards Serena.

Gabriel looked Serena up and down, but said nothing. Stephen noticed that Margaux and Gabriel, despite being the elders of District Eight, where Serena claimed to have come from, didn't know her. He tried to get up, but Pierre pushed him back down. Black spots danced in front of him. Soon the auras of those around him became clearer and more colourful. He blinked and tried to sit up, but a stabbing pain behind his eyes made him wince.

'Just be patient. You'll feel better in a minute or two,' Pierre said.

Stephen slowly sat up and propped his back against the wall, his legs stretched out in front of him. Pierre's cool hands kept him upright. He exhaled sharply and closed his eyes, frustrated by the pain that stopped him from functioning at the most basic level. It dissipated gradually, to be replaced by a duller, more manageable ache. Eventually, he felt able to get to his feet. Pierre and Gabriel grabbed an arm each and helped him up.

'What happened?' Gabriel asked him.

'I had a vision—I think.' Stephen looked at Serena. He could sense that she was annoyed with him, although he wasn't quite sure why.

'Was it something to do with Anton?' Leon said.

'I don't know. I can't be sure.' Stephen turned to Pierre. 'Who's Charles Deighton?'

Pierre grimaced. 'He was a man I once knew when I was a human. That personality in there—*Benedict*—that's passing itself off as Deighton may just be an imprint of the person I once knew, but in Anton's body, it's no less dangerous than the real man.'

'How bad is the situation?' Gabriel asked.

Pierre half smiled. 'Bad enough. We could see there was a definite power struggle between Anton and the imposter. Anton still has the ability to control his own body, but that ability is weakening and limited.'

'So you're saying *Benedict* is in charge and Anton doesn't have a chance?' Gabriel said.

'No, not necessarily,' Pierre said. 'If Anton still has some control over his body that means his mind is active.'

'We have to use the Nexus to break the connection between them,' Arianna blurted out. 'It's the only way to separate them.'

Pierre patted her on the arm. 'Yes, you're right. The Nexus is where we find strength. *Benedict* isn't familiar with how it works. If we can channel the combined power of the Indigenes to Anton using the Nexus, he may be able to regain control from *Benedict*.'

'Then what?' Leon asked. 'What do we do with *Benedict* once he's defeated? Keep him inside the Nexus indefinitely?'

'No. We'd have to kill him,' Pierre said.

Leon began to pace the room. 'After Anton killed Elise, I asked his team to run some tests on him. They discovered a device—a tracer and recording chip—inside his head,' he said. 'The humans are recording everything my son does, everywhere he goes. Right now, the device isn't transmitting anything to anyone because the omicron rock is blocking the signals. But if the humans ever penetrate the omicron shield, they'll be able to upload the information from the device and have access to maps of our tunnels and the Nexus. He may be holed up in a room now, but he had plenty of time to roam around the district before the explosion.'

Pierre was staring at him. 'Why didn't you tell

me this earlier?'

'I tried—several times, but you didn't want to have anything to do with me. The best I could do was keep an eye on him.'

Pierre took a deep breath and released it. 'Let's assume they used the same device to transfer *Benedict*'s personality to Anton in the first place: if we destroy *Benedict*, the device may be rendered useless. He can't be allowed to transfer the secrets of our district to the humans.'

'So, do you want to connect in to the Nexus with him, or shall I?' Gabriel asked Pierre.

Pierre shook his head. 'I'd like Arianna to try.'

Arianna's eyes widened. 'Me? Why?'

'Because you're a strong empath. Elise spoke very highly of you,' Pierre explained. Embarrassed, Arianna dropped her gaze. 'And because you're a second-generation Indigene and the Nexus responds to you in a way it doesn't to us.'

'Why not use her?' Margaux said suddenly, pointing at Serena. 'You know she doesn't belong here.'

'Because Serena isn't an empath, Margaux,' Gabriel said, putting a hand on her shoulder. He turned to the rest of them. 'I'm sorry, she doesn't really understand what's going on.'

Margaux was staring up at the rough stone ceiling. 'They're up there. I can sense them.'

'Does she need a break?' Pierre asked.

Gabriel shook his head. 'She's fine. Life's never dull with Margaux around. She sees everything as a series of problems to be solved. She's not affected by emotions or feelings the way I can be. It's why so many others find it hard to understand her.'

Margaux was staring at Serena again. 'You

don't belong here,' she said to her. 'You belong somewhere else.'

'I know. I'm from District Eight,' Serena replied calmly.

Margaux chuckled. 'That's not what I meant. You don't belong *here*'—she pointed at the floor—'with us.'

Stephen felt the need to defend Serena. 'Whatever she is, wherever she came from, it's not her fault.'

Serena frowned hard at him. 'And where do you think I'm from?'

He turned to face her and grabbed her hands. 'I want to believe you're an Indigene but the images in your head, the way the Nexus reacted to you, it's all too strange. Plus Gabriel and Margaux don't know you and they're from District Eight.'

Serena shook her head. 'But I grew up in District Eight. I have memories of my childhood.'

'Are you somehow mixing up your memories with those of the child I saw in the picture?'

Serena stared at him. 'No! I mean I remember the child, the picture, but I also remember being in the district as an Evolver.'

No one moved or spoke.

It was Margaux who broke the silence. She placed her hand gently to the side of Serena's face and looked into her eyes. 'Child, I'm telling you you're not from here. But don't be sad. You're extremely important. They'—she gestured towards the others around her—'just don't realise how important yet.'

Gabriel pulled Margaux away. 'Come on, my dear. You're scaring Serena.'

Pierre looked at Arianna. 'Can you sense

anything about Serena?' Arianna shook her head, so he asked Stephen.

'I don't know. Something doesn't add up,' he replied.

'What about these images you saw—in her head?'

'They were her private thoughts. It's not my business to say.'

'And in the Nexus?'

Stephen explained to them what had happened to Serena in the Nexus and how it had reacted to her. They all looked shocked.

'What was your role in District Eight?' Gabriel asked Serena.

'I worked in one of the labs there. We had Indigenes come in for routine check-ups.'

'Does that sound like something you have going on there?' Pierre asked.

'You know it's not. Indigenes don't need check-ups.'

Serena looked worried. 'Well, why do I remember it like it was only last month?'

Margaux chuckled. 'Because they've manipulated your memories. Can't any of you see it?'

Arianna's eyes widened. 'You mean she was changed recently?' she whispered.

'It's the only thing that makes sense, given the timelines,' Leon said. 'She arrived in the district at the same time as Anton came home. My son was made into a spy and it's possible that Serena was too.'

'So what species does that make me?' Serena asked quietly.

Leon frowned. 'A hybrid, most likely. You may not remember Anton, but if you were changed on Earth, it's possible you have some of his DNA mixed in with your own.'

'So she's a third generation?' Arianna asked.

'No, not quite,' Stephen said. 'Pierre and Gabriel are first generation, created by the humans. Anton and I are second generation, born to two first-generation parents. Serena would be the first of a new kind of Indigene. I'm guessing she's part second-generation Indigene, part whatever new DNA mutations they gave her.'

'But she doesn't look any different to us,' Arianna whispered.

'No. It's possible the changes are mostly in her brain. We won't know unless we carry out some tests.' Stephen looked solemnly at Serena. 'Do you mind?'

She looked stunned and shook her head gently. 'No. I want to know, as much as the rest of you do,' she said.

Pierre leaned against the wall and pinched the bridge of his nose. 'Well, that would certainly explain the Nexus's reaction to her.'

'Could we convince the Nexus to accept her as one of our own?' Gabriel asked.

'The Nexus was rough with me, as if it was trying to possess me.' Serena cleared her throat and explained what it felt like. 'Stephen had to physically come and get me out. It didn't want to let me go.'

'It sounds like the Nexus is changing character too,' Pierre said. 'So the sooner Arianna tries with Anton the better.'

'But why not use Serena?' Margaux butted in. 'Why are you all ignoring what she is?'

'No, we can't use her,' Stephen said gently. 'The Nexus tried to hurt her, remember?'

'What about your visions, Stephen—can you

see if Arianna will be successful?' Pierre asked quietly.

'I don't know. They're definitely stronger with Serena around, but I can't control them, not yet.'

Pierre straightened up. 'Gabriel, fetch Anton tomorrow and bring him to the Nexus. Let's see what Arianna can do.'

'What can I do to help?' Leon asked eagerly.

'You can help Gabriel,' Pierre replied.

'Do you think there were other humans changed at the same time as Serena—who are possibly living in District Eight as we speak?' Gabriel asked.

The question hung in the air. No one had an answer to that.

Margaux locked eyes with Arianna. 'It's all up here with her, child,' she said, tapping the side of her head and nodding at Serena. 'It's the way she makes you feel when you're around her. But you already know that, don't you?' Arianna nodded discreetly. 'They're not open to the idea yet. But they'll figure it out soon enough.'

# 12

*Earth*

Daphne Gilchrist arrived back at the Earth Security Centre after the board meeting in Washington. She was still shaking.

Deighton had waited for her at the door as the board room emptied. She'd tried to make it clear to him she didn't have time to talk just then, but he hadn't given her much choice, blocking the exit with his arm.

'I won't keep you long,' he'd said calmly.

She'd known it was risky going against him in the meeting, but she wasn't going to be blamed for orchestrating Serena's and Anton's departure alone. She had just been following orders—his orders.

'I must dash, Charles,' she'd said. 'Please remove your arm.'

He'd smiled at her, that insincere, all-teeth smile she hated. 'Tomorrow. We'll talk then,' he'd said, relaxing his arm. 'In the foyer, here, at noon sharp. Don't be late.'

She'd been relieved. At least the foyer was out in the open.

Now, sitting in her office on Level Seven of the ESC, Daphne decided to bring herself up to speed with the information Deighton had sent about the latest prototype, Serena. If she was going to be automatically included in the alteration programme Deighton was proposing—to alter a select section of population now—she needed to understand the report; in particular, she needed to know what Susan Bouchard—*Serena*—had become.

Daphne tried to make sense of the information about DNA strands, mutations and nanoid delivery, but her distinct lack of scientific knowledge tripped her up. So she turned to the layman's report that Dr Caroline Finnegan had written before her death, hoping to find a clearer explanation there. But she struggled to find anything that made sense to her. She leaned back in her leather chair and blew out a long, frustrated breath. Even the layman's report was filled with too much jargon. Not for the first time she wondered if scientists, whose heads were filled with so much detail, had lost the ability to write anything in plain language. She activated her communication device as she considered calling the Galway Medical Facility to see if they could clarify some of the report's findings. But she quickly disconnected again when she realised that her call might be monitored by Deighton.

She tried to read the report again, but she couldn't focus. She kept thinking about her future and was filled with a sudden sense of dread. Deighton was moving everything along too quickly. She was worried about the ease with which the board members could be swayed, given the right incentives, to fast-track the alteration programme years ahead of schedule.

And what would happen to the ESC? Would it still exist once she had changed into her new skin? Who would they need protecting from if the new race was practically indestructible and far more intelligent? What would her new role be? After she had been altered, how useful would she be?

Daphne stood up and smoothed down her skirt. For strategic reasons, she had always sided with Deighton, but in the case of the alteration programme, her instincts were telling her not to. The board members hadn't given it enough thought. They were rushing the idea through because of the limited time left to them on Earth—and for profit. Even while the conservative board members in favour of keeping investment on Earth were voicing their objections, she could tell that the idea intrigued them and they were rapidly devising new ways to capitalise on the programme. She paced the floor as she tried to think it through.

There were still many things to consider. For example, how would the new breed of humans fit into a world like Exilon 5? And what about the humans who had already transferred to the new planet, or the building work that had been done there? What about the Indigenes and the world they had created for themselves? Was the plan to leave them where they were, to live among them or destroy them altogether?

The more Daphne thought about it, the more unsettled she became. The idea of living among the Indigenes worried her. She didn't know much about them as a race. Even though she'd supported the plan to create the first Indigenes, she'd never been an active partner; it had been the pet project of Cantwell Senior and Deighton. She admitted that the idea of alteration had seemed exciting to her back then, radical and revolutionary, refreshingly different to her strict upbringing in Osaka, Japan. But the novelty had worn off quickly.

She sat down again and glanced at the

unreadable report on her monitor. How could she make a decision about the rest of her life based on this?

A knock on her door broke her train of thought; her assistant's face appeared in the open crack of the door.

'I'm off to lunch. Can I get you anything, Ms Gilchrist?' he asked.

'No. I don't want to be disturbed,' she snapped back and she noticed her assistant flinch. She waved her hand at him and the door closed.

A thought crossed her mind and she leaned forward in her chair. She pressed a button on her communication device.

Her assistant's tinny voice came through the speaker: 'Yes, Ms Gilchrist?'

'Actually, there is something you can get me. Bring me Laura O'Halloran.'

'Now?'

She could hear the disappointment in his voice, probably because his lunch would have to wait. 'Yes. Now.'

Daphne stared for a while longer at the report on the screen in front of her. It didn't make sense no matter how often she read it. She pushed back from the desk and stood up. She cupped her hand around her red hair, patting it into place, and ran her hands down her suit jacket, brushing off invisible fluff. She leaned her hands on the desk. Image was important to her. She wondered if it was important to the Indigenes. Not if Anton was anything to go by. She shuddered as she thought about what she might look like after the alteration programme. It was always easier to stand back and pass judgement when change happened to other people, but Serena's existence brought closer the possibility of her own transformation. If they put her on the spot and asked her if she wanted to be altered, she really wasn't sure what she would say.

Daphne glanced at the clock and straightened up, obsessively running her hand over her suit once more and tugging at the bottom of her jacket. She pressed the button on her communication device again.

Her assistant's voice came through. 'Yes, Ms Gilchrist?'

'Did you find her yet?'

'I've just located her,' he mumbled. 'She isn't on Level Five.'

'Where is she?'

'On Level Two, in the Energy Creation room. She's just getting dressed now.'

Gilchrist's male assistant wasn't allowed inside the female changing room and Laura had been grateful for a moment to gather her thoughts. She had been running on the treadmill when he found her and he was clearly in a rush.

'How much longer will you be?' he had asked, pacing anxiously back and forth.

'Another ten minutes, I reckon,' Laura had said, stalling for time.

'The CEO doesn't have ten minutes. You need to come with me now.' He had grabbed her elbow and tried to pull her off the treadmill.

'What are you doing?' Laura gasped, struggling to stay on her feet.

'Gilchrist will kill me if you don't come!'

'*Fine*. Give me a second to get changed,' she'd

said as she had turned off the machine.

Once Laura had changed back into her Level Five uniform, she reluctantly followed the assistant to the door of Gilchrist's office. He didn't wait with her. Instead, he grabbed his coat and mask and practically ran to the turbo lift.

Tentatively, she knocked on the door and waited until she heard the familiar 'Enter' spoken in the ice-cold tone that all the higher level staff seemed to adopt. Laura pushed the door open and saw the CEO sitting in a luxurious leather chair, her legs crossed, one elbow resting on the table and her chin supported by her hand. Gilchrist didn't look up when Laura came in.

'Take a seat, Laura,' Gilchrist said sharply.

Laura bit her lip as she sat down in the equally luxurious leather chair opposite Gilchrist. Her eyes wandered around the office; it was filled with Japanese artefacts, bonsai trees and personal photos—from Gilchrist's home in Osaka, Laura presumed. She had never been inside Gilchrist's office before and, for a moment, forgot to be nervous about why she had been summoned.

Gilchrist took a while to focus and when she did, her eyes scanned Laura's face. Laura noticed how different the CEO looked—more jaded than usual. Her normally sharp, cold eyes seemed sunken and dead. But it was Laura's appearance that turned out to be the hot topic.

'You look different,' Gilchrist said unexpectedly. Her eyes narrowed as she studied Laura. 'Your eyes look brighter than usual—not so lifeless and dull.'

Laura frowned, not sure where Gilchrist was going with this.

'I envy your beauty,' Gilchrist said. 'All of you young people, in fact. You have your whole lives ahead of you. You're not scared of change. Have you put on weight?'

Laura's eyes widened briefly and she released her lip from between her teeth. 'Em, not that I've noticed. I've been eating more, if that's what you mean.' She placed a hand on her slightly rounded tummy.

'Well, that will do it.' Gilchrist tapped her finger on her pursed lips.

Laura frowned, then shook her head, finally understanding. 'No, the replicated food doesn't add weight—no fat or sugar, remember?'

Gilchrist nodded and grimaced. 'But the food at Cantaloupe does.'

Laura could feel herself blushing. She thought it best to say nothing.

'I think you know we've been watching you for some time,' Gilchrist went on.

Laura began to chew on her lip again.

'Do you think the sun on Exilon 5 helped you to beat that seasonal depression of yours?'

Laura gaped at her. 'I—er—what?'

'The reports I received back said you went a little crazy on the ship and again when you saw the sun. It must have been a fantastic experience for you. For people like you, natural light can be as addictive as Light Boxes are to technology junkies.'

Laura's heart beat loudly in her ears. 'I don't know what you're talking about.'

'Irene Clark—was that the alias you used? Don't bother answering. Harvey Buchanan has already filled us in on your little adventure to Magadan in Russia.'

*Us?* Laura swallowed loudly, her eyes flitting nervously around the room. She was convinced Gilchrist could hear her heart thumping. 'Why am I here?' she whispered quietly.

'Because I wanted to have a chat with you,' Gilchrist said calmly. 'I want to know where you went on Exilon 5, what you did.'

Laura slowly shook her head and clamped her mouth shut. She suddenly wished that Bill was with her. He was a much better liar than she was.

Gilchrist stood up and walked around her desk to stand behind Laura.

'I'm struggling with a personal decision and I need you to help me. You see, I may be asked to make a decision about my future shortly, and I have plenty of questions but no answers. Do you understand?'

Laura cautiously looked behind her. Gilchrist, hands clasped behind her back, was looking at a photo of herself with a group of Japanese business men.

'No, not really,' Laura said.

'I've lived my life surrounded by rules and regulations. I don't know anything else. Truth be told, I don't care much for change.'

Laura noticed a shift in Gilchrist's tone of voice—uncertainty, fear—and almost felt sorry for her.

'I came to work for the ESC because I believed in what we were doing,' Gilchrist went on. 'But things are changing at a faster pace than I'm comfortable with.' She turned around and the expression on her face—as if she might cry—caught Laura off guard.

Laura cleared her throat. 'I don't understand

why I'm here.'

Gilchrist examined her face for a long time. 'You have lovely hair. I always wanted to be a blonde, but I knew that with my skin colouring I could never pull it off. But your skin tone is perfect for it. Having said that, I think redheads command a bit more respect than blondes. People fear me more with this colour, don't you think?'

Laura nodded. 'I guess so.' She wanted to say it was Gilchrist's cold eyes that people feared, not the colour of her hair.

Gilchrist went back to her seat and sat down. 'I've always liked you, Laura,' she said clasping her hands together on the desk in front of her. 'You know what you want and you work hard to get it. That's very commendable.'

Laura tried not to lift an eyebrow: the CEO 'liked' her?

'You know the difference between right and wrong and you're willing to fight for it. So, I come to the reason why I've called you in today.' Gilchrist lifted her chin slightly, her mouth set in a tight line. 'How about you describe to me what the Indigene race is really like? And I don't want you to leave out any details.'

When Laura eventually left ten minutes later, she overheard Gilchrist talking to her assistant: 'Get me Tanya Li. Now.'

# 13

*Exilon 5*

Stephen waited anxiously with Pierre, Serena, Arianna and Margaux outside the tranquillity caves. It was so quiet he could hear the sound of the vehicles on the surface above them. A low vibration permeated the wall—a reflection of the Indigenes' mood and the rising tension among them. The rock seemed to be at its most responsive when the situation was tense.

From where they stood they had a clear view of the entrances to the two access tunnels, one on the left and one on the right. Their eyes were fixed on the right-hand tunnel just as Gabriel's and Leon's shadowy forms emerged. They were both panting from the exertion of pulling along a resistant Anton.

'Shut up!' Gabriel muttered to the prisoner.

'I'm only saying, it's what he's always thought about the Indigenes.' Anton—or rather *Benedict*—was taking a great deal of pleasure in winding them up.

'If you don't shut the hell up, I'm going to punch you,' Gabriel bellowed, raising his free fist, but Leon pushed his arm down.

*Benedict* smiled. 'Daddy here will look after me. Daddy, the bad man is being mean to me,' he said mockingly.

Leon didn't react. He kept his eyes trained on the ground, careful not to catch Pierre's eye.

Stephen was eager to understand why Gabriel was so stressed out, but it was Pierre who asked. 'What did he say to you?'

Gabriel shook his head, refusing to answer.

'Leon?'

Leon remained tight-lipped and Stephen could sense that he was just about managing to keep it together.

Stephen and Pierre helped them to pull Anton into the cave. Most of the individual units in the room were taken, but they found a couple of empty ones.

'You know, we could have used a couple of stronger males for this,' Gabriel complained as *Benedict* tried to pull away. 'Why are we wasting our energy dragging this senseless fool around?'

'Anton is in this state because of my decision to send him and Stephen to Earth,' Pierre said. 'And *Benedict* is here because I am.'

Standing close to the edge of a unit, Arianna explained her idea to them. 'I'm hoping the power of the collective energies in the Nexus will help to draw *Benedict* away from Anton. The Nexus should be able to deal with *Benedict*'s malevolent personality much more easily if they're separated.'

'It won't be that easy to get rid of me, Pierre,' *Benedict* taunted.

Stephen and Leon held on to Anton's right arm. Stephen could feel the struggle between Anton and *Benedict*, one pulling towards the Nexus and the other pulling away.

'Seems like Anton doesn't agree with you,' Gabriel said.

'Doesn't matter what Anton feels,' *Benedict*

hissed. 'He isn't the one in control. Most times, he's curled up in the corner like a little baby. Don't forget, I'm the one who put him there.'

Margaux suddenly strode forward and prodded the back of Anton's head with her finger.

'That's not helping,' Gabriel said, his voice strained.

'He's weak. I can feel it,' Margaux said.

'Yes, but Arianna is going to help Anton.'

'No.' Margaux smiled and shook her head. 'It's *Benedict* who's weak. But Arianna isn't strong enough. She won't be successful.'

*Benedict* in Anton's body tried to get closer to Margaux, but Stephen and Gabriel held him back, shaking him until he stood still.

'This isn't going to be easy,' Pierre said. 'Should we ask some of the other users to leave?'

'No,' Arianna replied. 'I need them to help me. I only require one unit and as much energy from those connected in as possible.'

They edged forward until Anton was standing at the edge of the unoccupied unit. Stephen suddenly caught a glimpse of Pierre's thoughts: Anton lying at the bottom of the ten-foot unit after Pierre had pushed him in.

Stephen's grip tightened on Anton's arm. He turned to look at Serena, who stood back from the unit, her arm linked by Margaux's. 'Will you be okay?' he asked her. 'I have to help Arianna.'

'Of course,' she replied. 'I wouldn't be much use to you. You're more experienced than I am.'

'I want to go in,' Leon demanded.

'No, Stephen and I will be enough,' Pierre said with authority.

Leon scowled at him but said nothing.

Arianna jumped into the unoccupied unit while Pierre and Stephen pulled Anton down the stone steps into the hole.

'Please help me!'

Stephen's head whipped round when he heard the pleading. He stared at Anton, expecting to see the best friend he remembered. 'We're going to try to get you out of there, Anton. Don't worry,' he said reassuringly.

Arianna grabbed Anton's hand and squeezed it. 'It's okay, we're here. We're going to separate the two of you. You'll be free of him soon, I promise.'

'Pierre, I'm scared,' said Anton, his face screwed up in terror. 'Make him leave me alone.'

'Don't worry, it will all be over soon,' Pierre said firmly.

The look of horror on Anton's face turned into a smile as the act melted away. 'Wow, I'm getting really good at that,' *Benedict* said, screwing up his face again and mimicking Anton's voice: '"*Pierre, please help me.*" You stupid old fool. You're much more gullible as an Indigene than I expected. Good to know—might come in handy for the future.'

Stephen could sense the anger building inside Pierre. 'It's not the real Deighton,' he reminded him. 'If you harm him, you harm Anton. Let Arianna try to separate them.'

Pierre took a deep breath and quickly released it. He turned to Arianna. There was unsteadiness in his voice. 'Are you ready to try?'

She nodded.

'You don't have to do this. We have other empaths.'

'But none as strong as I am.' She lowered her voice. 'Besides, I feel like I owe Elise to try. Plus

Anton is my friend.'

Pierre could hear *Benedict* laughing behind him. 'So very touching, all of this. The Indigenes have feelings. Who knew!'

Before Stephen could do anything about it, Pierre had launched himself at Anton. A quick, hard knock to Anton's jaw with his fist was enough for Anton to slump unconsciously to the ground. Pierre stood there, his breaths coming in short, sharp bursts.

'Pierre!' Arianna gasped.

'Well, it's about time someone shut him up!' Gabriel said, smiling down from above. 'He was really getting on my nerves.'

'See? He's more cooperative this way,' Pierre said grimly, propping Anton up against the wall and checking his pulse. 'Let's get this over with.'

Arianna sat cross-legged on the floor beside Anton and grabbed his hand.

'Be careful in there,' Pierre said, patting her arm, before he and Stephen stood back.

Arianna's breathing slowed and she reached her arms out in front of her. Stephen knew that in Arianna's mind, the unit's solid wall had become an orange and gold web of light, and that soon, a tendril from the Nexus would reach through for her.

Arianna's and Anton's bodies jerked forward as the Nexus latched on to their energies and pulled them inside. Pierre and Stephen watched with concern when Anton's body twitched. The collective minds channelling their energies through the Nexus were trying to separate him from the darkness. Arianna's face was strained and beads of sweat had formed on her brow. She was muttering to herself. A few minutes later, Anton looked like he was beginning to stir on the floor of the unit.

'How long do we wait?' Pierre said, leaning back against the opposite wall of the unit.

'Until *Benedict* is gone,' Stephen replied. He looked up at Gabriel, Serena and Margaux who were peering down into the unit.

Another five minutes passed, and the longer they waited the more strained Arianna appeared to become.

'She needs to disconnect,' Pierre said sharply. 'I can't afford to lose another of my charges.'

Stephen placed his cool hand on Pierre's shoulder. 'We need to give it a bit longer. We don't know what's going on in there. She could be making headway.'

'It should have been me who connected in,' Pierre insisted.

'No,' Stephen said firmly. 'She needs you and me to bring her out of it if anything goes wrong.'

Before Pierre could say anything more, Arianna's and Anton's bodies shuddered. The Nexus was releasing its hold on their energies, pushing Arianna out with such force that she took a sharp breath.

Pierre hunkered down beside her and felt her pulse. 'Are you okay? What happened?'

She looked over at Anton, who was still unconscious. '*Benedict*'s right about one thing—he has control over Anton,' she said panting. 'Anton has regressed so much that he's become an Evolver again. He's helpless and looking for direction. The only one he can talk to is *Benedict* and that soul-sucker is feeding him a bunch of lies to keep him powerless.' Her breathing began to steady.

'But did it work? Were you able to free him?' Pierre asked eagerly.

Arianna shook her head. '*Benedict* has taken control of his rational thought processes and left him with only fear. Anton isn't going anywhere.'

'But the other energies!' Pierre shouted. 'Surely you had enough help—'

Stephen shot him a look.

She straightened up. 'I'm sorry, Pierre.' She looked up at the others. 'I'm sorry. I know you wanted me to succeed. I tried everything I could. The Nexus was protecting Anton, wrapping him up in some sort of webbing. The energies from the other Indigenes couldn't get close enough to help.'

Pierre shook his head and paced the floor of the unit. Stephen stared at the wall. The Nexus had always worked to protect the innocent, and Evolver minds were the most innocent of them all.

'Can we keep Anton in the Nexus permanently?' Stephen asked.

Arianna shook her head again. 'Extended periods of time in the Nexus are counterproductive. Over time, his mind would have trouble distinguishing between what's real and what's not.'

Anton began to stir. He groaned, sat up and rubbed his jaw, but it was *Benedict* who spoke. 'Ouch, Pierre. That hurt.'

Pierre pulled him to his feet and locked eyes with him. 'Anton, if you're in there, we're going to free you and kill *Benedict*.'

'I'd like to see you try,' *Benedict* said, laughing and rubbing his jaw.

Pierre leaned forward. 'And when I meet the real Charles Deighton in person, you're going to wish you were already dead,' he hissed in *Benedict*'s ear.

Pierre pushed Anton towards the stone steps and prodded him until he climbed out of the unit.

Gabriel was at the top, waiting to greet the prisoner and lead him back to his quarters. Stephen, waiting for Arianna below, noticed for the first time that Anton was limping.

Arianna looked tired after her ordeal and got up slowly. But Stephen detected a growing sense of optimism in her. 'What is it?' he asked.

'I think Margaux was right. I need to speak to Serena. She might be able to do what I couldn't.'

'No! The Nexus will kill her,' he protested.

Arianna said nothing. She climbed out of the unit and disappeared over the top.

'Pierre, talk some sense into her,' Stephen called out. He quickly climbed up after her but when he reached the top, Arianna and Serena had already left. 'We need to stop her!' he shouted.

Pierre grabbed his arm. 'Arianna has been through enough today. Let them have their chat and we'll talk about it tomorrow.'

# 14

*Earth*

At noon the next day, Daphne arrived promptly at the World Government foyer for her meeting with Deighton. She had her briefcase in one hand and her DPad in the other, a finger poised over the silent alarm that would alert her assistant that she was in danger. Her genetically modified personal bodyguard, who towered over everyone else, was waiting outside. The foyer was packed with eager new recruits, as it always was every day of the week.

Deighton emerged from the turbo lift, his hands clasped behind his back, his paper-thin lips puckered as he whistled a tune. As he surveyed the recruits in the foyer he seemed bemused, but when he saw Daphne, the look in his eyes gave way to a hard, intense stare. A chill coursed through her body. She recognised that look from her childhood; it was the same one her father had right before he taught her mother a lesson. Unlike her mother, Daphne had learned never to show weakness in front of him. The beatings had been so routine that she had always been able to see them coming, but her mother had never been as smart as her. Even now as a grown woman, her father nothing but a distant memory, Daphne shuddered at the host of feelings that the sadistic look in Deighton's eyes evoked. It was a warning, telling her that she was right to be worried.

As Deighton walked slowly towards her, Daphne pretended to rifle through her briefcase. She could play men at their own game—working in Osaka had taught her how use discipline to overcome fear—yet Deighton unsettled her more than any Japanese businessman ever had. Somehow, he made her feel like that little girl again, helplessly watching from the corner of the room while her father used her mother as a personal punchbag. The main difference between Deighton and her father was that Deighton seemed better able to control his temper than her father ever had.

Daphne tapped her index finger on the back of the DPad. She took a deep breath and held her chin up. *Come on, Daphne. You've dealt with far more difficult people. Charles Deighton is just another overachiever hell-bent on perfection.* She wanted to believe it, she really did, but Deighton scared her. He may have fooled the board members with his charm and his smiles, but she sensed that he needed something—she wasn't quite sure what—and that he wouldn't stop until he got it. She brought her eyes up to meet Deighton's.

He gestured towards the revolving door. 'Let's talk, my dear. We have some important things we need to discuss.'

Daphne nodded curtly. 'Of course, Charles. Another place. Shall I ask Carol at reception to book a table at Les Fontaines?'

She thought she saw something in his eyes—a flicker of surprise—as he turned away from her. When Deighton held his gel mask to his face, she noticed his shoulders shaking. When he turned around again he was laughing.

'That won't be necessary,' he said. 'I have everything planned.' The mask made a sucking noise and became airtight on his face. He connected the oxygen feed line that ran from the canister on his hip through the tiny hole in the mask.

Daphne gripped the DPad tighter, her finger still poised over the silent alarm. She fished her gel breathing mask out of her bag and held it over her face, waiting for the gel to conform to her contours. Then she put her communication device in her ear.

Several new recruits, recognisable by their eager grins, entered the building, drawn in, no doubt, by the countless recruitment advertising campaigns. Wide-eyed and mouths agape, they pirouetted on the spot, drinking in the ostentatious decor that was the World Government headquarters interior.

'Lovely, isn't it?' Deighton called to them, his words muffled behind the airtight seal. 'Make sure you speak to Carol at the desk about the many opportunities we have here.' He jabbed a finger at them, making it seem like a warning rather than a suggestion.

The new recruits smiled at him just as Deighton turned to her. 'Mark my words, they won't make it past the aptitude test.'

Daphne stepped past Deighton and entered the revolving door. She felt her body shudder as she passed through the force field surrounding the World Government building, and began to shiver as she left the regulated temperatures of the building for the frigid air outside. Deighton's bodyguards were waiting. She looked around for her own, but he was nowhere to be seen.

Deighton shoved his communication device in his ear. 'This way,' he mumbled and led the way through the crowds.

She followed him as they weaved and dodged their way along the streets. A quick glance behind her confirmed that Deighton's genetically modified bodyguards were coming too. There was still no sign of her own personal security. Little arms reached out for her DPad, which she was still carrying in her hand. The thieving arms kept coming until she finally shoved it into her briefcase. Triggering the silent alarm would no longer be an option. As they walked on, Daphne clutched her briefcase to her. Of course, if the beggars got their hands on the DPad, it wouldn't work without her chip, but the parts would fetch some money on the black market, while the inconvenience of requesting a new one and having it re-synced to her DNA would be a hassle.

She chewed her lip as she wondered where they were going.

Suddenly two town cars pulled up. The genetically altered men stood by the second car, their extraordinary height and bulk enough to keep the gawkers at bay. Deighton yanked open the door to the first car. Daphne hesitated and considered running back to the safety of the offices. This was not what she had had in mind when she suggested they talk in 'another place'. Les Fontaines was perfect, the quirky French restaurant close to the offices, with plenty of witnesses.

Deighton seemed to detect her mood. 'Come on, my dear. We're going to the river.'

Going against a powerful instinct telling her to run, Daphne smiled and got in. The two cars arrived shortly afterwards at the bank of the Anacostia River near the old Washington Navy Yard. When they stepped out of the car, Deighton pointed to a waiting yacht.

'I need to get away from land for an hour,' he hastily explained. 'It's too claustrophobic here.' He ordered the bodyguards to stay by the cars.

It took a while for the yacht to break away from the shore and sail along the river that had become highly toxic to humans. The water was littered with debris of all sorts. Daphne watched the cityscape shrink the further from land they sailed. The captain changed direction, sailing along the shore's length until the buildings hugging the water's edge became more uniform. She could see the new, taller buildings in the distance punching through the clouds. Washington D.C.'s skyline had always been low, but the need for more apartments had turned it into a carbon copy of every other city in the world. Among the skyscrapers stood the tallest and most impressive one of all, the World Government building. It stood out with its black windows and sleek outline. Daphne's eyes were immediately drawn to it.

The river was almost black and the clouds that hovered close to human habitation were thick and grey, giving the constant feeling that a storm was approaching. The feeling of being out on water was strange to Daphne. She took a moment to settle the queasiness that rose in her stomach. Sitting seemed to help with that. The bustle and noise of desperate people living in an unforgiving city was only a murmur on the river—nothing more than a background distraction. The toxic water looked deceptively calm and harmless, and she enjoyed listening to it lapping up against the side of the yacht.

Remnants of house boats floated like dead bodies on the river, the evidence of early failed solutions to the problem of overpopulation. Families had tried to make lives for themselves on the boats, but the lack of clean food and water, along with dwindling supplies of fuel, forced them back onshore. The World Government put a stop to travel by river or sea when spacecrafts became the easiest—and most convenient—way to move people and cargo.

As the yacht passed by one of the derelict boats, Daphne examined a pair of rusty chairs on deck and the blue curtains hanging inside the cabin window. A small teddy bear lay at the entrance to the cabin door. The snapshot of some family's abandoned life was ghostly; she wondered if they were still alive. A deep sorrow consumed her and she turned her head away.

The yacht came to a stop where the Anacostia met the Potomac River. One of the smaller docking stations was visible where the old Ronald Reagan National Airport used to be. Along the shore, the houses looked ragged, the city jaded, spent, and ready for a break from humans. Daphne wondered if she was also ready for a break from humanity in general. If Tanya was to agree to Deighton's plans, she might get a break sooner than she had planned.

It was only when they anchored that Deighton spoke. 'Care to tell me why you went against me in the meeting?' he said calmly.

Daphne didn't look at him, but she could sense his anger. Her father used the same approach right before he beat her mother—asking her a question, but already deciding her fate before the answer had been given. Daphne remained composed; to show weakness would be fatal, like the cries of a wounded animal that winds up attracting its predator. She would never admit it, but Deighton frightened her.

'Charles, you misunderstood me,' she said,

trying to placate him with an even smile as she turned to face him. 'In a roundabout way I was agreeing with you. I apologise if that wasn't clear in the meeting.'

She looked away and concentrated on the sound of the water lapping up against the side of the yacht, but all she could hear was Deighton beside her breathing thickly into his mask. 'Think about it for a minute,' she continued. 'The board members are on the fence about your idea of bringing the alteration programme forward. But we'd progress more quickly if we gave people a choice—ask them if they want to be altered and leave behind those who don't want to be a part of it. I'm sure the more conservative members would support you with that idea. With fewer people living here and more room to expand business premises, industry could thrive even more.'

Deighton's uneven breathing turned raspy. 'It wouldn't work, Daphne. We need a clean DNA baseline on which to conduct the tests. If we give people a choice, who knows what misfits of society we'd carry through to the next generation?' He shook his head. 'We need to force change on those who are worthy—those who deserve a second chance.'

But Daphne hated the idea of such rapid change. With great difficulty, she brought her eyes up to meet Deighton's. 'Charles, the board members will only consider it if you present a viable alternative for those left behind. They still have quite a bit of money tied up in industries here.'

'Well, that's not my problem,' Deighton said sharply. He relaxed a little and clasped his hands together tightly. 'We can't alter everybody, Daphne.'

She thought she detected a hint of sadness in his words. 'I'm not suggesting that you do. Natural selection will prevail in the end. It won't be too difficult to convince the entire board of that. They've already said they don't want the headache of transferring the entire population. I just think we need to think through all possible options, especially for those who will be left behind.' *People like me*, she wanted to say. Her heart hammered loudly in her ears. She was walking a fine line with Deighton by disagreeing with him, but the situation she could soon be forced into meant she needed to challenge him.

'I need your support on this,' Deighton said.

'Of course, Charles. You have it.'

'Besides the fucking conservative members, what other obstacles are in our way?'

Daphne released a quick, soft breath. 'I spoke to Laura O'Halloran recently and I've noticed she's been acting very strangely lately.'

'What—since their trip to Exilon 5?'

'It would seem so.'

'Strange—how?' Deighton was hunched over, his eyes trained on the floor. He unclasped his hands and examined them carefully.

'She's more jittery than normal. Her eyes are constantly shifting, like she's over-thinking some problem in her head.'

'Maybe she's thinking about how she can help her new friends.' The sarcasm in his voice was plain to hear.

'No, this is different. She was unsettled after viewing the contents of the micro file, but she kept her composure. She's bothered about something else now. I wouldn't have known anything was up if it hadn't been for her recently odd behaviour.'

Deighton shrugged. 'If her behaviour is such an issue, just ask her. And what the fuck was Tanya's suggestion all about—to include Taggart? I want you to ask that Laura one what she and the investigator are up to.'

'There's nothing to indicate she and Taggart are planning anything. I mean, realistically, what can they do?'

'Not much.' He smiled briefly. 'Serena is proof that alteration can work. She's adapted so fast to life on Exilon 5, it's as if she were born there. We don't have to wait years for the new batch of Indigenes to settle on the new planet, like we did with the first generation.'

All this talk of big change made Daphne intensely anxious and she could feel her heart thudding in her chest. 'By my reckoning, Bill Taggart is still an issue, more so than Laura. What should we do with him?'

'We need him,' Deighton said, sighing heavily. 'Tanya's right, as much as that pains me to admit. Taggart has a relationship with *them*. It's better that he's on our side rather than on theirs. If we cut him loose now, we give them an ally. We need to get in close to them somehow.'

Daphne tried to think of a way to protect herself, to stop Deighton from dragging her down to his level. She didn't know Tanya Li well enough to know if she could pull Deighton into line. Li allowing the issue with her granddaughter to distract her was exactly the reason why Daphne believed some women didn't belong in power.

'Any news of the explosion on Exilon 5?' she asked.

'Apparently ground troops in the area reported a tremor.'

She frowned. 'Is the intended target dead, do you think?'

# Crimson Dawn

He shrugged. 'I'll find out soon enough. Did you know that the Indigenes evolve faster in the face of real danger? Just think what we could do to speed up evolution if we kept the new generation—the ones we select—in a state of perpetual fear. Can you imagine the change we would see? We would probably wind up hitting an evolutionary wall at some stage, but that's when we would begin new tests—to better the best of ourselves.'

Daphne clenched her jaw as she thought about a life lived in perpetual fear. Her mother immediately came to mind. She nodded with a forced politeness as Deighton continued.

'What I don't know is if they've figured out yet how fast they can change. We need to get in there while they're still a fraction of the species they could be.'

The queasiness in her stomach rose as she turned on the charm. 'In that case, I look forward to being part of our new future. I for one am sick of this ageing process.'

He turned to face her, his voice gentle. 'It is possible to live forever.' His eyes sought out the jaded cityscape again. 'Very possible.'

A silence hung in the air between them.

'Tell me, my dear, do you know a good seamstress?' Deighton suddenly said.

When he saw the puzzled look on Daphne's face he grabbed his jacket with a shaking hand. 'My favourite suit jacket has a tear underneath the arm. It was the very suit I wore to my CEO interview, so it's special to me.'

Daphne, noticing the tremor in his hand, studied him carefully and noticed a twitch in his right leg. Did this shaking have something to do with his insistence that the alteration programme be brought forward? It intrigued her enough to investigate more. 'Have Carol drop it over to my office,' she said, smiling. 'I have a tailor friend who is absolutely marvellous.'

The yacht set sail, heading back to where they had left the cars. One of Deighton's bodyguards was waiting to help them ashore. Daphne was quietly relieved to have made it back in one piece. She had been worried that Deighton was going to ... but no, it had just been a chat. She would work out a way to find something on him, something she could use as leverage. She clutched her briefcase tightly, her DPad inside, the silent alarm not triggered. It seemed that she wouldn't need it after all.

Deighton walked ahead of her and arrived at the car first. A second bodyguard opened the door for him and Deighton whispered something to him as he climbed in.

Puzzled, Daphne started to walk around to the other side of the car when the first bodyguard came up behind her and ripped the mask from her face. Her chest suddenly tight, she swung around. She dropped her briefcase and groped at her face, feeling her lungs strain to get oxygen.

'What are you doing?' she gasped, her eyes wide.

The car window lowered and Deighton, still wearing his mask, stuck out his head. 'This is where we say goodbye,' he said.

Daphne sank to her knees, clutching at her throat. The strain on her lungs was unbearable. Her chest tightened even more.

'Charles, please.' It came out as barely a whisper.

'You should have kept your mouth shut,' he snapped.

She fell to the ground, pressing her hand on her chest as if she could somehow get air in. The first bodyguard, still cradling her gel mask, hovered over her, his face expressionless. She could feel the energy drain from her body as her eyes rolled back in her head.

The pain in her chest exploded.

Then she felt nothing.

# 15

*Earth*

Bill walked briskly from the bullet train station to the International Task Force office in London, on his way to the briefing he hadn't been invited to. They were starting up investigations again on Exilon 5, but he had been given no more information than that. Simon Shaw had been cagey about filling him in; Bill couldn't work out if it was because Simon didn't trust him or because he didn't think Bill was ready to return to full duty—maybe it was both. But he was more than ready to get stuck into something—anything—to distract himself from the problems that were quietly simmering away.

Bill pushed through the invisible force field surrounding the ITF building. Once his body had been scanned and his identity confirmed by his security chip, he strode down the blue-carpeted harshly lit corridor towards the open-plan office. As he passed Simon Shaw's office, he quickly glanced inside; he had a habit of doing it lately. Simon wasn't there, as expected.

The idea suddenly occurred to Bill that he could be in and out of Simon's office in a flash; no one need know. Just as he took a step towards the office door, a roving camera came through its own special entrance into the white corridor and began to sweep the area. Bill bent down and pretended to tie his shoelaces until the camera disappeared the way it had come. He stood up and kept walking; it wasn't the right day to snoop around Simon's office.

Bill turned left past the office into a narrower corridor, ignoring the doors on either side. Ahead of him, a dividing door separated the hallway into two sections. He pressed his thumb against the flat security plate and the door released, making a sucking sound like the door of a refrigerator. He walked past several briefing rooms until he reached the second last door on the left. He heard voices coming from inside. He pushed the door open a crack and peered in. Simon Shaw was standing at the top of the bright room while Team Eleven sat around a rectangular table in front of him. Bill burst in, noting the look of surprise on Simon's face.

'Sorry, sorry, sorry,' Bill said raising a hand. 'My alarm didn't go off this morning.' He took off his coat and draped it round the back of a chair near the door. He tucked his shirt into his trousers and straightened his tie before sitting down.

The creases on Simon's forehead deepened. 'You weren't scheduled to be here for this briefing, Bill.'

'Oh, wasn't I? Well, I'm here now. Who knows the Indigenes better than me, right? I mean, wasn't I in charge of profiling the little buggers not that long ago?' Bill glanced around the room, recognising a few faces: Caldwell, Jones, Page—in fact several of the team that had served under him at the time of the original investigation into Stephen. 'Caldwell, what brings you here?' Bill asked, folding his arms.

Caldwell stood up and squared his shoulders. 'That's Commander to you now.'

Bill smiled and looked at Simon, waiting for the punchline that never came. He shrugged and played along. 'Okay ... Commander. How did that happen, Simon? Was it a typing error?'

'Sorry, Bill. This is a closed briefing,' Simon said sharply. 'I'm going to have to ask you to leave.'

'Leave?' The smile vanished from Bill's face along with his pretence. 'You're fucking with me, right? It's my investigation, Simon—always has been. If I'd had my way, these losers wouldn't have got within a mile of Exilon 5.'

'Well, things have changed since then. Commander Caldwell will be handling things from now on.'

Caldwell leaned forward and placed his hands on the table. 'Sorry, Bill. I guess you weren't the right person for the job after all,' he sneered.

Bill pointed a finger in his direction and smiled. 'I haven't forgotten what you did, Caldwell. You'd better watch that you don't fuck this one up too.'

A few sniggers drifted aimlessly around the room. Clearly the story about their commander's decision to go against Bill's orders to stay hidden from the target—Stephen—was common knowledge. Caldwell's cockiness dropped away along with his sneer.

Bill stood up when Simon approached him. His boss placed his hands gently on his shoulders and ushered him towards the door. 'I'll speak to you later, Taggart.'

'Too right you will,' Bill said through gritted teeth. He lowered his voice. 'You've got some fucking explaining to do.'

Outside the room, he was about to walk back towards the main corridor when he noticed that he could still hear the voices inside the room; Simon hadn't closed the door properly. Bill went back and, with his back pressed against the wall beside the door, he listened.

Caldwell was delivering his report with a smug whine that set Bill's teeth on edge. 'While we were recording previous patterns in Indigene activity on the surface, the ground shook briefly as if there had been some kind of earthquake. We now suspect it may have been an explosion of some kind. Indigene hunting has intensified over the past couple of days and I can't say why. We can't find any obvious pattern to their movements and they're surfacing at all hours of the night. I recommend we investigate the tunnels that aren't used by bullet trains to see if something happened there.'

Bill smiled to himself. He had told Stephen to make sure their movements were erratic. He had known it would confuse the military who would be searching for behavioural patterns.

'I won't tell you again, Commander—your orders are to observe only,' Simon snapped.

'I get that, but my men are sick of waiting around. This isn't exactly our type of work—covert operations. We aren't trained to observe.'

Bill had always been against military support on what was supposed to be a delicate mission to observe Stephen. It seemed that his instincts had been spot on.

'Let us get stuck in there and see if we can't pull one of those freaks out of their hiding place,' Caldwell went on. 'Then we can talk about observation.'

It would be clear to Simon now that what had gone wrong during the original Indigene investigation hadn't been Bill's fault; he'd had no control over the military. Bill desperately wanted to get back on the case and find out exactly what was going on, but his orders were to man a desk and he was sure it was Deighton who had ordered it.

'What about their hunting numbers?' Simon asked.

'A slight increase, that's all.' Caldwell's voice had an edge to it. He's pissed off that he doesn't have full control over the mission, thought Bill.

'How many of them did you see?' Simon asked.

'Well, there was a sharp drop off directly after the earthquake or underground explosion,' Caldwell said. 'Within a few days, the normal hunting party began making its nightly appearance again.'

'I asked how many of them you saw.' Simon's tone sharpened. 'Deighton wants confirmation.' The hairs on the back of Bill's neck bristled.

'The usual, except—' Caldwell began to say.

'Except what?'

'Well, there was somebody else out there with them—a female. I haven't seen her before.'

Bill cocked his head to one side, as if it would amplify their voices.

'Describe her for me,' Simon demanded.

Why was he asking for a description? An unusual request, thought Bill.

'Tall, attractive, in that weird freakish kind of way.' Bill imagined Caldwell shrugging in a bullish military manner that indicated he didn't get the importance of the question. 'I don't like those bottom-feeders—ugly fuckers, the lot of them—but this one? Well, she was all right looking. Nice blue eyes. They called her Serena.'

# Crimson Dawn

Bill's heart was thumping loudly in his ears. He hadn't met Serena, but he recalled Stephen telling him about a newcomer to their district. At the time, he hadn't thought there was anything unusual about it, but Simon's line of questioning—his interest in Serena—suggested that her presence on Exilon 5 was no accident. Was she a World Government plant, Bill wondered.

Suddenly Bill's communication device rang and he shot a hand over it. 'Shit,' he hissed and walked towards the connecting door, glancing behind him. The briefing room had gone silent.

'Bill, can you hear me?' It was Laura calling.

'Say nothing,' he whispered.

As voices started up in the briefing room again Bill thought of something and walked back.

Simon's face appeared at the partly open door. 'Bill, I thought you'd gone,' he said curtly.

Bill smiled at his boss. 'I had, but I forgot my coat. Excuse me.' He pushed past Simon and retrieved his coat from the chair just inside the door. Simon gave him a look.

'I said I'm going!' Bill replied and left. This time he heard Simon close the door properly behind him.

Bill made his way back up the narrow corridor, and once he was through the connecting door he darted inside the first empty room he could find.

'I suppose you heard all that?' he said quietly into his communication device.

'Hard not to,' Laura replied. 'Trouble?'

'Nothing I can't handle. What's up?'

'We need to talk—urgently. Can we meet later? I can be there this evening.'

# 16

Bill waited for Laura at seven that evening outside the docking station that had once been London City Airport. Its interior was masked by a large set of dark doors. When she exited from the building, the confusion and terror on her face told him all he needed to know.

'Come on,' he said. He hooked his hand through her arm and pulled her in the direction of the bullet train station. 'I could have come to you, you know.' The lines on his forehead deepened.

'No, I needed to get out of Sydney for a couple of hours, and this time I don't care if they miss me,' she said.

Laura remained silent on the short trip to Stratford and Bill didn't want to push her just yet. They went to Mick's Bar on the high street, a fairly new place that had become popular because of the bootleg alcohol it sold. Bill had discovered it just before he'd been assigned to work on Exilon 5. At that time of night, the bar wasn't too busy. Dark wood dominated the interior. Bright lights more suitable for interrogations hung overhead. The smell of unclean drinkers was pervasive. There was something old-world about the bar, as though it and the smells had been bottled two hundred years ago and only cracked open the day before.

Mick, the owner of the place, was leaning on

the long wooden bar. He straightened up when he saw Bill arrive and nodded to him. Bill nodded back and Mick filled two tumblers with amber liquid, waving away Bill's offer of payment. Bill nodded curtly and Mick went back to leaning on the bar, watching the Light Box news feed on the wall with the other punters. He and Mick had an unspoken arrangement: *Don't tell me, because I'm not asking*. Mick's past was chequered, but he understood who the good guys were and knew which side he was on.

Bill carried the tumblers of whiskey to a quiet snug at the back of the bar, Laura following him. Her low-heeled shoes clacked on the dark wooden floor. The two men sitting at the bar looked round, suddenly interested in the woman who had come in. Laura pulled her coat around her tighter. They sat down and Bill handed her one of the tumblers. He took a large gulp, then another and the glass was empty.

Laura took a sip of hers and made a face. But a second later, she visibly relaxed as the alcohol hit the spot.

'You were pretty vague when we spoke earlier. I take it Gilchrist called you in?' Bill said after a few minutes.

Laura looked up at him, surprised. 'You haven't heard?'

'Heard what?'

Laura lowered her voice. 'Gilchrist is dead.'

'What!? You're joking! What happened?'

'They found her by the Potomac River in Washington. Her gel mask was in her hand. Her hair was wet. They say she drowned.'

'Shit!' Bill said, rubbing his hand down his face. 'But that's not what you wanted to talk to me about, was it?'

Laura shook her head. 'Gilchrist pulled me into her office yesterday. She pretty much told me she knew about our trip to Exilon 5, and to Magadan.'

'And you're only telling me this now?'

'Sorry. But we already had our suspicions.'

'So who gave us up?'

'Harvey Buchanan.' Laura took another sip of the whiskey, swallowing loudly.

'Son of a bitch.' Bill slammed his fist down on the table, although he wasn't sure why he was surprised that Harvey would betray them. Harvey wouldn't have wanted to risk damaging his business relationship with the World Government.

'Look, maybe it's not a bad thing that Harvey spilled his guts,' Laura said, taking another sip of her drink. 'I didn't get the impression that Gilchrist was reprimanding me. She was asking me questions about the Indigenes and it sounded like she was asking for personal reasons. Perhaps there was a rift developing between her and some of her colleagues on the board. Maybe that's what got her killed.'

'Deighton's the most likely candidate.' Bill rubbed his chin. 'Yeah. I told you before, Simon has been acting strangely ever since I returned. Now I'm fairly sure he wants me to know something, but he can't tell me directly.'

'This is all getting rather dangerous. I wasn't Gilchrist's number one fan, but now she's dead, I'll admit I'm scared.'

Bill smiled wryly. 'It's been dangerous since the day you followed me in Sydney and told me about the micro files. Gilchrist's death isn't going to change anything. The fact that we're not lying in some pool of water just proves that they need us. It's very easy to kill people these days. We need to keep searching for the truth.'

Bill was sick of the lying. He wanted to openly challenge them to make a move—arrest him, reassign him, do something other than have him sit around waiting for them to make their move. He had considered asking Deighton himself, but he squashed that idea on the journey home from Exilon 5. It wasn't just his own safety he needed to think about any more—there was Laura's too, especially with the news of Gilchrist's death.

Bill heard Laura's stomach rumble as she took another slow sip of the whiskey. Her face contorted and she shivered. 'Can we get something to eat? Even with everything going on, I'm starving.'

'Sure,' he said. 'There's a replication terminal not far from here.'

'Can't we go to Cantaloupe again?' Her eyes were pleading with him.

'Replication terminal or nothing, I'm afraid.' As much as Bill liked Cantaloupe, he couldn't afford to visit it regularly, not without putting it on the World Government tab.

In the communal eating area of the nearby replication terminal Bill and Laura chose a spot as far away from others as they could get, at the white counter that ran along the back wall. The replication terminal was busy as workers prepared for the back-to-back shifts that would run right through to the morning.

Bill took a bite of his chicken sandwich and turned his nose up at the taste. 'This is disgusting.'

'Tastes fine to me,' Laura replied. 'We can still go to Cantaloupe, you know.' On the counter, Laura had laid out a sausage and gravy pie, a tuna sandwich and a half litre carton of tomato soup.

Bill looked at her spoils. 'If you want to go to Cantaloupe again, be my guest, but you're paying. Do you know how many portions there are in what you've just replicated? We don't want the ESC to get suspicious when they see your account. They'll think you're meeting more than just me.'

Laura frowned. 'Well, I need it after everything that's just happened. And right now, I don't care.' She lifted a fork to her mouth and shoved a large helping of the sausage and gravy pie into it.

'This comfort eating is getting out of hand. What's got into you lately?'

'I'm just sick of everything.' Laura mumbled scooping up another helping of pie with her fork.

Bill could see the steam rising from its gooey centre. That must be uncomfortably hot, he thought as she shoved the hot food into her mouth without a second thought. If she was bothered by it, she didn't show it. 'Your appetite seems to be increasing,' he said. 'Do you think it's a side effect of Stephen's treatment?'

She shrugged. 'Possibly,' she mumbled through a mouthful of food. 'I used to think about my depression all the time and look for ways to control it. Now I barely give it a second thought. I feel as if I've just got my appetite back. I can't explain it, but all food tastes wonderful to me. Maybe I was just hungrier than I thought.' She picked up the soup and poured half of it down her throat in one go.

Bill gently took hold of the carton and guided it away from her mouth. 'Easy there, lass. You're going to drown yourself in soup.'

'Sorry.' She wiped her mouth with her hand and swallowed. 'I'm finished. I promise.' She pushed the rest of the food to one side.

# Crimson Dawn

Bill looked around the terminal. The place was busy and noisy, and he was confident their conversation couldn't be overheard.

'What did you tell Gilchrist about the Indigenes?' he asked Laura.

'Nothing. I gave her some waffle about how we observed them from afar. I didn't tell her that we met them or about all the other stuff that happened.'

'I'm as curious as you are to know why she called you in. You said it seemed as if she was asking you questions for a personal reason. Were the two of you alone?'

'Yes. She called me into her office. She seemed distracted. At one point, I thought she was going to cry.' Laura looked around the room, then at Bill again. 'So what now?'

'I hate to say it, but we're getting nowhere with our investigation. We may have to check in with Stephen—see if there's anything happening at their end. How would you feel about another trip to Exilon 5?'

'I don't know. Maybe,' Laura said unenthusiastically.

Bill raised an eyebrow. 'It wasn't that long ago you were biting my hand off to get on that passenger ship.'

'Well, even if we *are* allowed to leave the planet, I doubt that they'd let us go a second time. And I'm running out of ways to explain my lengthy absences from work. Anyhow, the absence of sunlight on Earth doesn't bother me anymore. In fact, I kind of prefer it now.' She glanced down at the counter where the food was.

'Are you serious?' Bill gently took hold of her chin and turned her face so he could look her in the eye. 'You hate this place.'

'I still hate it, but the darkness isn't an issue. Stephen cured me of my seasonal depression.'

Bill took another bite of his sandwich as Laura eyed up the remaining food.

He sighed deeply. 'Come on. You're far too distracted here. Bring it with you.'

They bagged up the food and walked the short distance back to the bullet train station. Laura kept checking the food in her bag; with her mask in place, she wasn't able to eat it.

Keen to avoid his ITF-owned apartment in London that he knew was bugged, Bill decided to bring Laura to his private apartment in Nottingham. When they arrived, he advised her to finish the food so that they could talk properly. He sat down on the sofa and watched Laura pacing round the room with a half-eaten tuna sandwich in her hand. He shook his head. She was acting so strangely, and it was getting worse. He put it down to the news of Gilchrist's untimely death. He suddenly regretted telling her about his theory that they were being watched.

When the food was all gone, Laura calmed down marginally. 'That was the best meal I've had in a long time—except for Cantaloupe, of course.' She rubbed her belly in approval and continued to pace around the room. Bill stared after her.

Laura stopped moving and stared back. Her tone sharpened. 'Why are you looking at me like that, Taggart?'

Bill was surprised. 'You're not usually this abrupt with me.'

Laura smiled grimly. 'Are you going soft on me? Did my comment hurt your feelings?' she cooed in a baby voice.

'You would have to say or do a lot more than that, trust me,' Bill said slowly. 'Why don't you sit down? You're making me edgy.'

Laura's face softened and she suddenly looked embarrassed. 'I'm sorry. I don't know what came over me. I've no business speaking to you like that.'

'Please, I'll feel better if you sit down.'

'I'd prefer to stand. I have bundles of energy,' Laura said, pacing the floor in a figure of eight. 'So, where do we go from here?'

'Let's just say, for argument's sake, that the World Government knows everything that we've been up to,' Bill said. 'And we know they're up to something too—they're too calculating not to be.' Laura snorted. 'In order for us to help the Indigenes, we need to know what the government has planned.'

'I agree. So how do we do that?'

'We have to talk to someone who knows. I want to ask Shaw outright.'

'I thought we'd ruled out going through the front door,' Laura protested. 'You were going to try profiling him first.'

Bill looked at her. 'And I still can. What happened to the courageous girl who gave two fingers to the world and charged a questionable amount of food to her account?'

'I don't feel that way right now. Why Simon? We still don't know if he can be trusted.'

'There's no one else to ask. Simon has always stuck up for me in the past. Besides, I still have a feeling there's something he wants me to know.'

'What if he reports back to Deighton?'

Bill shook his head. 'We can't do much about that—it's a risk we'll have to take.' He rubbed his stubble with one hand. 'Believe me, if there was an easier way, I'd be doing it, but I think it's time to go on the offensive. Gilchrist must have known something, otherwise why would she have ended up dead? There seems to be bigger things going on here.'

'What kind of things?' Laura asked. She sat down beside him on the sofa.

'I don't know, but I feel like we're wasting our time, time that the Indigenes might not have, by going around in circles. We need to bring this to a head so we can help them in the right way. And I think the new Indigene that I was telling you about—Serena—is connected somehow.'

Laura examined Bill's face closely. 'Okay, then—go talk to Simon Shaw,' she conceded with a sigh. There was a new edge to her voice. 'But you'd better be right about him.'

# 17

*Exilon 5*

'I should have gone after them yesterday,' Stephen said. 'Where are they? What are they doing?'

He was pacing anxiously outside the Southern Quadrant tranquillity cave where Gabriel, Margaux, Pierre, Leon and Anton were all waiting for Serena and Arianna to show up. Leon had Anton gently but securely pinned against the wall.

'Calm down, Stephen. They'll show,' Pierre said.

Stephen stopped pacing. 'I want Anton back as much as anyone, but I'm telling you now that Serena isn't going anywhere near the Nexus until we have a better understanding of how it reacts to her.'

It had been Margaux who'd convinced him the day before not to go chasing after them. 'Serena's an influencer,' she'd explained. 'She can control the Nexus—she just doesn't know how to yet.'

After twenty minutes of waiting for the females to show, Stephen finally had enough. He could see Anton was getting restless. Leon was having difficulty controlling him, even with Pierre's help.

'I'm going to look for them.' Without waiting for a reply he started towards the tunnel. He stopped when he heard Serena's voice. She and Arianna emerged, smiling and at ease in each other's company.

'Sorry we're late,' Arianna said. 'We had something we needed to try.'

A stab of jealousy caught hold of Stephen when he saw how at ease Serena was with Arianna. He couldn't help how possessive of Serena he felt. He also wondered what had changed Arianna's mind all of a sudden—it hadn't been that long ago that she'd admitted to not trusting Serena.

'What's going on with you two?' Stephen demanded.

'I'll fill you in later,' Arianna said. Then she turned to Pierre: 'We all need to connect in so we can help Serena.'

'I said no!' Stephen grabbed her arm roughly. 'It's too dangerous. She needs to stay with me.'

Arianna twisted out of his grip and glared at him.

'I'm sorry, Stephen, but as elder I must insist Serena tries,' Pierre said. 'We don't have a lot of time.'

Serena reached out and touched Stephen's arm gently. He felt her warmth, different to the cold of the Indigenes, pass through his skin and in an instant, a feeling of calm washed over him. 'I know you're worried, but I have to try,' she said. 'If Anton's really a part of me, as you've suggested he might be, then I need to do this for him. I don't know much about this other life of mine, but maybe he helped me in some way.'

Suddenly, Stephen felt ashamed for putting Serena's happiness above Anton's chance to escape *Benedict*. 'Get him back,' he said, his lips barely moving.

Inside the tranquillity cave, Gabriel cleared a

row of units by rousing the occupants and asking them to come back later. Groggy at first, they snapped awake when they saw Pierre in the room.

'We need to remember which unit everyone is in so we can find each other inside,' Arianna said.

Gabriel helped Margaux climb into the unit at the end of the cave. He jumped in after her.

'Leon, you'd better stay with Anton,' Pierre suggested. 'Stephen, you're in the next one.'

Stephen didn't move.

'Come on. There's a chance this will work if we all connect in,' Pierre said.

'It's not that.' Stephen's eyes shifted warily.

'Then what is it?'

'I'd like to stay with Serena. I was with her before when the Nexus ... reacted to her.' He noticed Arianna gripping Serena's arm tightly and he saw red: it was him she trusted. It was he who knew her secrets and it was he who should be the one to protect her.

*Benedict* taunted him. 'Ah, listen to the pale-faced lovebirds—can't bear to be away from each other. They'll make some ugly children together.'

'I want to stay with Serena,' Arianna said firmly, ignoring Stephen.

Stephen narrowed his eyes and his temper flared. 'But you don't trust her!'

'Of course I do!' she said defensively. 'I can help her.' The colours of her aura told him that she was undecided.

'So can I!' He moved towards Arianna, his feet twitching on the stone floor, ready to challenge her if necessary.

'I'll be fine, Stephen,' Serena interrupted.

Pierre created a barrier between Stephen and Arianna. 'Okay, that's decided then. Stephen—unit—

now! You two in this one.' He pointed at Serena and Arianna.

Stephen growled at Arianna and jumped into the unit without looking. The awkward landing sent a tremor through his legs. He rubbed away the sensation, sat cross-legged on the stone floor and waited impatiently. He heard Arianna jump into the unit with Serena and he ground his teeth together.

Pierre spoke. 'Is everyone in position?'

They answered him telepathically.

Stephen closed his eyes and tried to calm his aggravated breathing. He concentrated on the solid wall that, in his mind, slowly transformed into a shimmery golden and orange lattice. He could feel the Nexus awakening to his presence and reaching out its golden tendrils for him. But the Nexus hesitated to take him. With his breathing still erratic and his mind consumed by a slew of negative feelings, he inhaled deeply, put Arianna out of his mind and thought about Serena.

Instead of reacting calmly to him, the Nexus became excited by his thoughts. He remembered how strangely it had reacted to Serena when she'd used it. It tapped its tendrils on his arm instead of gently grabbing hold of his energy and pulling him inside. Stephen briefly opened his eyes but the wall in front of him was as solid as ever. He closed his eyes, and this time the golden lattice replaced the solid wall. Through his closed eyelids he could see its brightness, powered by the energies of the other Indigenes already inside. But the Nexus was still tapping on his arm. In his mind, he could see it gesturing to him. Stephen held out his hand and grabbed the tendril. It jerked and pulled at him aggressively the more he thought about Serena.

Inside, Stephen's energy drifted towards the giant Nexus and he stuck himself to it. He turned around so he could get a better view of the individual units. Pierre was already inside. Leon had managed to coax an unwilling Anton inside. Anton's colours were distorted inside the Nexus. No longer could he see faint blues, yellows and reds hidden behind murkier colours; instead his aura was reddish orange, vermillion and yellowish green as if the murky colours had merged with bright ones. A small, bright ball of energy—Anton's—had separated from *Benedict*'s large distorted one and nestled in a corner far away from everyone else. The Nexus cocooned Anton's small and weakened energy in a web as if to protect it.

Margaux's unclear energy came through next, followed by a strong, but inconsistent energy from Gabriel. The Nexus was rough with him. He remembered Gabriel being angry at Anton in the tunnel yesterday when he and Leon had brought Anton to the cave and Arianna had tried to connect with him. Whatever *Benedict* had said to him was still on his mind. Stephen committed to memory what their energy signatures looked like.

Next, he pushed along the Nexus's pulsating wall, feeling its energy grow, looking for Serena. He looked at the unit where Arianna and Serena should be. But where was Serena? He started to panic, suddenly wishing he hadn't allowed Arianna to stay with her. What if Arianna was hurting her, preventing her from helping Anton? But that didn't make sense. Why would she hurt Serena when Anton, her friend, was relying on her—on both of them—to help?

The Nexus rippled behind him, trying to dislodge his energy and send him into the bottomless chasm below. Stephen hung on and changed his attitude fast. The Nexus stopped and rippled again, this time in a gentle, throbbing manner, more like a heartbeat. He studied the units, trying to see where Serena and Arianna might be. In the distance, two energies emerged and he panicked when he saw a Nexus tendril shoot out from the wall towards Serena's energy. She fought back but the Nexus wasn't giving up. It wanted her. A pang of jealousy caught hold of him; he didn't want the Nexus to have her. The Nexus rippled again and tried to dislodge him a second time.

Then Stephen saw something that gave him pause. Arianna had put herself between the Nexus and Serena, and was using her energy to absorb the worst of the repeated attacks. He noticed Serena hesitate as Arianna put to work a plan they had obviously come up with together. Stephen instantly regretted how he had spoken to Arianna, and sought out the others to help.

The others were hanging back. Pierre was the furthest away; he broke from the group and drifted towards Serena and the Nexus tendrils that continually swiped at her. The energies from other users closed in on Arianna, trying to give her the strength to protect Serena and fight the Nexus. Suddenly, the Nexus spun a golden web in front of them, and no one could get any closer.

Arianna's energy oscillated weakly and was struggling to hold on. Stephen could see other energies, less helpful ones, abusing her empathic ability and drawing power away from her. Tiny wisps drifted away from her energy ball and latched on to theirs. He thought of Elise and wondered if it was the same experience for all empaths inside the Nexus.

How draining it must be when energies added and drew away strength, and not always in equal measure. No peace, no solitude, no escape—even inside the Nexus. Just a continuous stream of interruption.

As Pierre neared the commotion, the Nexus trailed a new tendril out and blocked his approach. It danced with him as he tried to get around it. He changed direction and attempted to climb over the tendril. It bucked and rippled like a bull with a rider on its back. Pierre was thrown backwards towards the giant Nexus. His energy fell and hit the illuminated ledge just below it. He launched himself again in Serena and Arianna's direction.

Stephen was torn between remaining where he was and drifting to where the first tendril was attacking Serena and Arianna. He was about to do the same as Pierre when they all heard a distorted 'No!' coming from Arianna.

Pierre slowed his attack.

'Serena needs to do this,' Arianna said in a weak and altered voice.

Pierre turned around and drifted back to the wall.

The Nexus tendrils fought to get around Arianna to reach Serena, but Arianna's fading energy kept it at bay.

'You can have her, but not like this,' she said.

It took Stephen a moment to realise who Arianna was talking to. The golden tendril receded, as if it was waiting for her to tell it what to do. The energy flattened a little as the Nexus calmed down. Arianna reached behind her and grabbed Serena's energy. She led her to the front. The Nexus popped and rippled and licked its tendrils at her again. Arianna used her weakening energy to block the advances. This time, the Nexus seemed to obey. She guided the tendril to touch Serena's arm gently. It curled around her more politely than before. Arianna peeled its grip away from Serena and the Nexus complied. Then she told Serena to try.

Serena's energy moved in closer to the thick, rippling golden tendril and touched it. It responded to her, but more respectfully than it had done before. Then she drifted past the tendril, which mirrored her movements over the large chasm between the Nexus wall and the individual units, and floated towards Anton. The thick golden tendril followed her. Pierre floated towards Serena. Suddenly, the Nexus wound around her tightly as if it possessed her.

'Command it!' Arianna shouted, her voice strange and tinny.

Serena looked briefly at Arianna, then pushed against the tendril. It held fast until she pushed harder. 'Let go of me!' she insisted.

It relaxed enough for her to slip out of its grip. It retreated slightly and followed dutifully behind as Serena greeted Pierre.

It was the first test. The Nexus didn't react.

Stephen moved closer to watch. Serena floated to where Anton's tiny energy ball was protected behind a webbing of the Nexus's own making. Barely recognisable as a live energy, Anton was weak, and the longer he was kept away from the healing power of the others the more he lost strength.

Serena touched the webbing and it sparked. She turned around and spoke to the tendril: 'Let me in.'

The giant wall rippled and the fine net over Anton's energy dissolved. Serena grabbed what was left of Anton and drew him out. She brought his energy to the wall and held him against it. Stephen did the same with his own energy and watched as the others copied his move. With everyone in place on the wall, Serena kept Anton there with her hand.

Pierre struggled to bring *Benedict*'s muddied energy to the wall.

'Help him,' Serena commanded the Nexus.

The golden tendril wrapped around *Benedict* and moved him in a downwards direction towards the open chasm.

'No. Not yet,' Serena ordered. 'Beside me.'

The Nexus slammed *Benedict*'s energy against the wall and held him in place. The wall brightened as it drew energy from the connected Indigenes and fed it into Anton. As Anton grew stronger, *Benedict* shrank. Eventually, all that remained of *Benedict* was a small dull nugget.

The energies of each exhausted Indigene disconnected from the wall face. Stephen watched as the Nexus curled around what remained of *Benedict* and dropped him into the chasm. The nugget smacked against the sides of the seemingly endless hole all the way down.

'Good riddance,' Pierre said, staring after it.

Arianna instantly became alert as the web designed to keep other users at bay vanished. 'I need to get out of here. The other energies are coming for me.'

They each floated to their respective units as thousands of energies sought out Arianna to steal what little remained of her energy. The Nexus no longer protected them; they were on their own. The others climbed out first. Stephen waited until Serena was out. It took all her strength to pull Arianna out of the grip of the other Indigene energies. Stephen exited last.

On the floor of his unit he lay on his back, exhausted from the effort of dealing with this new and evolving Nexus. He had never experienced it in such a raw form, and for the first time, it struck him how young the Nexus probably was. It was possible that it existed only because the Indigenes did—it wasn't the ancient, finely tuned, healing network that had existed for centuries after all.

Stephen heard voices above him—Pierre, an excited Margaux, Gabriel, Anton—Anton! He clumsily navigated the stone footholds leading to the top of the unit and pulled himself up the final few steps. Out of the unit, he found himself surrounded by a crowd of tired, but happy faces.

But Stephen's attention was drawn elsewhere. He concentrated on the colours of Anton's aura: they were plain green, yellow and grey, representing calm, confusion—and something else.

Pierre and Leon were standing on either side of Anton holding him up. His skin was ashen-coloured and had lost its vibrancy. Stephen hoped that his bright energy would soon return to him. He had been without his friend for too long. He looked forward to the day when they would go hunting together again and argue over new designs, like they used to do.

Anton looked at Stephen and smiled weakly. 'There you are, you idiot! I've been trying to speak to you for weeks.' He shuddered violently, perhaps a delayed reaction to the Nexus's influence and his body's attempts to clear out any lingering bad effects from *Benedict*.

Stephen grasped Anton's face with both hands and examined it in detail. Anton made a face that made Stephen's heart dance.

'Next time, how about we leave the stupid

ideas to the humans?' Stephen said. 'That was a dangerous thing you did in the docking station. I almost went after you.'

Anton's body shook again and Stephen felt the tremor run through his hand.

'You know full well you wouldn't have,' Anton said. 'I'm much braver than you—admit it.'

'Stupid, brave idiot,' Stephen said and let go of Anton's head. 'How are you feeling?'

Anton's eyes met Stephen's. He was shifting from one leg to the other as if he was in some discomfort. 'I've a thumping headache, but it's good to be home,' he said. Then he turned to Pierre. 'I'm sorry about what happened to Elise. If I could have controlled him I would have—please don't blame my father.'

'Don't worry about me.' Leon's voice was full of emotion. It's you that he shouldn't be blaming.'

Pierre glanced uneasily at Leon and whispered. 'I don't.'

Stephen thought he saw Leon thumb a tear away. Arianna and Serena came closer and he turned to them. 'How did you know how to control the Nexus like that?' he asked Arianna.

She shook her head. 'It wasn't responding to me. It was Serena. Elise had told me something—that the more she used the Nexus, the more it started behaving like an unruly Evolver. It got me thinking that the Nexus probably wasn't trying to hurt Serena but saw her as a playmate. It was actually Margaux who helped me to understand.'

'Margaux—how?'

'She noticed how it was all up here with Serena'—Arianna tapped her temple—'the way she makes people feel when they're around her. I felt jealous ... not of your relationship with her, but of her, like she was affecting my mood somehow.'

'That must be what Margaux meant when she said she's an influencer.'

Gabriel said, 'So, the Nexus was grabbing her arm—'

'—like a small Evolver would to grab someone's attention,' Arianna went on. 'It saw how vulnerable Anton was so it tried to protect him. It wasn't interested in *Benedict* at first and was concentrating on keeping Serena all to itself and on keeping the other energies away from *Benedict*.'

'But like Elise, you weren't successful in controlling the Nexus either,' Pierre said sadly.

'That was because the energies were too busy attaching themselves to me, as they do to any empath that uses the Nexus,' Arianna said. 'On the inside, Serena is more powerful than we are, but the Nexus wasn't interested.'

'In what?' Gabriel frowned.

It was Margaux who answered the question. 'In her ability.'

Stephen frowned. 'What is an influencer, exactly?'

'We're all different inside the Nexus,' Arianna explained. 'Take your ability to see auras in colours, for example. Your energy allowed me to see the muddy colours around *Benedict*. The Nexus opened your ability up and shared it with those around you. Serena doesn't remember much about her human past but I'm guessing that people were naturally drawn to her in the same way the Nexus was. She seems to be a bit of all of us—part empath, part envisionary.'

'She can influence those around her,' Leon added. 'It's a rare skill, but some tests on her brain activity should clarify which parts she's using and to what extent.'

'Her influence doesn't work on everybody though,' Arianna continued. 'For example, she had to work hard to get me to see things her way. Stephen was easier to control.'

Stephen's heart beat faster. Was that all it was—control?

Anton cleared his throat and everyone turned to look at him. 'So if Serena is part envisionary, why was Stephen's ability not enhanced?'

They stared at him. 'Were you able to hear us?' Stephen whispered.

'It was mostly *Benedict* I heard, but on occasion I was able to listen in.'

'Stephen's almost there with the envisioning thing,' Serena said. 'He just needs to learn how to control it. With a little more time …'

Leon shuffled around excitedly. 'I'd like to see if we can remove the device from my son's head.'

Pierre nodded curtly. 'Let Anton rest and we can try then.'

'While he does, I'd like to run some tests on Serena, if she doesn't mind,' Stephen said.

Serena nodded. 'Can Arianna join us?'

As Stephen hesitated, she rushed to explain. 'You need to understand why she was so willing to change her mind about me.'

# 18

*Earth*

It was 10 a.m. at the London ITF office and Bill was busy dealing with a call that had been forwarded to him from one of his colleagues. He listened as calmly as he could while the person whined about a car accident—an out-of-control self-drive taxi in Suffolk and twelve injured pedestrians. Bill calmly told the person to hang up and call emergency services.

As he disconnected the call, several of the officers in the room burst out laughing. Their annoying shrieks burrowed deep under his skin. Next time they deliberately diverted a wrong call through to him, he would tell them to go fuck themselves. Sitting with his head in his hands and his elbows propped up on his desk, he didn't notice Simon Shaw suddenly appear in front of him.

'I've booked a table at Involution,' he said. 'Let's get lunch there at 1 p.m.' The surprise on Bill's face prompted Simon to add, 'We can talk about your future at ITF.'

Two of Bill's colleagues sitting behind him sniggered. One of them was Dave Solan.

Bill frowned. 'I have some things to do, things outside the office.'

Simon nodded and walked off. 'Fine. Take the morning. I'll see you later.'

'Looks like the golden boy has fallen from grace,' Dave said. The room erupted with new laughter.

Bill stood up slowly from his desk and turned around. Dave was only a few feet away from him, close enough for Bill to punch him in the face again. Instead, Bill addressed the room: 'How many of you have been invited to dine at the most exclusive restaurant in town?' The laughter faded. Bill snatched his gel mask off the desk and walked over to grab his coat. 'I didn't think so. Enjoy your soggy sandwiches and lukewarm coffees, gents,' he said and left the room.


Bill's thoughts about the real reason for the meeting prompted him to walk around London for a while to clear his head. At 1 p.m. he headed to Involution to meet Simon. At the restaurant, he flashed his ITF badge and a waiter showed him to a private booth at the back. Simon had not yet arrived.

Involution was bigger than Cantaloupe and had tempered glass tables and black and cream covered seats. Diners sat stiffly in business attire, pretending to enjoy the company they were with. The place had an unusual atmosphere, as if something was about to happen. But it wasn't anything physical. It was the air of pretentiousness and the fact that those who went there never really relaxed. The restaurant was popular among the elite, but it wasn't one of Bill's favourites—steak and chips were too lowbrow for them.

While it was usual for high-level ITF staff to frequent the place, it was the first time Simon had invited Bill to dine there with him. As Bill sat alone in the booth, he wondered why.

The waiter brought him two digital menu cards. Bill ordered a coffee while he waited. As the waiter turned to leave, Simon came through the front door, fussing with his coat and looking flustered. Bill noticed Simon had changed his tie.

While he watched Simon walk the short distance to his table, he remembered Laura's suggestion that he try profiling him. Bill counted three people that stopped Simon to say hello and shake his hand on the way past. While Simon shook the first man's hand with the confidence of someone in charge, Bill noticed the smile slip away slightly. After the second handshake, Simon ran his fingers through his mousy brown hair signalling that he was distracted by something. On the third handshake, he could barely look the other man in the eyes. Bill noticed other revealing signs: the fleeting touch to his face, the subconscious tug on the end of his jacket.

Simon pushed through the small crowd standing at the bar, drinks in hand, and reached Bill's booth. He took the seat opposite Bill but didn't look at him. Instead, he smoothed down the red tie that had been a grey one just three hours ago. Simon rarely wore the red tie, except when he wanted to impress Deighton or Gilchrist. With Gilchrist out of the picture, that left just one person.

'Nice tie, Shaw,' Bill said flatly.

Simon straightened it. 'I had a meeting.'

Bill eyed him more closely. He couldn't figure out if the mention of a meeting was a red herring designed to distract him, or if he was telling the truth.

'Have you ordered yet?' Simon asked.

'No, I was waiting for you.'

Simon grabbed the digital menu card and,

barely looking at it, glanced uneasily around until he found a waiter hovering within earshot of their table. He called him over and ordered a Waldorf salad.

Bill's coffee arrived. Suddenly, he had lost his appetite.

'Aren't you eating anything?'

'Not hungry. Same as yourself, it would seem.'

Simon shrugged. He rubbed his hands together slowly. 'Bill, things are getting a little difficult at work. I can see you're struggling with the desk job and I know you would rather be out there fighting the good fight. It has always been your forte.'

The waiter came back—a little too quickly—with the Waldorf salad. Simon picked up a fork but waited for Bill's response before he started to eat.

'Yeah,' Bill said flatly. 'It's no secret that I hate what I'm doing. So why am I still doing it then?' He took a quick sip of his coffee. The caffeine jangled his nerves, but in a good way—it was a decent blend.

Simon forked through the salad that had been arranged neatly in a swirl in the centre of his plate. He looked up and smiled at Bill, but it was forced. Bill's defences went up a notch; for some reason Simon was trying too hard.

'I'm starving,' Simon said, but didn't make a move to eat anything. It was almost as if he needed to fill the void of silence.

Was it a delaying tactic? He watched Simon's hands as he played with his food. They were rock steady.

'Are you sure you don't want anything to eat?' Simon asked, gesturing with his fork, as if he was inviting Bill to have some of his.

'No thanks. I'm not in the mood.'

Simon turned around and called the waiter over again.

'Is there something wrong with your food, sir?' the waiter said haughtily.

'No, it's fine. Can I get a gin and tonic, please? Bill, do you want something?'

Bill lifted his coffee cup to indicate he was happy with his lot. 'Gin and tonic, Simon? It's a bit early for a liquid lunch.'

Simon cleared his throat. 'Things are a little crazy at the moment and I need some Dutch courage.'

Bill's defences went up another notch. Dutch courage? What did he need Dutch courage for? Was Simon here to get rid of him? Or worse, was he to be banished to Earth for the rest of his life? Bill suddenly had a change of heart. He snapped his fingers at the waiter. 'Actually, that sounds good. I'll have the same.'

The waiter returned with a silver tray on which were two cut crystal glasses and a bottle of tonic water. He set the tonic and the glasses, jangling with ice and gin, on the table. Bill splashed some tonic in his glass and downed the contents in one. He pulled a face as the sharpness of the gin hit him. Simon slowly poured some tonic on top of his gin, swirled it around and took a measured sip.

Fuelled by the alcohol, Bill decided to challenge his boss. 'Come on, Simon, don't keep me in suspense. Why don't you just tell me why you invited me here? I'm assuming you had a meeting with Deighton. So how does he want to do it?' He pictured Gilchrist being held under water, trying to get some air in her lungs.

To his surprise, Simon smiled again, this time more genuinely. But still he said nothing.

'Okay, cut the crap and tell me why you brought me here.' Bill couldn't bear the suspense. 'Are you looking for witnesses to say I was on the edge before my …' He couldn't bring himself to say *fake suicide*.

Simon took a couple more sips of his drink. 'Bill, if only you knew the kind of morning I've had.' He stared into his glass.

'Why don't you enlighten me? Was I right about who you were meeting?'

'Maybe,' he said sharply.

Bill swallowed hard. He had been right about Simon, in particular about why he was wearing that tie. 'Is Deighton watching me? … Why was Gilchrist killed?'

Simon took another mouthful of his gin, a stalling tactic, Bill thought. He'd wait it out; he wasn't in any hurry to hear his fate. Finally his boss put down the glass. 'It's not just Deighton—they're all watching you.'

Bill swallowed again. 'The board members?'

'They're especially interested in you.' Simon swirled the contents of his glass.

Bill leaned forward and spoke almost in a whisper. 'Well, you'd better fucking tell me why.'

His boss sighed loudly. 'I like you, Bill—always have—and if I could have influenced the outcome, then I would have. But Deighton is adamant.'

'About what?' Bill was getting frustrated now.

'Look, I was instructed to tell you some things if you ever got close to the truth: Deighton—which also means the board members—knows about your recent contact with the Indigenes. They also know about the micro file.'

Bill narrowed his eyes. 'So is that why they tried to kill us in Magadan?'

Simon shook his head. 'No, they'd no intention of killing you. They were just letting you know they were around. My orders were to have troops issue non-lethal force.'

Bill's face darkened. '*You* ordered the hit on me?'

'No. I ordered them not to harm you.'

'Well, tell that to the back of the car we were travelling in. Their laser almost cut me in half.' Bill sat back hard into his seat.

'I'm sorry, Bill. Their instructions were to scare you—nothing more.'

'Who else are they watching? What about Laura?'

Simon nodded.

Bill thought of Jenny Waterson. 'Anyone else?'

'No.'

Bill had no reason to disbelieve him. He leaned forward again. 'Did you know Daphne Gilchrist called Laura in for a meeting the day before Gilchrist died?'

'No, I didn't. What for?'

Bill pursed his lips.

Simon spoke in a low voice. 'You can trust me. I'm on your side. But if you ever tell them I said that, I'll deny it.'

Bill chewed on his lower lip, keeping his dark eyes trained on Simon's every move. 'Essentially to tell her the same thing—that she knew about her trip to Exilon 5. Was Gilchrist instructed to interrogate her like that?'

'Not that I'm aware of.'

Bill released a long breath, still staring at

Simon. 'Why was Gilchrist killed?'

Simon shook his head gently. 'I don't know.'

Bill slammed his fist down on the table. 'So why haven't they made a fucking move to get rid of me yet?'

'Because they view your friendship—or whatever it is you have with the Indigenes—as something positive, as something they may be able to take advantage of.'

'So you're not here to order me to my death?'

Simon laughed quietly. 'No, quite the opposite. Deighton needs your help.'

Bill picked up a jug of clarified water and poured some into a glass. His hand was shaking.

'Well, what was the debriefing about? I thought all the investigations were on hold.'

'They *are* on hold.' Simon looked him straight in the eye, but Bill noticed him touch his sleeve. He was lying—the investigation was continuing, but why? His heart beat faster.

'Why did they send the captured Indigene, Anton, back to Exilon 5 with a bomb?' Bill asked.

Simon's gaze drifted away to look at the wall behind Bill's head. He briefly pinched the end of his nose.

'You assumed I didn't know that, didn't you?' Bill said. 'Where the hell did you think I was at the time?'

Simon composed himself a little. 'Deighton had a score to settle. I overheard him telling Gilchrist.'

'A score? With whom?'

Simon leaned in closer. Bill could feel his warm, alcoholic breath waft over him. 'I don't know. He just said it was an old friend.'

'So why am I here? What does Deighton want

with me?' Bill asked impatiently.

'The board members are considering calling for a truce with the Indigenes. They want you to be involved—to be the friendly face that the Indigenes trust. I asked you to lunch because they wanted me to report back on your willingness to help them.'

Bill hesitated as he remembered a detail he had overheard from the briefing. 'Who's Serena?'

Simon said nothing, just filled his empty glass with water.

'Why are they so interested in her?' Bill persisted. 'I heard you mention her.'

Simon took a drink of water.

'How do you expect me to trust you when you won't answer my questions?' Bill said sharply.

'Why do you think you were brought back to work?' Simon said eventually. 'Do you think I forgot to close the door to the briefing room after you left? You know more than you think. Try working it out for yourself.'

Bill threw his hands up in the air. 'At least give me something to go on.'

Simon paused for a moment. 'I don't know specifics, but I do know that the transfer programme numbers have picked up again.'

'That's it?'

'That's all you're going to get from me. The World Government is asking you to travel to Exilon 5 so they can negotiate with the Indigenes,' Simon continued. 'Think about whether you want to be on the inside of that important discussion, or on the outside, unable to help.'

Bill stood up to leave.

Simon grabbed his arm. 'Don't waste your time worrying about Gilchrist's death. You need to focus elsewhere. Things are beginning to happen. Look closely at the recent transfers to Exilon 5—times and dates. The numbers never lie.'

# 19

*Earth*

In his private World Government office on the minus fourth floor, Deighton read through the medical files his doctor had given him, files that explained his condition.

It was something he'd had since his late sixties. As genetic improvements moved away from ever finding a cure for it, he'd had to rely on treatments at the clinics—muscle-stabilising shots or gene-producing dopamine injections into the brain—to mask his condition. The mutations in his genetic code stopped the nanoids from fixing his defective genes permanently. If the severity of his condition was ever discovered, it would mean the end of his plans to live in a different body, or on Exilon 5.

Before the clinics had come into existence, he'd tried every type of black market treatment he could get his hands on. His life had been similar to the animals they tested on, but instead of being trapped inside a cage, he was trapped in his own body. The tremors, already noticeable enough, would be what others would judge him on, even though his mind had not changed. So he controlled the disease as best as he could. He read the report again:

*Parkinson's disease results*

*from mutations in the LRRK2, PARK2, PARK7, PINK1, or SNCA gene. It is characterised by a deficiency in dopamine. Some genes may try to alter themselves, although we have not been able to identify how or why. The nanoid treatments have so far only been successful in fixing some mutations in other patients, but point zero one per cent of the population still show symptoms of this rare disease.*

Deighton held his hands out in front of him. They were steady enough now but they wouldn't stay that way for long. At least the worst of the tremors were confined to his hands, but he could feel new twitches beginning in his arms and one leg. Hiding his condition when he was forced to sit still, like at one of the board meetings, was a struggle. When the tremors began, the only way to stop them was to sit on his hands or clasp them together so tightly it hurt. So far, nobody had noticed how fucked up his genetic structure really was. He knew well enough what happened to those unsuitable for the alteration programme. Perhaps the conservative pro-Earth board members would let him live as he wished on Earth. Or maybe he would be confined to one of the Infirmary clinics, the places run by the autobots the residents called the *tin can men*.

It was why Daphne Gilchrist had to die. He had been unable to hide his tremors in front of her. He'd noticed her curiosity. He couldn't afford to have her uncover the truth. She had already shown her disloyalty by openly disagreeing with him in the meeting.

He stared at the file showing the double strand helix of his genetic structure and zoomed in to look at the defective genes. Instead of fixing the problematic genes, the nanoids merely patched them up. The alterations were only temporary, meaning the underlying problem still remained.

There was really only one solution that he could see, only one way out of this: to change into an Indigene before the board members found out that the new code wouldn't work on him. And he needed to make his 'change' appear natural and pre-determined, not one he was forced to aggressively manage. He knew exactly what happened to those with incompatible genetic structures—he was the one who ordered their terminations.

Deighton tightly gripped the edge of his mahogany chair with one hand and with a long bony finger of the other pressed the call button on the monitor. A face appeared.

'I need to see you urgently,' he said. 'I'm running out of time.'

'I'll be in London on business tomorrow. I can arrange to meet you at one of our safe houses,' the man replied.

'Fine. Send the details to my DPad.'

Deighton disconnected the call.

# 20

*Earth*

Bill travelled to Sydney to see Laura after telling her about his meeting with Simon Shaw. When he arrived at her apartment block, he hesitated. Did he want to increase her involvement with the World Government? Would she be safer away from the mess—away from him? He could do it on his own if he had to. As he thought of reasons not to include her, he was already inside the foyer of her building and pressing the button for the lift that would take him to her floor.

*Turn around, Bill. Don't involve her.* He silently repeated the words as he stood outside her apartment door. He raised his hand and rapped on the door. A smile formed on his lips when she opened it. His need for her overwhelmed any other thoughts he had in his head. *Let her decide for herself if she wants to be involved.* But he knew what her answer would be. She closed the door behind him.

Out of habit, Bill removed the disruption device from his pocket and attached it to her Light Box's hardware unit. He sat down on Laura's sofa and crossed his legs. She stood, hovering over him uneasily. It wasn't that long ago that the roles had been reversed—she would have been the calm one and he the one who hovered.

He gestured at the nearest seat. 'Sit,' he said.

Laura did as he asked, but she had a strange expression on her face. She clasped her hands together tightly. Bill uncrossed his legs, her mood suddenly putting him on edge.

'Well, don't keep me in suspense. What did you find out?' Bill asked her.

She shook her head as if snapping out of a daze. 'There wasn't really anything specific or unusual in the reports about the transfer numbers, but there was something odd about the time it took for the people to arrive on Exilon 5.'

Bill frowned. 'Odd—how?'

She turned to face him. 'The timing was all wrong. We know the trip takes two weeks. But the recent transferees—the ones selected based on their genetic code—arrived three days later than that.'

'So what happened in those three days?'

Laura smiled grimly. 'You mentioned that Stephen said a new Indigene arrived at the same time that Anton returned home. You also said that the military were now interested in someone called Serena.' Bill nodded. 'It's quite possible they created her in those three days.' Her expression hardened. 'What did you learn from Simon?'

Bill laughed cynically. 'To be honest, I was busy preparing for the worst—that I would be carted off for termination.'

Laura stood up and began to pace the room. 'No, you can't think like that.'

He watched her and recognised the same figure-of-eight pattern she had traced when she was last in his apartment in Nottingham. His eyes narrowed. 'The World Government has asked me to help them.'

Her head snapped around quickly. 'Help how?' she asked, staring at him intensely.

'They want to discuss a truce with the Indigenes and they want me there, centre stage, to provide a friendly face.'

'And you're going to do it,' she said. It was more of a statement than a question.

'Well, I wanted to hear what you thought.' He leaned forward and looked at her again.

Laura thought about it for a moment. A strange look crossed her face. 'I think I'm hungry.' She padded in her bare feet across the floor to the kitchen. Minutes later, she returned with a pile of food stacked high on a plate and placed it on the table near the sofa. On the plate were various cuts of cooked chicken, steak and pork. She forgot her manners and started eating with her hands. Bill couldn't hide his surprise.

Laura stopped eating and stared at him for a moment. 'I'm sorry, did you want some?' she asked.

He shook his head and she carried on, shoving food into her mouth, barely chewing before swallowing.

He waited for a natural break in her eating before continuing. 'Simon confirmed that Anton's bomb was courtesy of Deighton.'

Laura slammed her fist down on the table. 'I knew it!' The table rocked with the force.

Bill jumped. 'Laura, what the fuck has got into you?' he asked. Her behaviour really was quite strange.

'Nothing—I feel fine. I'm just happy to hear it confirmed that we were right all along.' She eyed the remaining food on the plate.

'I have a feeling that I can trust Simon.'

Hearing himself say the words out loud made him smile. 'I never thought I'd say that about him.'

'Who?' Laura had a chicken leg in her hand and was tearing at it with her teeth.

'I was talking about Shaw—' Bill realised he might as well have been talking to himself. He couldn't bear Laura's distraction with the food any longer. 'Can you stop eating for a minute, please?'

Swallowing, she dropped the chicken leg on the plate and looked down at her hands, confused. 'I don't know what's going on—I'm just so damn hungry all the time.' She wiggled her greasy fingers at him. 'Excuse me, I need to wash these.' She left for the kitchen and returned a moment later, towelling off her wet hands. She took a seat beside him. 'Sorry, I'm all yours.'

Her expression softened and, in that moment, Bill noticed how bright and green her eyes were. She turned towards him until their legs were touching. Bill felt a tiny shock run down his spine at the physical contact. It took him by surprise. Her perfume lingered in the air between them and he was finding it hard to concentrate. He held his breath. She was too close. Bill sighed just as Laura turned her face, but he couldn't look at her. He could feel her soft, sweet breath on his neck.

'So what else did Simon tell you about your involvement?' Laura sounded more like her usual self now.

Bill cleared his throat and kept his eyes to the front. 'Not much else. I expect they'll let me know in their own good time.'

She shifted in her seat. Suddenly, he was acutely aware of every movement she was making. Her knee grazed his and Bill felt that spark again. His body felt like it was on fire, sensitive to her every touch. 'I don't know if the World Government really want a truce or if they're simply using me to get close to Indigenes,' he said.

'Possibly both,' Laura said, shifting her position again. Her hand casually grazed the back of his.

'Laura, I don't think that's a good idea,' he whispered hoarsely.

'Sorry.'

He moved up the sofa and turned towards her, resting his arm on the back of the seat. He wondered where her new confidence was coming from. But he was suddenly drawn in by her bright, green eyes.

'There's not much room here,' he said clearing his throat. 'Maybe I should sit somewhere else.'

'Well, I'm not stopping you,' Laura said softly, her eyes falling on his hand that sat on the back of the sofa. 'There are plenty of chairs.' She grazed his hand lightly with her fingers.

Her touch coursed through him like a bolt of electricity and his mouth went dry. 'What are you doing?' he asked, but instead of moving his hand away, his fingernails dug into the soft sofa. He urgently wanted to drink the sight of her all in. His breath caught when her mesmerising green eyes looked straight through him.

'You haven't ever thought about it? I've seen the way you look at me sometimes,' she said softly.

Yes, he found her attractive—what red-blooded male wouldn't? But did he want to ruin their friendship by going there? He wasn't sure.

She was still looking at him, her eyes soft and sensual, her lips and mouth inviting him to come closer. There was a change in her expression again, a fleeting one, but enough for him to wonder if the change in her behaviour was to do with something else. First there was the cough, then the excessive eating, then the restlessness, and now this uncharacteristic flirting, all since she arrived back on Earth. Bill frowned. What had Stephen used to treat her Seasonal Affective Disorder with?

Laura looked at him, puzzled. 'What's the matter?'

Bill could feel his body twitch in reaction to her proximity. He grabbed her hand and rubbed it between his. 'Laura, this can't happen. We're friends and I really don't want to ruin that.'

'It's only ruined if we don't think this is the right thing to do. It feels right to me.'

'But that could be the—' The touch of her soft lips on his silenced him.

'Laura, we're just friends—' he mumbled as his free hand grabbed the back of her neck and pulled her in close. His mouth found her lips a second time and he pressed harder, more urgently. 'We shouldn't be doing this—' His tongue teased her mouth open, then found its way inside.

His breathing came in short, sharp bursts and he felt his excitement build. He thought about pulling away, but he didn't really want to. A raw, animal need was driving both of them and it was addictive.

He stood up and pulled Laura up with him, unable to take his gaze off her beautiful, bright eyes. Had they always been that green? He tucked a strand of blonde hair behind her ear, then leaned in and kissed her soft, smooth neck. She moaned with pleasure, pressing her body into his. Hungrily, he searched for her mouth once more. Her leg curled around his until there was barely an inch of space between them. He cupped his hands underneath her ass and she jumped up to wrap her legs tight around his waist. He carried her into her bedroom.

Her room was a mess. The last time he'd seen it was just after meeting Stephen and it was tidier then. She didn't seem to be bothered by it so neither was he when he threw her onto the clothes-littered bed. They were in the moment—that heavy, sweating, achingly sweet moment. With shaking fingers, Bill slowly undid each button on her white blouse. But Laura had no patience; she ripped it open with a strength that didn't match her size and buttons scattered around the room.

'I have other ones,' she said smiling when she saw the expression on his face. She grabbed fistfuls of his shirt and tore it apart with ease, sending the buttons flying in all directions. 'Now we're even.'

She undid the buckle on his belt. Bill stood over her and opened the buttons himself, eager to save his trousers. Then he removed the rest of his clothes until he was standing naked in front of her. He watched Laura's eyes travel the length of his body, suddenly feeling self-conscious in front of her. He hadn't been with anyone since Isla. But he forgot his self-consciousness when he saw Laura smile and motion for him to come closer.

She still had her trousers on. Bill fiddled with the zip, careful not to break it. Laura wiggled from side to side as he pulled them down. 'Hurry up!' she whispered, clawing at the ends to help him. Bill tossed her trousers aside and watched, wide-eyed, as Laura removed her underwear. Any lingering feelings of self-consciousness vanished.

He hovered over her on the bed, slowly kissing her stomach, her breasts, her neck, twisting his fingers in her long golden hair. His lips found hers just as he entered her. She bit his lip and drew blood. As she began to lick the wound, he pulled away. Was she tasting him? Her moaning made him forget everything. His vision blurred and he gave in to his animal instincts. He wanted her so badly he felt as if he might explode.

He lifted her up and pushed against her. She arched her back with pleasure. Closing his eyes he shuddered as a rush of satisfaction coursed through his body.

# 21

The next morning Laura woke to find Bill lying beside her in the bed. She turned to watch him, his chest, partially uncovered, gently rising and falling as he slept. There was a faint smile on his lips.

She smiled too as she propped her head up with one hand, while her other hand hovered over his chest. She wanted to entwine her fingers in the small curls of hair that perfectly covered it. Instead, she lightly traced the contour of his face with a finger, and felt the heat of her own face where his stubble had rubbed against her delicate skin like sandpaper. She could feel herself blush as she recalled the night before.

'Oh my God, what have we done?' she whispered, smiling harder.

She felt like a naughty child. She had wanted him for a long time, and last night there was the strongest of urges to do something about it. She was both embarrassed and empowered that Bill had wanted it too. But how would he feel about her this morning?

Bill stirred beside her and stretched before finally opening his eyes. He blinked. 'Hey, what the hell did we do last night?' he said softly.

Laura's shyness returned. 'I don't know what got into me,' she said, lying down and pulling the covers up around her chin.

Bill laughed gently and pulled the covers back down to her waist. He stroked her naked stomach with his fingers.

'It's a bit late for modesty, don't you think? Do you regret it?' he asked.

Laura relaxed into the pillow and turned her head towards him. 'I—no. Do you?'

'No. I wonder why it took us so long.' Bill smiled, his eyes shining. Then he became more serious. 'Is our friendship ruined?'

Laura smiled devilishly. 'We weren't that close anyway.'

Bill laughed. 'You seem to be back to your old self this morning.'

'Yeah, I feel a little different than I did last night.'

Bill smiled.

'What?' Laura said, arching her eyebrows, a smile playing around her lips.

'Want to try again? We really should see if this was a one-off.' He tried to look serious as he continued to stroke her stomach. 'I mean, we owe it to ourselves to check for the sake of our friendship.'

'Last night could hardly count as a one-off!' Laura said giggling.

'You know what I mean. All the times we did it last night count as one try in my book.'

'Well, why don't you come over here and find out?' she said, summoning him to her with a hooked finger.

That morning their lovemaking was more powerful and sensual than the frenzied sex of the night before. They held each other for a while afterwards, talking about anything that came to mind.

A little later Bill suggested they have some

coffee. He got out of bed, Laura watching him as he fished around the floor for his underwear.

She propped herself up on one elbow and mock-scowled at him. 'You know I hate coffee. How about a cup of tea? I'm parched.'

Bill turned and smiled at her, but it vanished in an instant when his eyes darted from her face to the pillow. He scrambled back into bed and reached a hand out behind her. He held large clumps of blonde hair in his hand.

'Since when did you start losing your hair?' he yelled at her, holding the hair out for her to see.

Horrified, Laura got up and went to the mirror. Yes, her hair was falling out but it wasn't as bad as it first looked. Bill came up behind her and tugged on her hair, but it didn't yield more than a few wispy strands.

Laura felt as if she was an experiment subject as Bill poked and prodded her. She tried to laugh it off as she pulled on her underwear. 'Don't worry about it. I've been losing my hair since we were confined to perpetual darkness. It's nothing to be concerned about.' But she could tell he wasn't convinced.

'Well, what about your eyes, then?' he said. 'They looked different last night. This morning and in the light of this room, their colour seems exaggerated.'

Laura turned to the mirror and examined them. 'They've always looked like this. I see nothing unusual about them. You're worrying yourself over nothing.' Suddenly, she whipped her head around so fast, her hair fanned out and hit Bill in the face. 'I'm hungry. I need to eat.' And with that she rushed off to the kitchen, leaving Bill to stare after her.

In the kitchen, she yanked open cupboard doors and pulled whatever she could find out onto the counter. In her haste, an open box of cereal fell to the floor. Ignoring it, she punched numbers into the replication machine. Some didn't work, so she tried again. Eventually, she had replicated enough food to satisfy her. Armed with the food, she went back into the living room, her bare feet crunching the cereal into the floor.

Bill was partially dressed and hunched over his DPad at the table, reading something intently. He didn't look at her straight away. She placed the food on the other side of the table and picked up an apple. Her loud crunching made Bill look up, but only briefly. He tapped the screen and scanned it. Laura moved closer and saw one name she had hoped never to see again: Harvey Buchanan.

'Why are you looking him up?' she asked.

'I'm taking you to see him.'

Laura felt the panic build from the bottom of her stomach. 'No, Bill! Don't you remember what happened last time? ... And he betrayed us to the World Government ... And what about those replica identity chips you gave him, the ones that wouldn't work? I'm sure he's figured out that you were keeping something from him.'

'But Laura, there's something wrong with you and I can't think of anyone else who can help. Harvey has experience with nanoid technology. If he's working for the World Government, then he's most likely working on genetics.'

'We can't be sure that he can—or will—help. Besides, I feel fine.'

'You're far from fine, Laura.' Bill's voice was stern. 'We have to do *something*—and he has access to medical equipment. Don't argue with me.'

Laura turned away as Bill continued to examine his DPad. She touched her face; her skin was ice cold. She turned back again to see Bill studying a 3D map he had pulled from his DPad. She could see a tiny red light flashing. 'Is that his chip?'

'I'm using ITF software to track his movements. He's leaving Warsaw and is on the move.'

'So, where's he going?' She leaned over him.

'Judging by how quickly this dot is moving, I'd say he's on a Mag Lev train. There's only one place that particular train is heading at that hour.'

'Where?' Absentmindedly she picked up a carton of tomato soup she'd replicated and tipped it to her mouth.

'London,' Bill replied.

At first, Laura couldn't hear him clearly but the fog in her mind lifted enough for her to understand and to realise that Bill was opening the door to her apartment.

'I can't do this—I have a shift today,' she protested when he pushed her along. 'Besides, I'm not even dressed.'

'You are dressed, Laura.'

She looked down at what she was wearing: black trousers, a cotton shirt and a pair of black flats. Her hair was tied up. Why didn't she remember getting dressed?

'Call in sick. This isn't normal,' Bill said. He ushered her out the door.

Laura felt the hunger pangs strike again. She twisted out of his grip and grabbed a sandwich from the table. Bill shook his head.

Bill and Laura arrived at the docking station in London and hailed a self-drive taxi to King's Cross station, where the Mag Lev train from Warsaw was due to arrive. Bill paced up and down the platform until the nose of the train came into view. A loud whoosh sounded as the train slowed with the help of giant magnets positioned on the station wall. Almost instantly, the train came to a stop.

They waited by the entrance to the platform, watching as thousands of people alighted from the train. Bill checked his DPad, which showed that Harvey was coming towards them. Bill craned his neck trying to see him, but there were too many people. Then he spotted him, surrounded by his bodyguards and a man who looked very similar to Vladimir, the driver who had picked them up in Magadan. Harvey slowed when he saw Bill.

'Well, well, what a surprise!' Harvey said, his eyes narrowing as he got closer. He glanced at Laura who was fidgeting with her gel mask. 'I see you've brought your pit bull with you. Lovely to see you again.' The sarcasm was evident in his voice; he clearly hadn't forgotten that Laura had threatened him with a laser scalpel.

They stood on the platform in silence, throngs of people pushing past them, until it was almost empty.

'There are no witnesses now, Bill,' Harvey said coolly. 'Just let my men break your jaw, a few bones in your body and put you in hospital for the rest of your life. That should make up for you giving me those dud replica chips.'

'We need your help, Harvey,' Bill said urgently.

Harvey raised an eyebrow. 'You mean this is an official visit? I'm touched.' His eyes travelled up and down the length of Laura's body. 'I seem to remember her looking a little better the last time we met. What's wrong with her?'

'That's why we're here. We don't know what's wrong. I need you to run a scan on her genetic code.'

'Where—here?' Harvey said, fanning out his hands dramatically.

'You must have a safe house in the city where they allow you to "practise" your medicine?'

Harvey wagged a finger and briefly closed his eyes. 'Not for you to know, Bill.'

Bill noticed movement out of the corner of his eye and quickly grabbed Laura's hand to stop her from wandering off. 'Look, Harvey, will you help us or not?' he said.

Harvey clucked his tongue. 'You know … I've been looking for you, Bill Taggart. What did you expect me to do with dud replica chips?'

'I'm sorry. I was under strict instructions.'

'And now it seems you need more from me than I need from you.'

Bill nodded curtly. 'I'll show you how to get the replica chips to work.'

Harvey laughed, as did his companions. 'That will do for a start,' he said and walked on. When Bill didn't follow immediately, Harvey turned around. 'Are you coming, or not? I have a car waiting and you're welcome to a lift, but there are some conditions.'

Outside the station, Bill and Laura were blindfolded and bundled into the back of the car.

'This doesn't feel right,' Laura whispered anxiously.

'I know, but I need him to check you out. He's an expert on nanoid technology. Besides, there's no one else to ask,' said Bill, reaching up to adjust the blindfold.

Someone slapped his hand away. 'Tut, tut. No peeking!' said one of Harvey's associates.

Bill leaned back in the leather seat and tried to count how many turns the car had taken since they'd left King's Cross. If they hadn't taken any false turns, then they should be in the middle of Finsbury Park. But he could hear water, which meant it was more likely they were close to the former reservoir, now a sewage and water processing plant, near Seven Sister's Road.

The car stopped abruptly and the door opened. A hand reached for Bill and pulled him out. He landed on his knees. Behind him, he heard Laura struggle with one of the associates, then a man screaming, 'The bitch bit me!'

Bill smiled to himself. He climbed to his feet and the smell outside seeped inside his gel mask—an overpowering stench of sewage that confirmed their location. With the blindfold still firmly over his eyes, he was pulled down a flight of stairs and pushed into a lift. When the lift door opened again the smell of medical-grade antiseptic hit him. Screams filled their ears and Bill felt Laura grope around to find his arm. After walking a few hundred yards, a door closed behind them and the blindfolds were taken off. The overhead light was harsh, and Bill and Laura squinted until their eyes got used to it.

'Now, what is it you want done?' Harvey's tone was brusque.

'I told you—I need you to analyse Laura's genetic code,' Bill said. As his eyes adjusted to the artificial light, he noticed how ghoulish Laura's skin looked in it.

Harvey narrowed his eyes at her. 'Looks like there's a little mutation going on. Problems at one of the genetic manipulation clinics?'

'I need specifics,' Bill said, getting frustrated.

'One thing at a time.' Harvey removed a small square box from his pocket and opened it. Inside, sitting on a small pad, were the three chips Bill had had to part with in order to secure new identities for him, Laura and Jenny Waterson. 'Why don't you tell me how these babies really work?' Harvey said.

'Fine. But only after you check Laura over,' Bill said.

Harvey laughed cynically and pushed his hands through his sandy hair. 'I don't think you understand how this works.' He reached for the waistband of his trousers, pulled out a knife and turned it in his hand, the blade glinting in the overhead light. 'Considering this one'—he pointed the blade at Laura—'tried to kill me last time, think of it as an added security measure.'

Bill froze when he recognised the antique knife. It was similar to the one Larry Hunt's henchmen had used on him years ago. He had been profiling Larry Hunt, a major player in the food replication business, and his follow-up surveillance of Hunt's staff had linked Hunt to the crime of producing and selling fake replication machines. Hunt's henchmen had followed Bill through the streets of London, trapping him like an animal and sending him a 'friendly' warning. Bill touched the spot on his shoulder where they had plunged the knife in.

Harvey's eyes widened. 'Ah, so you remember.'

'Remember what?'

'What happens to you when you screw with my people? Larry Hunt was a client of mine before you sent him to jail, and I lost half of my business overnight.'

So it had been Harvey's men who had chased him that night. Bill sighed. 'Fine. What I didn't tell you about the chips is that you need to "mark" them—they must sit in a sample of the host's blood to make a connection. Without the "mark", they won't work.'

Harvey took the knife and sliced it across his thumb. Blood dripped to the floor. He grabbed a Petri dish and squeezed out enough blood to cover the base of the dish. Then he sat one of the chips in the blood. 'How long?'

'It depends,' Bill said.

'Well, in that case you'll be here for as long as it takes.'

'I've done as you asked,' Bill said sharply. 'Now I need you to analyse Laura.'

Harvey stared at him for a long time, then shrugged. He motioned for her to sit in the chair. When she didn't move, he yelled, 'SIT, NOW!'

Laura promptly sat down. Harvey produced a swab, told Laura to open her mouth and took a sample from the inside of her cheek.

'You're not checking her blood?' Bill asked.

'Cheek swabs, blood—it's all the same. It all contains her genetic code.' Harvey snipped the end of the swab and dropped it into a solution. He put a cap over it and placed it in a small machine.

'What does the machine do?' Bill asked.

'It splits open the nucleus contained in the cells.'

'I'm sorry, I left my genetics profiling handbook at home. In English please.'

Harvey sighed as if the answer was obvious. 'Well, without boring you, the DNA analyser first pellets the cells, then breaks them open to get at the nucleus, which is where the DNA is. Then the machine gets rid of any junk in the surrounding membrane that might break down her DNA when we release it. It then extracts it by breaking open the cell membrane using a mixture of heat and alkaline. We give it one final spin, and voila!—we have our genomic DNA!'

'The what DNA?'

'Genomic—the set of DNA that holds her entire genetic data.'

'How long will it take?'

'About five minutes.' Harvey opened a file on his monitor. 'Now, we should have her normal genetic code on file at the ESC.' He opened the file and a picture of her original code came up. When the machine finished, it fed the new results to his monitor. The two images were side by side.

'There's definite mutation in her code all right, but it's continuing as we stand here,' Harvey said, fascinated. 'Whatever this is, it didn't happen at one of the genetic manipulation clinics. They have controls in place so only certain genetic code is altered. But inside her, it's like a free-for-all. What happened?'

It was Laura who spoke. 'I was given a cure for my seasonal depression. It contained Indigene genetic code.'

Harvey turned to look at her. 'Where—on Exilon 5 or here?'

'Exilon 5.'

Harvey laughed. 'So the rumours are true. You're more than just passing acquaintances with those freaks.'

Bill noticed Laura bristle at his description of the Indigenes as she got out of the chair.

Harvey pushed the hair out of his eyes and looked at the monitor. 'There's a mini war going on inside you. Your body is attacking the nanoids and genetic copies that are trying to replace your originals, and that is kicking your immune system into overdrive. It's a bloody mess in there!'

'Just tell me if you can reverse it,' Laura said stiffly, standing over his shoulder and staring at the code.

Harvey shook his head. 'Not here. You're going to have to talk to your Indigene friends. Your body doesn't recognise the new code. We only use a mix of human and Indigene code so that the body accepts the changes slowly and naturally. I don't have anything to counteract what this stuff is doing to you.'

'Clearly you've dealt with this kind of change before, and you know how to transform a human into an Indigene,' Bill stated.

Harvey smiled. 'I told you. We use a very specific DNA sequence to encourage the body to accept the changes. But this is a full, no-holds-barred dose of real Indigene in her system. What I don't understand is why they would mutate her genetic code quickly like this without safeguards in place.'

'They were trying to cure her Seasonal Affective Disorder. I don't think they were fully aware of how their altered code would affect her,' Bill said.

'Sorry, but you are just going to have to wait.' He stroked Laura's hair. She jerked away from his touch and glared at him. 'And you, pretty lady, are in a whole heap of trouble until then.' Harvey turned away and fiddled with something on the counter. He turned around quickly and jammed a syringe in Laura's arm but didn't push the contents.

'What the fuck are you doing?' Bill shouted.

Harvey walked backwards, holding Laura with one hand and the syringe with the other. Laura flinched and tried to pull her arm away, but Harvey was too strong for her. He kept his thumb on the flat top of the syringe. 'It's filled with destructive nanoids, worse than the ones in her body. These ones kill anything they touch. Didn't you hear the screams on the way up?' He smiled cruelly. 'We're going to wait here—all of us—to see if that chip you gave me accepts this supposed "mark" you keep telling me about. Otherwise, your girlfriend gets a dose of something that will ruin her insides forever. And if that happens, you're going to wish the genetic mutations were her only problem.'

Harvey glanced briefly at the time projection on the wall.

'Are we keeping you from something?' Bill asked.

'I have to be somewhere in an hour. So hurry up and tell me everything else about the replica chip or your girlfriend gets the Buchanan special.'

'The "mark" *is* everything,' Bill said hotly.

'Well then, pull up a chair,' he said. 'Because you're not leaving this room until I see it in action.'

## 22

*Earth*

Deighton stepped out of the docking station and into London's icy air. A town car waited for him, courtesy of Harvey Buchanan. He climbed in and the driver spoke softly to the dashboard. The car began to move.

'Mr Buchanan is expecting you,' the English driver said briefly.

Heat spread through Deighton's body and face. He tore his mask off. 'Yes, I know. I just spoke to him an hour ago. Cut out the chit-chat, young man, and concentrate on what you're supposed to be doing.'

Buchanan's driver narrowed his eyes as he peered at Deighton in the rear-view mirror.

Deighton hit a button and a black partition separated them. He felt the tears begin again and he squeezed his eyes shut. But it didn't stop the tears from falling. Deighton took a white handkerchief from his pocket and dabbed at his eyes. He pulled a mirror down from the roof of the interior and checked his face. The light wasn't great, for unlike the World Government cars that projected pleasant scenes on the side windows and shut out the nasty real world, the glass in Buchanan's car windows let in little light but allowed him to see outside.

When the car turned left on to a smaller street,

it slowed down. The crowds were denser here than at the docking station, and the military, in toughened black suits holding shields close to their bodies and weapons at the ready, lined the streets.

Deighton released the partition separating him from the driver. His tone was abrupt. 'How did they know I would be here? Who told them?'

'Mr Buchanan thought it would be best to notify the police. Otherwise the streets would be a nightmare to navigate.'

Deighton leaned back and looked out the window. So much for privacy. This wasn't a trip he had wanted announced to the world. 'Are the roads like this the whole way in?' he asked.

'No. Barricades have been set up to isolate our approach to the hospital.'

'Good. I need privacy.'

He stared at the Londoners gathered by the roadside, all of them struggling to keep still in the frigid temperatures. Deighton grimaced a little when the car pushed through the crowds as if the people on the street weren't there. That was how Deighton felt at times among his peers—as if he were invisible in Tanya Li's presence. With Peter Cantwell, he had had control, but with Tanya in charge that control was no longer there. He desperately needed the alteration programme to move beyond the talking stage to help him transcend his miserable life and become great again in the eyes of those that mattered.

Deighton had been to see several doctors about his condition, but had only seen Harvey Buchanan twice before. The first visit had been about ten years before; his body had rejected the additional genes that would mutate his code. But Deighton hadn't been concerned—the Indigene race was still evolving and he was confident he could try again. The second visit was a couple of years ago, around the time the military had captured a young member of the Indigene race. As Deighton had studied the young male's genetic code, fresh desires surfaced for a longer life. Even with a cleaner sample of genetic material from the young Indigene to mutate his code, the second time had been no more successful than the first. Harvey had explained to him the reason why: on top of his condition, the extra work carried out in the genetic clinic over the years had screwed with his code. And because of his age, Deighton was no longer a viable candidate. But this time, he was coming to Harvey with two fresh samples and renewed hope.

The car passed through the barricades and pulled up outside a cordoned-off neighbourhood—one of the no-go areas in the city. It had been used as a temporary refuge for migrants travelling down from the colder countries. But London was now cold itself and the air made it too dangerous to live in makeshift houses—accommodation needed to be sealed to keep out the harmful air. The migrants had since moved on. Now, tall electrical gates surrounded the neighbourhood. When they had discovered a hospital inside the zone, the exclusion area had been widened to include the hospital.

Several genetically altered men in heavy beige coats with fur collars and gel masks arrived at the gate. They weren't as large as the board member bodyguards, but the buttons of their coats still strained in the middle. Deighton wondered if they had missed an opportunity by not altering the bodyguards' lungs so they wouldn't need the gel masks. But he realised it wouldn't have made any difference; they'd have needed to use the masks inside instead.

The military scanned the car first, then turned off the electricity that surged through the gates. The heavy gates swung open and the car moved forward. The giant men stood to attention, staring straight ahead of them as the car passed by. Then the car pulled up outside the white-washed hospital, one of the many places the World Government had kitted out to hide the black market's experimentations with failed prototypes.

With a shaking hand, Deighton slapped on his gel mask. He held his hand out to see how bad the tremors were. After he'd seen Harvey, he would stop at one of the manipulation clinics to get another muscle-stabilising injection in his hands. He didn't want to reveal how bad his tremors were to the man he planned to nominate to run the alteration programme as soon as it was approved. It was silly vanity really—his genetics were on file; Harvey could easily see how bad his genetics had become.

At the door, Harvey Buchanan waited for him just inside the force field. He proffered his hand. 'Mr Deighton. It's a pleasure to see you again.'

'You're a hard man to track down,' Deighton said, wagging his finger at him. They shook hands.

Harvey smiled politely. 'As I should be, Mr Deighton. Shall we chat upstairs where we will be more comfortable?'

Deighton pulled off his mask and shoved it in his pocket. He walked with his hands clasped tightly behind his back. On the third floor, Harvey showed him into his office. Inside, there was a small round table and two chairs, and along one wall a white bench with a DNA analyser and a monitor on it. The space was small, but it was neat and tidy. Deighton liked that. He hated untidiness and loose ends. He thought about the Indigenes; they were effectively loose ends—survivors of the original explosions that had been allowed to live. They should have been wiped out there and then, when they were at their most vulnerable.

Harvey showed Deighton to a seat and sat on the one directly opposite, smiling pleasantly. Deighton felt a pang of jealousy at Harvey's ability to control his emotions so easily. Or was it that Harvey was well protected and not fearful of anyone, including him?

'You said over the communication feed that you wanted to discuss your alteration again,' Harvey said. He leaned forward. 'Mr Deighton, I have to be honest here. The older you get, the less likely the change will work. And with your condition, it makes success much less likely.'

Deighton stood up and removed his coat without meeting Harvey's eyes. 'I understand that, but I want you to check me over again,' he said.

Harvey looked at him and blinked a couple of times. 'If you insist, Mr Deighton,' he said eventually. He pulled a swab from a drawer and took a buccal sample from Deighton's cheek.

Deighton watched Harvey prepare the sample and place it in the DNA analyser. The process only took five minutes but it felt much longer than that to Deighton. The analyser made a buzzing noise and Harvey activated the monitor.

'Okay, Mr Deighton. The results are as I expected. You still carry several genetic mutations. The dopamine treatments at the clinic have done a good job of temporarily stopping the Parkinson's in its tracks, and the muscle-stabilising shots have helped, but nothing has been successful in fixing the mutated code. If anything, your code has worsened since your last visit.'

Deighton nodded. He reached into his pocket and produced two vials. 'One of these contains genetic material from Anton, the adult second-generation Indigene,' he announced. 'The other is from a new Indigene called Serena that we created from the first Indigene's genetic matter.' He held the vials up higher. 'I want you to isolate the corresponding code and use it to fix mine.'

Harvey took the vials from him and placed a sample of each in the DNA analyser. After a long five minutes the results appeared on the monitor. He smiled, pointing to the left image. 'I assume this one's from Anton? Interesting. I can see why you spent so much time catching the bugger in the first place.' He pointed to the code on the right. 'The specific mutations in Serena's genetic material look quite different to what we've seen up to now.' Harvey stood up, his expression suddenly grim. 'But there's still no guarantee that it'll work for you.'

Deighton rolled up his sleeve and held out his arm. 'Try it.'

Harvey drew a sample of Deighton's blood and combined it with a sample from each of the vials. He then added nanoids to each mix before injecting them back into Deighton one at a time. With the first mix, Harvey waited for the nanoids to get to work, then took a new sample from Deighton's cheek. Then he did the same with the second mix. He ran the results through the DNA analyser and examined each of the changes. The DNA from Anton's sample had joined with Deighton's code, then separated and died. The sample from Serena's had done the same, but separated after a longer spell.

Harvey tapped the bench top with his finger. 'You know, I examined an interesting patient at the safe house near Finsbury Park just an hour ago.'

'Who?' Deighton's eyes widened.

'Laura O'Halloran.'

The curiosity in Deighton's eyes faded. 'So?'

'She was presenting with mutations in her code as a result of Indigene DNA. Her mutations are erratic and her body is fighting against them as it would an infection.'

Deighton blinked slowly and stood up. 'When did that happen? From her time on Exilon 5?'

Harvey nodded. 'It would appear that one of the Indigenes treated her with nanoids and slammed in copies of his own genes for good measure.'

'So? How does that affect me?' Deighton asked coolly and sat down again.

'Because with the right DNA sequence, we may be able to *force* your body into accepting the changes,' Harvey explained. 'We may even be able to turn you fully. If the copied Indigene genes are stronger than human genes, then think of it as simple evolution—the stronger genetics, and their mutations, will prevail. But the sample needs to contain pure Indigene code.'

'I assume you have a sample from her?' Deighton smiled and held out his arm. 'I want you to test me immediately.'

Harvey pushed Deighton's arm away. 'Not yet. Laura's body was fighting the change. All I have from her is a confused genetic mess. The sample needs to be pure—no human genetic material present.' Harvey pointed to the vials that Deighton had brought with him. 'These are no good. They're only partial because they've been contaminated at the laboratory, mixed with human genetic code for testing, I presume. I would need a pure sample, from Serena if possible. Her code might work.'

Deighton felt the tears coming. In a fit of rage and frustration, he stood up and upended the table in front of him. Harvey slid his chair back in time. Deighton stood there, panting hard, trying to keep the tears from falling. He'd had the perfect opportunity to take what he needed, but his obsession with changing Susan Bouchard into Serena had drawn his attention away from his own needs. They had taken pure samples from Anton—several of them—but had combined his code with Susan Bouchard's so that Susan's body wouldn't reject the changes. He had presumed that taking a DNA sample from Serena would be enough. If Harvey was telling him that both samples were contaminated with human genetic material, then Serena had not fully changed into an Indigene and was still technically human when they took her sample. 'What the fuck am I supposed to do, Harvey? She's not on Earth anymore.'

Harvey stood up. 'You need to get a pure sample, Mr Deighton. There's no other way to check if we can fix the mutated code that gives you Parkinson's.'

Deighton sat down on the chair, breathing heavily, and put his head in his hands. His mind raced. A journey to Exilon 5 was his only chance to get a pure sample from the Indigenes. If he spread word of his impending arrival among the military there, it was bound to get back to the Indigenes. And maybe that would be enough to draw them out of their hiding place.

Deighton jumped to his feet, grabbed the vials

from the bench and left the room, not hearing Harvey call after him to offer his help. Outside, he climbed into the town car with a renewed sense of determination. The only way to play the Indigenes at their game was to play a game of his own, in a place where the humans had the advantage—out in the open on the surface of Exilon 5.

## 23

*Exilon 5*

Following his traumatic separation from *Benedict*, Anton slept solidly for two days. He was exhausted by everything that had happened since his return home and by his time spent in captivity on Earth. Pierre ordered that he receive no visitors while recuperating. A frustrated Stephen, eager to speak with his friend, spent the time working with Serena to see if he could control his envisioning ability. When he didn't fight the visions so hard, he could feel them strengthening in her presence. But what was interesting him even more was what Margaux had said about Serena being an influencer.

He arranged to meet Serena in one of the testing labs. When she arrived, he wasn't entirely surprised to see Arianna with her. Why had Arianna changed her mind about Serena? Had Serena persuaded her to?

Stephen said nothing about it and motioned for them to come in. There was a long work bench stretching along one wall. On it were items that had been stolen from the surface—a laser scalpel, a monitor and a DNA analyser. He had laid out some cheek swabs.

In the centre of the room was the largest item they had taken: a 3D body image scanner with a flat bed attached for the patient to lie down on. The scanner had been sitting outside the docking station, ready to be moved to another destination when the Indigenes had taken it in the middle of the night before the humans knew anything was missing. With a few modifications, the Indigenes had been able to use the body scanner to detect and analyse new metals as well as the ones it was programmed to.

It was the first time Serena had seen the lab and Stephen noticed that her aura colours were tinged with grey, a sign of her uncertainty. She ignored the body scanner and instead went straight to the bench. She picked up the laser scalpel, turning it over in her hands.

'Where did you get this?' She frowned.

'From one of the human labs on the surface,' Stephen replied.

'I think I recognise it,' she said quietly and quickly put it down. 'Come on, let's get to work. I want to know as much as you about what's going on in my head.'

Arianna stood close by, careful not to get in the way of Serena and Stephen. On the bench, Stephen had set out what he needed to take a sample of Serena's DNA. He turned on the DNA analyser. 'Come stand next to me,' he said.

He took a cheek sample from Serena and processed it through the DNA analyser.

'Where did you learn to do all this?' she asked while they waited for the results.

'I watched the scientists when I was young. I seemed to have a natural aptitude for it and picked it up quite easily. The rest—well, let's just say lots of mistakes were made along the way.' Stephen smiled.

'What are you hoping to find today?' she

asked, sounding a little unsure.

'I honestly don't know.' His attention was drawn to the monitor when the DNA analyser hummed and then went silent. 'We know what Indigene DNA looks like. I want to see what's different about yours.'

'And if it looks the same?'

'Then with your permission, I'd like to do more tests and delve into your brain functionality.'

Serena motioned for Arianna to come closer. They all studied the images of Serena's genetic material on the monitor.

'It's not that different to our DNA,' Arianna said quietly.

'Different enough,' he replied, pointing at the screen. 'Look at the mutations here. They're what make her the way she is. The change is natural in you and me, Arianna, because we are second-generation Indigenes. But in Serena—and first-generation Indigenes—the change was forced, probably aggressively so in Serena's case; the mutations are more obvious. They may have been in a hurry when they created her—and braver! They seem to have gone further with the changes.'

'And my mother?' Arianna asked.

'As a first-generation Indigene, Anna was probably given longer to transform. She wouldn't have been in any discomfort.' Stephen paused for a moment. 'Is that why you changed your mind about Serena, because of your mother?'

Arianna nodded. 'My mother was Elise's assistant when she was human. Elise wouldn't tell me about it so I "walked" her mind. She tried to hide it from me, but she couldn't in the end.' She dropped her eyes to the floor, then looked up at Stephen again.

'Even if Serena has been planted, none of this is her fault. But she probably has better control over what they did to her than Anton does.'

'You could be right. She's one of a kind.' Stephen smiled softly at Serena and gestured at the 3D body imaging scanner. 'I need to scan your brain to see how the neural pathways work.'

Serena lay down on the bed attached to the scanner and Stephen positioned the device over her head. The scanner hummed and reproduced a 3D image of her brain. The image floated in the air and Stephen rotated it with his hands.

'What do you make of this?' he asked, pointing to the areas that were the brightest.

Serena sat up and frowned. 'Why are there so many active areas?'

'You don't know?' Stephen said, puzzled. 'You said you were a scientist in District Eight. What about the lab I saw in your memories? And when you came in here first, you seemed to recognise the laser scalpel.'

'I ... I wish my memories were clearer,' Serena said. 'I remember moments, things, being in places, but not how to do anything. Please explain it to me.'

Stephen nodded briefly. 'You're using all parts of your brain simultaneously. Margaux may be right about you being an influencer.' He pointed at a specific area. 'To influence effectively, we must be aware of our own thinking and that of others, and be able to act outside our preferred thought style. It's called Whole Brain Thinking. There are several areas involved in this. The left and right sides of the cerebral cortex are responsible for logical and holistic thoughts, and the left and right sides of the limbic brain are used in planned and emotional responses.'

Serena frowned as she studied the image.

'Usually we have our preferred thinking style—a bit of one, a bit of the other—but in you, all areas of influence are extremely active.'

'So you're suggesting I can influence who I like just by talking to them? I know enough to know that's not possible.'

'Well, you have a hold over me and most of the males in this district,' Stephen said quietly.

'But not the females,' Arianna added.

'Why not?' Serena asked frowning.

'We know that the skills in our first generation are an extension of who they were as humans. The skills they already had have been enhanced by the mutations to their code. It's probably the same for you. Whatever role you had as a human probably involved influencing people in some way. You probably found that people were naturally attracted to you.' Stephen gave her a quick glance.

She looked hurt. 'You think that's why I'm with you—because I have some sort of hold over you?'

'The thought had crossed my mind.'

'It couldn't be further from the truth,' she said angrily. 'If I have this ability, it's not a conscious thing.'

'It isn't, Stephen,' Arianna said. 'But she can learn to control it. I was the most resistant to her influence at the beginning. She could practise on me.'

They all turned when they heard a noise. Gabriel was suddenly standing at the entrance to the lab. 'It's time,' he announced. 'Leon is bringing Anton over. We need to see if we can remove the device in his head. I've rounded up some help.'

Stephen persuaded Serena and Arianna to go to the Gathering Room so Serena could practise controlling her influencing ability. Deep down he knew Anton wouldn't want an audience.

He waited nervously for Leon to bring Anton to the lab. He wondered about the tracer device and the reasons the humans had put it there in the first place. If they ever got their hands on it, what had they planned to do with the data? The device had been underground with them now for a number of weeks, yet the humans had not tried to come to District Three. The omicron rock had probably rendered the device useless, preventing any signals from reaching the surface.

When Anton finally arrived, Stephen caught his breath. The deterioration in his physical appearance since Stephen had last seen him was shocking. Anton was still incredibly weak after his ordeal and looking much older than his thirty years. He had also developed a pronounced limp. Leon followed slowly and patiently behind him, his expression confirming what Stephen was thinking—that his continuing weakened condition was not normal. Stephen wondered what terrible things the humans had done to Anton. He saw Leon nod at him as if he too had been thinking along the same lines. Three of Anton's old research team had arrived; their auras were mostly shades of grey and dark green and they were struggling to hide their discomfort at seeing Anton in this way.

Behaving more like an elderly human, Anton pointed to the body scanner and his research team rallied around. Leon hooked his arm under Anton's and helped him onto the bed. Anton groaned and grimaced as he lay down. One of the research team positioned the machine over his head where they knew the tracer device was located and switched it on. The giant machine whirred into life. Stephen waited for it to produce a clear 3D image of Anton's brain, but then the scanner started running the length of Anton's body. Stephen frowned. Why were Anton's team looking at his whole body?

Anton turned his head slightly and smiled weakly at Stephen. 'I'm in a lot of pain right now. *Benedict* knocked me around a bit. And then there were the experiments on Earth. I need to know exactly what they did to me.'

Stephen nodded, swallowing hard, and watched the scanner run up and down the bed while in the space above, a 3D replica of the inner workings of Anton's body was produced. Everything looked normal until the scanner mapped out the lower half of his body. Stephen and Leon gasped together when they saw it.

The image clearly showed that Anton's hipbones and fibulas had been broken in several places and then reset incorrectly. They could see where the body had tried to fix the breaks and knitted the sections of bone back together, but because the breaks had not been clean, the bones had reset at jagged angles to each other and were pressing on his sciatic nerve.

Stephen winced as he considered the strong possibility that the humans had deliberately allowed the bones to reset badly to see how Anton's body would cope. We aren't that different from humans, he thought angrily. We still feel pain. He counted fifteen separate breaks in each leg. The tears welled up in his eyes.

'How bad is it?' Anton asked gently, unable to see the lower half of his body in the image.

Stephen coughed to steady his voice. 'How bad is the pain?' he asked.

Anton grimaced. 'It hurts like hell when I walk.'

Leon motioned two members of the research team over. 'Get me some painkillers,' he whispered to one. To the other, he spoke telepathically.

The second Indigene left and returned with a small piece of wood in his hand and some soft materials. Leon wrapped the soft materials around the wood and held it in place with some gauze. He leaned over Anton. 'Here, bite down on this. This is going to hurt—a lot.'

Stephen quickly realised what Leon was about to do. 'Stop! You can't! We need to wait for the medication,' he yelled.

Leon struggled to keep the emotion out of his voice. 'There's no time. I need to start resetting the breaks now.'

Stephen was about to argue some more, but Anton had already clamped the wooden mouthguard between his teeth. The research team gathered to hold Anton down. Anton reached out to Stephen, who gripped his hand tightly.

Stephen could barely watch as Leon twisted Anton's left leg. The Indigene let out a blood-curdling screech and arched his back. The 3D image showed his heart beating faster while further down his body, the first of the deliberately offset breaks began to align correctly. Leon worked as quickly as he could, tears dripping from his eyes onto Anton. Stephen could only now see the extent of the damage to the outside of his left leg. There was no bruising, no swelling, but the skin was no longer translucent. It was ashen grey and in the first stages of necrosis; the skin cells were dying after what must have been a continual infection. Stephen suddenly understood the reason for Leon's urgency.

The next break was worse for Anton and harder for Leon to perform. Stephen steeled his grip on Anton's hand. Anton clamped down on the piece of wood and arched his back a second time. His fingers turned white as they squeezed Stephen's hand. He only relaxed when the reverse break was complete. Stephen suddenly visualised Anton on a similar table while the humans made the original breaks. He felt bile rise in his throat.

The third break was the worst; it was the main break in Anton's leg. Leon didn't pause between resets. He twisted Anton's leg in the opposite direction to how it was lying. A guttural noise rose from the back of Anton's throat as he squeezed his eyes shut and bared his teeth. The noise was unbearable. Stephen pulled his hand away and shot both hands over his ears. He watched Anton grab a fistful of the female Indigene's tunic as she struggled to hold him down.

'Let go of his arm!' he yelled at her, suddenly picturing the humans doing the same thing to him when he had been their prisoner. She removed her hands; Anton immediately let go of her tunic.

The Indigene returned with the pain medication. 'I'm sorry, it took me so long. I couldn't find it.'

Leon grabbed it and injected it into Anton's arm. Anton instantly relaxed and the rhythm of his heart began to slow. As each of the breaks were made and reset correctly, the skin on Anton's legs began to return to its normal colour.

'Shouldn't we be giving him something for the infection?' Stephen asked.

Leon shook his head. 'The infection's been and gone. All we can do is wait to see if the necrosis reverses itself.'

Leon reset the last bone as a heavily medicated Anton slept. He took a deep, shaky breath and released it. 'Okay. That's the worst part over.' Then he rotated the 3D image of Anton's head. 'Let's see what's going on with this device.'

The image showed a small black disc attached to Anton's hippocampus, the area of the brain that stores memories. Leon pulled the image apart with his fingers and examined the device more closely. As he did, a pulsing red light became visible.

'Pierre was right. It's trying to send a signal,' Leon said. He moved away from the table and breathed out heavily. 'The humans are tracking us and using my son as bait.'

'But they haven't found him or the device. The omicron rock is dampening the signal,' Stephen said.

'But it's only a matter of time,' Leon said. 'We need to get your envisioning ability working. Then we'll be better prepared for whatever the humans have planned.'

'But I can't control it properly yet.'

'You mentioned that one vision came through while you were with Serena,' Leon said.

'Yes, for some reason Serena's presence really helps. I think Margaux was right about her being an influencer. Her brain activity in those areas is off the charts.'

'Well, let's test that theory and bring Serena back in.'

Leon sent one of Anton's researchers to get Serena. When she arrived, Arianna, Gabriel and Margaux followed her in.

'How is Anton?' Gabriel asked.

Leon explained the extent of the damage to his legs and his hope that the necrosis would reverse itself. He was close to tears.

Gabriel patted him on the back. 'Don't worry. He'll get through this.' He smiled. 'Margaux and I wanted to witness the geniuses at work. I've heard a lot about Anton's research team. Leon, I hear you taught Anton everything he knows.'

While Leon and Gabriel discussed Anton, Serena and Stephen took a few steps back. As their eyes met, Stephen felt a sudden rush of warmth pass through him. He wondered how much of it was due to her ability to influence him.

'Are you sure you want to get involved with us?' he asked her. 'There's still time to back out.'

'Well, if my brain is working the way you say it is, shouldn't we put it to good use?'

She grabbed Stephen's hands and he closed his eyes, focusing on the darkness in his mind. He tried to relax, to keep his mind open, but nothing happened.

'Let it happen naturally. Don't force it,' Serena said.

Stephen studied the flickers of visions that began to appear. He tried to latch onto one of them, pulling gently as if he was tugging a rope, but there was resistance. It felt like a word on the tip of his tongue that was just out of reach. He opened his eyes just as another ache began inside his head. He noticed Anton had roused from his sleep and was watching him.

'Okay, I felt the visions that time,' Serena said.

She gripped his hands tighter. 'Arianna told me that for my influencer ability to work, I need to concentrate on who I want to influence, think of the outcome I want and transfer that outcome into the minds of those I'm concentrating on.'

'So you're effectively changing their minds?'

'Something like that. I don't actually do anything to change their minds. I just prey on their susceptibilities and doubts so it seems as if they've thought of it themselves.'

Stephen closed his eyes again and tried to latch on to the visions just out of his reach. Serena did something—he could sense it—and suddenly he was tugging the rope and there was less resistance this time. One final tug and the visions knocked loose. Everything came rushing forward the same way they had when Anton returned home. Stephen staggered backwards, but Serena kept hold of him and he quickly steadied himself.

Multiple visions whizzed past him from events that had already happened and were no longer relevant. His closed eyes darted from left to right as he scrolled through the visions at breakneck speed as if he was searching through a storage device. When the visions became more relevant, they slowed down enough for him to see. The first was of them standing inside the Southern Quadrant tranquillity cave just before they freed Anton from *Benedict*'s power; the next was of Anton lying down on the bed right before his scan and then Anton awake with Arianna watching him from a short distance away, nervously chewing on her thumb; finally, there was the vision of him and Serena standing together and him almost falling over. Then the visions vanished.

Stephen opened his eyes and blew out a short,

frustrated breath. 'It's not working. I can only see the past and present.'

'You need to shut everything else out,' Serena urged.

He closed his eyes again, and the vision of him just having opened his eyes and blowing out a breath came easily to him. But then slowly, other visions appeared—Gabriel finding Margaux sitting cross-legged among a group of young Evolvers in one of the teaching alcoves; Arianna and Anton gazing at each other the way Stephen looked at Serena. Another vision, different from the rest, appeared in the distance and Stephen gasped when he saw who was in it. He opened his eyes and smiled. 'I can't believe it worked!'

'I knew it would,' Serena said, squeezing his hands and looking relieved.

Gabriel and Leon had joined them now.

'You're not going to like what I've just seen,' Stephen said to Gabriel. 'I think you'd better get Pierre. His old friend is coming.'

'Who? ... What did you see?' Gabriel asked anxiously.

But Stephen's attention was drawn back to Serena. Her eyes were wide and she looked as if she was about to scream.

## 24

The change in Serena's expression prompted Stephen to look into her mind, to invade her thoughts. He saw a series of random images, memories she had not yet learned to keep private. Through her eyes, he could see that she was in a large dark room with thousands of humans trussed up in bucket-shaped seats with large metal restraints across their middles. She looked down at her own body, unable to move her arms because of the wrist clamps. She looked up again at a young man opposite her—blonde hair, blue eyes—and Stephen saw several tubes sticking out of the top of his arm.

Serena stepped back, placing a hand over her mouth. 'What am I looking at? When was I restrained? Was it here?'

'It looks like one of the human stasis rooms on board the passenger ships,' Stephen said.

Serena was staring into space. 'Are these memories of my time before they ... changed me? Was I human then?'

'Possibly.'

'Why am I seeing these now?'

'Maybe by unlocking my ability to envision you've inadvertently unlocked your own memories.'

Stephen saw another memory in her mind. She was in a different room looking up at the ceiling. She turned her head to the right and Stephen gasped when he saw Anton lying on a table beside her. She looked away from Anton and the face of an old man came into view. Stephen instantly recognised him—he had just seen him in his own vision a few moments ago.

'Who is he?' Serena whispered. 'Was he responsible for my … my new form?'

'Possibly. All I know is that the humans are coming—several of them—and the man in your memory is the same man who is coming. I can't be sure it's Charles Deighton but Pierre will know.'

Anton turned on his side. 'Did he have black hair and eyes lacking emotion?'

Stephen nodded.

'Then I'm afraid it's him.'

Gabriel became agitated. 'I think we should leave Pierre out of this,' he said.

'Why?' Stephen frowned. 'He's our elder. And he says he knew Deighton when he was a human. He has a right to know that Deighton is coming.'

Gabriel threw his hands up and stormed silently out of the room.

Stephen frowned at Leon. 'What was that about?'

'It was something *Benedict* said to Gabriel … about Pierre,' Leon explained.

'What did he say?'

'That Pierre couldn't be trusted. That he had once been human.'

'So? We all were.'

'That's not what concerned Gabriel,' Leon said sharply. '*Benedict* said that he and Pierre used to work together and they'd both considered the Indigenes to be vermin. He said that soon, Pierre would come round to that way of thinking again—that the Indigenes were of no use to humans anymore and should be destroyed. *Benedict* also claimed that Pierre had already reverted back to his secretive behaviour, making decisions without others. Eventually he would pick a side—the humans' side. He said Elise's death was planned so that Pierre's true personality would rise to the surface.'

Stephen blinked. 'Why do you think *Benedict* said all that? Why give away so much information?'

'I'm guessing *Benedict* wanted to plant the seed of doubt in Gabriel's mind.'

Stephen shook his head. 'We've both known Pierre for decades. He's not capable of that.'

Leon rested his hands on the edge of the scanner bed. 'But you don't know who he was as a human. None of us do and if he's linked to Deighton …'

'Pierre has worked tirelessly to help the Indigenes. He wouldn't go against us, not after what *Benedict* did to Elise in Deighton's name.'

'You need to keep an eye on him—we all do,' Leon said, moving away from the table and standing in front of Stephen. 'None of us know how this will play out. That's why we need your visions.'

Leon turned to speak to Serena and Arianna behind him. 'The humans are coming and we don't know why. It could be for you'—Leon nodded at Serena—'or it could be for Anton. Pierre may be the elder of District Three, but all our lives are at stake here, and not just in this district. Pierre's been secretive ever since Stephen and Anton left for Earth. And he refused to consider finding a way for us to rescue Anton when he didn't return.'

'Doesn't mean he wasn't trying to help,' Stephen said defensively.

Leon sighed. 'Look, it's no secret that Pierre

and I no longer see eye to eye when it comes to the welfare of my only son. He didn't even bother to check on him today. But if Pierre has started to recover some of his human memories, I don't trust him to guide us anymore. Surely it's safer to give *Benedict* the benefit of the doubt and all be a lot more vigilant.'

Suddenly Stephen heard a noise behind him and he turned round. Anton had got off the scanner bed and was standing up. He looked much stronger, but not quite his old self. 'They're probably after what's inside my head,' he said. 'Use me as bait.'

'Bait for what?' Pierre was standing at the door.

After a few moments' silence, Leon spoke. 'Stephen had a vision that the humans are on their way.'

The continuing lack of trust was evident between the pair when Pierre could barely make eye contact with Leon. 'Can you remove the tracer device in his head?' he asked.

'Not without killing him,' Leon replied sharply. 'They've attached it to his hippocampus. It's too deep inside his brain.'

'They've come at us before. With Stephen, we'll be ready,' Pierre said.

Stephen shuffled uncomfortably. 'My visions are unpredictable. I was only able to see something tangible with Serena by my side.'

Pierre's eyes flitted around the room. Stephen studied him closely; he could see nothing alarming about the colours of his aura. 'We'll manage, we always do,' Pierre said. 'They won't get a chance to come at us like they did before. Something tells me things will work out the way they should.'

'Pierre, you should know that I saw an old man among them—thin, gaunt, thick black hair, dead eyes.'

Pierre nodded solemnly as if he already knew. 'When are they due to arrive?'

'I don't have a time frame, but we could maybe work that out by hacking into their passenger ship database,' Stephen suggested.

'I could do that,' Anton said.

'Are you sure?' Pierre asked. 'You've been through a great ordeal.'

'I need to do something to make my time away count for something other than the deaths of innocent people.'

'Okay, but take Stephen with you. And keep me updated on every detail,' Pierre said.

'I'll work with Serena to help improve her influencer ability,' Arianna said. 'I'd also like to see if Margaux can help.'

'So what's left for me to do?' Leon asked sharply.

'You can help Gabriel and I figure out what to say to the district,' Pierre said. 'We're going to need volunteers when the time comes.'

# 25

*Earth*

In his London apartment, Bill sat and stared at the half-empty coffee pot on the table in front of the Light Box. He was waiting for a call. It had been twenty-four hours since he'd spoken to Simon Shaw and demanded an audience with the board members. He was running out of time to help Laura. He needed to get her back to Exilon 5 for treatment. It killed him that he'd had to leave her in Sydney on her own, but Simon said they would only make the call to Bill's ITF-owned apartment because the communication feed there was secure.

He stood up and paced the floor behind the sofa, stopping briefly to check the time projection on the wall. Simon had said he needed to convince the board members to talk to Bill directly. Bill knew an audience with the board members was a long shot but he had to try. He really hoped he wouldn't have to speak to Deighton. The thought of asking for help from the person who had ordered his wife's death didn't sit well with him, but Laura's worsening condition trumped everything. He needed their help and there was no one left to ask.

At 3.15 p.m., his Light Box trilled loudly. This time, there was no need for the sound disruptor—he wanted everyone to hear what he had to say. His hands shook as he smoothed back his short grey-flecked hair and straightened his black tie. He remained standing behind the sofa. If Simon, acting as the board members' go-between, said no to his request, he would need to find another solution. He hoped it wouldn't come to that. They owed him a favour, after what they'd done to his wife.

Bill addressed the large image of a rattling telephone on the Light Box and a female face appeared in the screen.

'Yes?' he said cautiously. He'd never seen this woman before.

'Hello, Bill Taggart?'

Bill nodded.

'My name is Tanya Li. I'm the Chair of the World Government board. We haven't had the pleasure of speaking before now.'

Bill had prepared exactly what he wanted to say to Simon Shaw, but seeing an unfamiliar face threw him, and some of the anger that had gathered while he waited for the call dissipated.

'Mr Taggart?' Tanya looked puzzled. 'You were expecting me, were you not?'

'To be honest, I wasn't expecting a board member to call me back. I'm a … little surprised, that's all.'

Tanya nodded, her mouth pursed tightly the way he had seen Gilchrist's on occasion. Her Asian face was pulled back so tightly that it was line free. Her eyes, sharp and focused, did not betray her true age. It was how she sat that did, the way she interlocked her fingers and propped up her chin—like a schoolteacher. Tanya looked at him as if she were peering over a pair of glasses.

'Mr Taggart—may I call you Bill?'—he gave

his permission with a wave of his hand—'I hear you need something from us and that you believe it's in our interests to give it to you.'

Bill frowned at this open and caring World Government figure before him. 'You've changed your tune,' he said sharply.

'I beg your pardon?' Tanya said, raising her eyebrows.

Bill's eyes blazed. 'Well, first you have me believe that my wife was killed by the Indigenes, which she wasn't. Then you pull me off my mission so I can come back to Earth and twiddle my thumbs. You didn't seem too concerned when I recently disappeared off Earth for the guts of five weeks. In fact you seemed to approve of my trip to Exilon 5. I've worked for the World Government for many years and not once have I ever spoken to a board member. But here you are now, eager to offer me help.' He stepped back and released a quiet, controlled breath. He berated himself; he should be thinking about what Laura needed, not airing his own grievances.

Tanya continued resting her chin in her hands, seemingly unperturbed by his anger. She shifted a little in her chair. 'You must believe that I'm sorry for what happened to your wife. She got caught up in something that was beyond my control.'

Bill pointed an angry finger at the screen. 'Don't you talk to me about Isla! You have no right. She didn't deserve to die for what she believed in.'

Tanya sighed then dropped both hands and laid them out flat on the table. 'We are not living in sane times. Things happened that I wish I could take back. But I wasn't in charge then—Peter Cantwell was. I have only been in the position for a year.'

'Well, that was long enough for you to come clean about my wife's whereabouts. Instead, you seemed to be happy to let me run around in circles searching for the truth about her disappearance.' Bill took a deep breath and calmed down a little.

Tanya blinked several times. 'Again, what happened to your wife was not my fault. But I do accept responsibility for not telling you the truth. I have been a little ... preoccupied. A family matter. I'm sure you can understand.'

Bill remembered reading a private memo concerning one of the board members, about a recent death. 'It was your granddaughter, wasn't it?'

'How did you know about that?' Tanya snapped.

Bill smiled smugly. 'I have my sources.'

Tanya touched her nose briefly with her index finger. 'We can't change the past, Bill, but maybe we can talk about what you need now. I assure you my intentions today are honourable.'

Bill came round to stand in front of the sofa. 'I'm still a little confused that you're making this call and not Simon.'

Tanya looked bemused. 'Because Shaw said you needed to speak to me urgently.'

Bill paced back and forth. 'Part of me wants to trust you, for Laura's sake. Another part is sceptical and wondering what your angle is. If I can't trust you, I'll find another way to get Laura to Exilon 5.'

'Of course you can trust me.' Tanya leaned forward, her hands disappearing out of sight. 'Do you think I'm lying to you now?'

Bill smiled. 'Probably. It's highly unusual for a board member to drop everything to speak to one of its employees. But that's not the issue. I'm more interested in why you decided to call me personally.'

Tanya leaned in closer to the screen. 'I'm more interested in these lies you think you see. Where are they hidden—in my face, in my expression, in my posture? I want to know.' She leaned back and her hands came back into view.

Bill stood to one side of the Light Box to get a better look at Tanya. 'Well, for starters, your efforts to keep your hands on the table seem false. What you like to do most is rest your chin on top of your hands. It gives you control. You look at people as if you used to wear glasses. I'm guessing you did once and you liked the way you could hide behind them. But you can't anymore. So when you're not resting your chin on your hands and you feel the need to assert yourself, you do so by angling your chin downwards and examining people as if you're looking over a pair of glasses. You touch the end of your nose when you're lying, which I've seen you do once already. But you didn't do that when you spoke about my wife, or when I mentioned your granddaughter.'

Tanya placed her elbows on the table and brought her hands up to make a bridge. She was smiling as she rested her chin on them again. 'Perhaps you could teach me how to hide my feelings in front of a profiler. Yes, you're right. I am calling you for a reason other than the one you want to discuss.'

Bill folded his arms across his body. 'So, why don't you tell me what you want from me, and I'll see if hell needs to freeze over first.' He couldn't help it, being confrontational. Something told him he needed to be vigilant; he wasn't about to risk Laura's safety. If necessary, he'd put her into stasis until he could figure out another way to get help for her.

Tanya laughed, a perfectly natural laugh. 'I'm

afraid, Bill, you might be eating your words soon. The devil is looking for a new place to live.'

'You and I know he's already on Earth,' Bill said, thinking of Deighton. 'What happened to Gilchrist?'

'She committed suicide.'

'Are you sure about that?'

Tanya nodded. 'There's no reason to think otherwise,' she said. She straightened up and placed both hands flat on the table once more. 'Okay, Bill. I think you deserve a straight answer.'

'I'm listening.'

'We wish to meet with the Indigene leaders and we would like your help in approaching them.'

Bill was a little taken aback. 'What makes you think they'll agree?'

'Well, that's where you come in. If you travel with us, we'll not be perceived as so much of a threat. You're an ally of theirs, no?'

Bill wondered how much he should tell the Chair of the World Government about his relationship with them. He suspected she already had an idea. 'I wouldn't go that far,' he said, deciding to keep certain facts hidden for now.

'Well, you haven't dismissed the idea outright, which I'll take as a positive sign. Tell me what you think.'

He tapped his lower lip with a finger. 'I'll consider what you ask—*if* you help me with my problem.'

'What do you need?' Tanya asked, splaying her hands out in front of her. Bill got the impression that she was making a concerted effort not to touch her nose.

'As I already said, I need to take Laura

O'Halloran to Exilon 5.'

'May I ask why?'

'She's not well.'

'Okay, if you help us I'll remove your travel restrictions once we have returned. You'll be given the freedom to go to Exilon 5 any time you like.'

'No, I need to take her there now.'

'You helping us doesn't come in exchange for unlimited favours, and certainly doesn't cover the two of you,' Tanya said flatly. 'What's so urgent about her condition? We have the best doctors in the world at our disposal.'

Bill shook his head. 'She doesn't need a doctor. She needs the Indigenes.'

Tanya leaned forward. 'I'm getting impatient, Bill.'

'It's not the kind of medical problem that human doctors can cure. She's been exposed to a pure sample of Indigene genetic code and I think she's transforming into one of them.'

Tanya looked surprised and mouthed the word *How*. Bill waited for her to ask but she never did. Instead, she said, 'We have the best doctors. Alteration is not something we need to be afraid of.'

Bill put one hand up. 'We've already spoken to Harvey Buchanan. He says it's not a normal alteration. The mutations are creating havoc inside her body and she's unable to deal with it. Her immune system is fighting the invasive genetic material and her organs are beginning to shut down. She's in a state of limbo—neither human nor Indigene. I'm not sure how much more she can take. We need the Indigenes. They'll know what to do.'

'Alteration is a straightforward process. There are no side effects,' Tanya muttered, leaning back in her chair.

'Yes, when you introduce the body to it slowly, when you use nanoids to bypass the immune system and deliver the human/Indigene genes directly to the DNA structure. Not when you slam a pure alien dose in there all at once and force the immune system into hyper drive.'

Tanya folded her arms and regained her composure. 'I'll consider your request, Bill. But I'm not promising anything. In the meantime, I think it would be best to bring Laura to one of the medical facilities. We can monitor her better from there.'

'Not an option. She needs help from the Indigenes—and I need to know now.' Bill was on edge. 'Are you going to allow her to travel to Exilon 5 with me?'

Tanya paused for a moment. 'I need time to discuss this with the others. I'll be in touch.' With that, she disconnected the call.

Bill's anxiety grew. He summarised their conversation in his head: Tanya hadn't dismissed the idea outright, but she hadn't agreed to it either. He quickly dialled another number. After several rings, a thin, gaunt, sunken-eyed woman appeared on screen. She was yo-yoing between too much energy and none at all. Laura was disappearing right before his eyes.

He relayed the conversation to her and she listened quietly. It seemed at times as if her mind was drifting and the conversation was of no interest to her. But Bill knew it wasn't her fault; she couldn't control what was happening to her. Eventually, she told him she needed to rest, and she hung up.


Laura was tired, but that wasn't the reason she ended

the call prematurely. She couldn't bear to see the pity in his eyes. She was getting it from all sides lately. Even her colleagues at the ESC had told her to go home after she blacked out at her desk.

Now, alone in her apartment, she struggled between the abundance of energy and the sickness that raged inside her. She popped another Actigen to counteract the tiredness, but all it did was fuel the out-of-control energy that pulled her in different directions. She staggered to her bed and lay down.

Sleep. No sleep.

She didn't know what her body wanted to do. The excessive hunger had passed, as had the cough she'd had at the beginning. Now, her body was shutting down and telling her food wasn't necessary. She no longer had an appetite. She had tried to eat a little cereal that morning, but it passed right through her, giving her body no time to draw out any of the nutrients along the way.

What was happening to her? Was she finally turning into an Indigene as Harvey Buchanan suggested? Shouldn't she feel stronger than this? Slowly, she climbed to her feet and stumbled to the bathroom, fighting against the weakness in her legs.

Laura examined her complexion closely in the mirror. She needed to see the changes for herself. Her skin was loose all over her body as the weight she had recently gained was dropping off again. Her usually thin face was gaunt, sickly looking, in the artificial light. She pulled at the skin around her eyes where dark circles now reigned. She stared into her green eyes. They had always been her best feature, she thought, but now, flecks of bright yellow were eclipsing the green pigmentation while her pupils were changing colour too, from black to dark grey.

Laura shielded her eyes from the overhead light with one hand. It was bothering her more than usual. She turned it off and continued to study her reflection in the mirror. With the door closed she could barely make anything out, but she could see the yellow flecks in her eyes, shining like reflective dots. She opened the bathroom door and went back to bed.

An hour later, she sat bolt upright. Suddenly she felt alive, as though she could get through an entire week's work without needing sleep. She also felt a bit hungry. Encouraged by this, she quickly checked her reflection in the mirror. What she saw made her gasp. Her hair was falling out in huge clumps. She pulled at the blonde strands that still clung to her scalp and they came away easily in her hand. Her skin was still grey and sickly; she certainly looked no better. Panicked by the loss of her hair, Laura ran to the kitchen and pulled open several drawers until she found what she wanted. With shaking hands, she clutched the tube of glue.

Back in her bedroom, she collected all the hair she could find—from her pillow, from the floor, from the bathroom sink—and standing in front of the mirror, she opened the glue and placed small dots of it randomly on her scalp. Then she gathered neat bunches of hair together and pressed it into the glue. When she'd finished, there wasn't a spare strand left in her hand. Laura stood back and admired her work with tears in her eyes. She looked like one of those cancer patients she'd seen in old medical textbooks.

Why her? Why was this happening?

She sank to her knees, still gripping the tube of glue tightly. Small drops of clear fluid leaked out and fell on her pyjamas. She didn't care when her sleeve stuck to her pyjama leg and she tore both garments trying to separate them. Her hair was gone. Her green eyes were fading. This was her punishment for trying to help the Indigenes, for thinking awful thoughts about her mother, for wanting something for herself—a cure for her seasonal depression. This was punishment for … no, she wasn't responsible for killing him. Her father took his own life.

She tossed the glue away and the tube hit the far wall. She clambered to her feet and wiped away her tears, careful not to catch another glimpse of her appearance in the mirror. She found the safety of the soft sofa and sank into it. For a long time, she drifted off into another world. When she came to, she knew what had to be done.

Grateful that she still had some energy, she went to the bedroom and stripped the sheet off the bed. Using the glue, she affixed it to the wall over the Light Box's shimmery facade. Then she grabbed a couple of towels and covered all the mirrors in her apartment. She could feel the energy sapping; moving around would be difficult soon.

In the bedroom, she stared at the dishevelled duvet on the floor and the clothes she had not washed for weeks. This room isn't right, she thought. She dragged the bedside tables out into the living room and pushed the bed over towards the wall. She grabbed the mattress and pulled it to the floor beside the bed. With her fists on her hips, Laura checked over her work. She was getting there, but it wasn't right yet.

She worked fast. The clothes, duvet, pictures of her family were all tossed out onto the living room floor. The small bedside lamp was relocated beside the mattress. She turned it on. Too bright. She placed it outside the door so that only a low light crept in under the door and cast an eerie glow inside the room.

Perfect.

She stripped out of her clothes and lay down on the bare mattress, just as the energy slump hit. Naked and curled up in a foetal position, she waited for her overheated body to cool down. She thought about getting up for some ice as the fever raged inside her, but moving about was too much of an effort now. Her fingers grazed the glued strands of hair. Then she closed her eyes and drifted into an uneasy sleep.

## 26

*Sydney, Earth*

With the access code to Laura's apartment block indelibly stamped on his memory, Bill made his way into the building and reached her apartment door. He banged his fist repeatedly on it making the doorframe rattle. A sick feeling circled around his stomach. He had tried calling her from the docking station as he'd waited for an available flight, but she hadn't answered. It had been several hours since they'd last spoken. His breathing heavy and his palms sweaty, he continued to pound away on the door. Faces appeared in the doorways of the other apartments on Laura's floor—an old man, a young woman, an older woman. It was the older woman who spoke to him after the others had closed their doors and disappeared from view.

'What'cha making all that noise for?' She didn't wait for an answer. 'Another one of them junkies, is it?' Her door opened a bit more. 'Well, I saw her only yesterday, wandering around in her pyjamas. Went out, then came back with a large bag. Hardly appropriate wear for decent folks to be lookin' at. Him next door has probably been gettin' quite the eyeful. Usually does. I tried to warn her, but she didn't wanna listen.'

Bill gritted his teeth and continued to bang on

the door. 'Laura? Come on, open up.'

'Laura? Is that the girl's name?' The old woman folded her arms now. 'As mad as a cut snake, but not as crazy as the old fart next door. You here to arrest her? 'Bout time.'

Bill placed his ear against the door and listened.

The old woman continued to chatter. 'There's no place for whingers like her in a decent block like this. You'd be better carting her off someplace else. You get me?'

A sudden prickle crept up Bill's spine as the woman's chatter drowned out his efforts to listen. 'She don't look well, sunken eyes, her hair falling out,' the old woman continued. 'I hate to be yabbering on but someone needs to point out the obvious. The girl needs professional help.'

Bill slowly turned around and, keeping his eyes locked on the old woman, strode towards her. He pushed her roughly inside her apartment and pulled the door closed. He could hear her release a string of expletives, then an inner door slammed.

Although he had the code to Laura's apartment, he was at a disadvantage without her security chip. He pulled out a small device and placed it over the lock, shielding it from the lens of the security camera up high on the wall. Random red numbers came up on the display of the device as it worked its way through the possible algorithms. Bill hit the override button and keyed in 4—1—3—6—8, the code Laura had given him to use only in case of emergency. He reckoned this qualified as one. The lock clicked open and Bill pushed his way inside.

He closed the door behind him. The sudden surge of adrenaline caused by what he saw rooted his feet to the spot: the upturned chairs, the bedside

# Crimson Dawn

lockers on their side, clothes strewn around the living room. And then there was the stench that prompted him to hold his nose tightly. He moved forward, slowly, uneasily. His chest tight, he struggled to catch his breath. With shaking hands, he checked under the mounds of clothes for the body. *Shit. I shouldn't have left Laura alone.*

The smell of rotting flesh drew him towards the kitchen. He closed his eyes then opened them again slowly, carefully sidestepping the mounds of debris on his way across the living room. He checked each pile, hoping that he wouldn't find anything more than furniture hidden underneath. But it was the smell coming from the kitchen that worried him most and he prepared himself to face his greatest fear—that Laura was dead.

Bill fought against the tears that threatened to fall and he blinked several times to dispel them. He couldn't help but think the worst, but he tried to tell himself that it was just his imagination running wild. He pushed through the swing door into the kitchen, quickly surveyed the scene and gasped loudly.

He wasn't looking at the spilled milk that had turned to lactic acid and gave off a metallic smell. He wasn't looking at the cereal on the floor nor the plate of barely touched lasagne. His eyes were focused on the dead body lying in a small pool of its own blood.

He willed his legs forward, forcing himself to look into its open, dead eyes, wondering what had happened to cause this—what had changed. He dropped to his knees and knelt beside it. Reaching out a hand, he grabbed the fur matted with blood and turned the body over; there was a large gash and a hole in the centre where its heart and intestines had once been. Bill gently laid the corpse down, grabbed a tea towel and wiped his hands on it. Frowning, he climbed to his feet, careful not to step in the blood of the white Persian cat that Bill assumed had belonged to Laura's mother.

He ignored the mess in the living room and walked more steadily towards the bedroom. There he found Laura, curled up on her side on the mattress on the floor. She was naked, her skin a strange sickly colour, her arms covered in scratches from the cat as it had fought for its life. Her hair was all but gone, except for patches where Laura had tried to glue it back on. Her breathing was shallow, her mouth bloody.

Bill lifted a sheet and threw it over her. He checked her pulse—it was strong, but too fast for her human heart to cope with. She was really beginning to look like an Indigene now, but the cuts and scratches on her arm that had not yet healed and her rapid heartbeat told him that the alteration wasn't going very well.

He put a hand on her shoulder and rocked her gently. 'Laura, wake up … Come on, Laura.' He slapped the cuts on her arm to evoke a different response.

Her eyes flickered open. She looked through him.

'Shit, Laura, what happened out there?'

She stared at the wall and licked her blood-caked lips. 'I was hungry.'

'So you killed your mother's cat?'

'It was the only place I knew to get fresh blood.'

'Come on,' Bill urged her and pulled on her arm to get her to sit upright. He lifted some clothes from the living room and dressed her. 'Come on, we need to go,' he said gently.

'Where to?' she managed to say as Bill carried her to the living room.

He placed her gently on the floor, then cleared the sofa of debris. He picked her up and set her down on the sofa beside him. 'First, I need them to see you,' he said.

Bill pulled down the sheet from her Light Box and activated it. Fourteen messages were waiting, all from her mother—looking for the cat, no doubt. They could wait until later. Bill air-punched a code into the virtual screen and Dave Solan's face popped up. Dave looked shocked to see Bill.

'What do you want?' he asked.

'Don't be a dickhead, Dave. Get me Simon,' Bill said sharply.

'No can do. Simon's in a meeting.'

'Then get him out of it.'

'I'm sorry, but that's not poss—'

Bill banged his fist down on the coffee table, his voice urgent. 'I'm not asking for your permission. Get him for me. Now!'

Dave blew out a breath and moved away from the screen. Bill could hear voices in the background. A minute later, Dave's face reappeared. He was more subdued. 'Simon's going to take your call in his office.'

A few seconds later, Simon appeared on screen, clearly unnerved by the impromptu call. 'What can I do for you, Bill?'

'It's not what you can do for me. It's what you can do for her.' He pulled Laura into shot and Simon's mouth dropped.

'What happened to her?' he asked.

'She's been infected by Indigene genetic code.'

'There are doctors here ...'

Bill could feel his face getting hot. 'Cut the bullshit, Simon. They don't want to help her. They want to study her.'

'What do you want from me?'

'She needs help from the Indigenes. Tell the board members I'll cooperate with them, do whatever they ask. They can assign a security detail to her if it makes them feel better. I need them to arrange for us to travel to Exilon 5 now.'

Simon rubbed his face. 'You're asking a lot.'

Bill's anger erupted. 'Didn't you hear me? I said I'll act as the go-between for both parties.'

Simon shook his head. 'I hate to say it, but it's Deighton you want to speak to. He has the Chair's attention, not me.'

'I wouldn't trust that fucker as far as—'

Laura tapped Bill on the arm. 'Let me say something.'

Keeping one hand on her back, Bill sat back to let her speak. She was shaking.

'Simon, Gilchrist was worried,' Laura said. 'She met with me the day before she died. She wanted to know what the Indigenes were like. You knew about the test subjects—you said the transfer numbers never lie. I think she was killed because she opposed World Government plans to change people into new Indigenes.'

Simon said nothing as he studied Laura.

'Please, help me,' Laura pleaded, her words slow and thick in her mouth. 'The Indigenes can help me in ways no humans can.'

Simon looked at Bill, horrified. 'She won't last the two-week journey.'

'She will if we put her in stasis. Harvey

Buchanan gave me a nanoid treatment to delay the alteration effects, but it's only temporary. The Indigenes have done this to her and they are the only ones who can reverse it.'

'Why not use the treatment on her now?'

'He only gave me enough to make sure I would remain dependent on him. I don't want to waste it,' Bill said.

'I can order him to give you more.'

'It's a temporary solution. It doesn't fix the underlying issues,' Bill said, his voice getting louder.

Simon stayed silent for a few minutes, but to Bill it felt like an eternity. He was holding Laura's hand now, and she was squeezing it so hard he thought the bones might break. Eventually Simon leaned in to the Light Box.

'Be at the docking station in Sydney tomorrow morning. I'll do my best to convince them,' he said.

'What are our chances?' Bill asked.

'The board members have been after you for a long time now. Deighton used your wife to make sure you took a negative interest in the Indigenes. No matter how standoffish the board have been about it, they're not about to miss out on this trip. Now Laura's turning into a new species. I think they'd prefer it if she stayed on Earth so they can study her, but if that isn't an option, they'll want her where they can keep an eye on her.'

Bill's chest tightened when he thought about Deighton using his wife. 'What was my real mission on Exilon 5?'

'Aside from telling us the exact location of the Indigenes?' Simon smiled wryly. 'To reveal their strengths and weaknesses, of course.'

'And I was pulled off, why?'

'Because you were beginning to side with them, to show them sympathy.'

'And now?'

'The board view your friendship with the Indigene as a way for them to get in close.'

Bill shook his head at the pack of lies they had fed him for so long.

'Inform them that we're packing our bags,' Bill said sharply. 'For once, Simon, you've chosen the right side.'

# 27

*Earth*

Charles Deighton arrived by town car at the docking station in Washington D.C. after a restless night's sleep. Reluctantly, he swapped the warmth of the car's interior for the cold early morning air. A second car pulled up and his two large, thick-necked bodyguards emerged. A string of lights approached them through the gloom, the light blinding him as the vehicles neared. Deighton shielded his eyes as the convoy of black cars—mostly security—pulled up to the kerb. A military vehicle brought up the rear of the group. The board members who had elected to come on the trip emerged from the last three cars. There were only three of them, including Tanya Li. That suited him perfectly.

He greeted each of them—Tanya Li, one conservative member and one liberal member—with a brief, stiff handshake. They stood as close as they could to each other without actually huddling, their thick winter coats wrapped tightly around them and their gel masks instantly filling with condensation. The oversized, inflated bodyguards talked into their micro-thin wires and paced up and down the stretch of pavement outside the docking station.

'Are we waiting for anybody else?' Deighton asked Tanya, his words muffled by his mask.

Tanya peered at him. 'This is it I'm afraid. Nobody else wanted to come. But don't worry, we have plenty of security.'

Deighton smiled briefly. He wasn't worried about security; fewer board members meant fewer people to convince of his plans for alteration. 'Are we meeting Mr Taggart and the girl on the passenger ship?' he asked.

Tanya nodded. 'I've arranged for them to travel to the passenger ship from Sydney by spacecraft. They have heavy security to accompany them.'

Deighton was tense on the journey to the passenger ship as he tried to work out a strategy to deal with Taggart. He wondered if there would be an opportunity to talk to Taggart privately and feed him some more lies. He viewed the investigator as the last obstacle to him getting what he wanted.

As the spacecraft manoeuvred into the hold of the passenger ship, Deighton squeezed his hands together. The tremors got worse when he was worried. His right leg bounced up and down uncontrollably. If he was lucky, the others would just view them as nervous twitches.

The craft doors opened and Deighton stepped cautiously into the cavernous hold of the ship. The second spacecraft had arrived and a security team was buzzing around them as Bill Taggart emerged with his arm wrapped around Laura. She was covered in a blanket. Deighton noticed that Bill's face was fraught with worry, his body stiff. When Laura stumbled, he immediately scooped her up in his arms. Deighton didn't understand relationships. Why inconvenience yourself for another person only to get so little in return?

Bill leaned in close to Laura's covered face and whispered something before frantically seeking out a member of staff. 'We need to put her in stasis, immediately,' he shouted. He handed one of the staff three vials. 'Give her one dose every four days. It'll halt her changes temporarily. Stasis should do the rest until we get there. Did you get all that?'

The staff member nodded while the remaining staff, flustered by the intense security presence, finally got their act together and wheeled in a mobile bed. Bill placed Laura on it and briefly glanced in the direction of the board members before disappearing through the doors that led to the main part of the ship. The tension evaporated in the hold and the board members, who had been quietly watching Bill, now began to move.

Personal attendants appeared as if by magic and relieved the board members of their luggage, while genetically superior bodyguards quickly ushered the board members through the doors as if they were delicate cargo.

The board members were housed in the same corridor, just a short distance from the cockpit. There were twelve plush rooms available, one for each of the board members to travel in comfort had they chosen to come. With only four board members travelling, they had their pick of the rooms. Deighton chose a room as far from the others as he could get.

The male attendant placed his bags on the cream carpet and closed the explosion-proof door behind him. Inside was a walnut four-poster bed big enough to sleep four people. Four wooden chairs, their seats covered in a soft cream fabric, surrounded a round marble table in the centre of the room. A chaise longue dressed in a similar cream fabric beckoned for him to lie on it and relax. He could smell the dark roasted blend coffee wafting from the sterling silver pot. Beside it there was a fine bone china cup and a plate of bite-sized lemon muffins. If it hadn't been for the shimmering Light Box on the wall that had activated as soon as he'd entered, he could have been in the 1920s.

Deighton thought about taking an hour to relax, but all he could think about was Bill Taggart poisoning Tanya Li with his lies. He would need to keep close to Tanya to stop her from having too much contact with Taggart—the wrong words from him could be Deighton's undoing.

He opened his bag and removed a syringe. He flicked off the protective top and jabbed the needle first into his leg and then into his arm. The muscle-stabilising shots would only last a few days before he'd need to give himself more.

He lay down on the chaise longue and closed his eyes. He soon dreamed about being locked in a room with poisonous snakes that were repeatedly biting him.

## 28

An unshaven Bill sat on the floor of the sleeping quarters, his back against the wall and his knees pulled up to his chest with his arms wrapped around them. There were twelve sleeping pods in the room, but aside from his own, the rest were unoccupied. He had not been offered one of the official rooms, so this was as close as he could get to privacy, and to Laura in the stasis room.

He could hear a clanging noise in the distance; the air conditioning was on the fritz again. The white wall he stared at opposite him conjured up images of Laura all alone in her stasis pod and only checked infrequently by unfamiliar staff; mostly, the onboard computer would monitor her vitals. He rubbed his eyes with the heel of one hand, breathing heavily. He had already tried to get in to see her, but he had been denied clearance to the corridor beyond the recreation room that separated the general population from the stasis rooms and the functional areas of the ship. What else could he do? Demand an audience with the board members? Yes, if it meant he could check that Laura was all right, and that her alteration process had stabilised for now.

The Indigenes came to mind. What if they couldn't reverse what they had done to her? What would he do then?

In one hand, he gripped the last vial that

Harvey Buchanan had given him to slow Laura's alteration. She'd already had one shot. He had given the ship's personnel three additional vials. He was holding on to the final one for when they arrived at Exilon 5 and stasis was no longer an option.

Bill's legs slid out in front of him and he let one hand drop to the floor while he kept the fist containing the vial close to his chest. His breathing finally slowed as he came to the realisation that he could do no more for Laura. He sat there for hours in the same position, thinking about how much he'd taken her for granted before their night together and wishing they'd got together sooner. Once, it had been Isla who filled his thoughts, but when he closed his eyes now it was Laura's face that appeared. It was Laura who made him feel good about himself and he wanted the chance to find out if they had a future together. A bitter pain caused his chest to tighten as he thought about the risks he had allowed her to take. But, he reminded himself, she was still alive.

A renewed sense of determination filled him when he thought about Laura as she got on the spacecraft: her patchy hair, sickly looking skin and sunken eyes. Even then, she'd managed to keep it together and had been able to give him one of her smiles. Throughout the alteration process, he could still see her—her unique character, her humour, her optimism—and was confident that everything would work out fine.

Bill's eyes roamed the floor, searching for the grey holder that the vials had come in. He stretched out for it and wiggled his fingers until he had a grip. He slid the remaining vial into the reinforced padded holder and put it inside the pocket of his green military coat. He stood up and brushed the dust off his coat and black combats. He'd have to sweet-talk Tanya Li if he was going to have any chance of seeing Laura. As he understood it, the board members were being guarded by the giant freaks, so storming her room wasn't an option unless he wanted every bone in his body broken.

He put his belongings in to his sleeping pod and locked it, then left the room. Outside in the corridor, two military men approached him.

'The Chair wants to see you,' one of them said.

'Well good, because I want to see her. Where is she?'

'We'll take you.'

They walked in silence with Bill sandwiched between the two men as if he was under arrest. He quickly tapped his hand over the breast pocket of his coat, checking for the vial and his breathing calmed once he was reassured it was still there.

The two military men led him through the recreation room, which was now filled with blonde-haired, blue-eyed people. They were dressed in white and were almost gleaming from what he assumed was some new mandatory disinfection of all transferees—the place smelled of fresh laundry. Not that long ago, passengers had been allowed to wear civilian clothes.

The blue-eyed people were indifferent to them as they passed through; the only noise in the room came from their three pairs of boots hitting the floor. It seemed odd to him that not one of them was interested in the dark-haired, scruffy man being escorted by military. But the glazed look in their eyes explained it.

'Why have they been drugged?' Bill asked one of the military men, thumbing in their direction. They stopped in front of a metal door leading to the non-civilian area of the ship.

The man shrugged as he scanned his security chip on the plate beside the door. 'Stasis?' he replied, just as indifferent to the blue-eyed passengers as they were to him.

The impenetrable door opened and Bill stepped through, eager to leave behind the group of blonde passengers that suddenly gave him the creeps. He was grateful that Laura's eyes were green and that she didn't match the current genetic criteria selection.

The smell of flowers hit him when the military men led him down a wide, opulent corridor. His heavy boots barely made a noise on the plush red carpet. Dark oak doors lined the corridor and rich lighting sconces guided the way. Gentle music reached his ears. This corridor belonged to apparently important people.

The military men stopped outside a large walnut door; one of them knocked then opened the door. Bill followed him inside the oval-shaped room. Two extremely tall bodyguards stood at military ease against the wall by the door, their heads grazing the ceiling. The board members were sitting on red velvet-covered chairs arranged around an oak table with a leather inset. There was one empty seat.

'Ah, Mr Taggart, you're here,' said Tanya Li patting the seat beside her.

Bill looked around at everyone; he recognised Charles Deighton, but the other two he didn't know. Tanya introduced them, but he forgot their names. All he remembered about them was that one was conservative in his views and the other was more open minded to settling on Exilon 5.

Bill raised an eyebrow. 'I thought more of you would have come.'

Tanya nodded, her expression grim. 'The others had difficulty finding people they could trust to look after things in their absence.'

Bill sat down on the seat Tanya indicated. From there, he had a good view of Deighton sitting opposite him.

'Would you like a drink?' Tanya asked. She rang a bell and a waiter emerged from behind a panel in the wall. 'Brandy, wine? Whatever you like. We have it all.'

Bill shook his head. 'Just water, thanks.'

Deighton picked up his glass and swirled the amber liquid around making sure Bill could see it. 'Come on, my boy. Try it,' he said, keeping his eyes fixed on the contents. 'It's vintage. You probably won't get another chance to drink something from 2133. There are only a thousand bottles left in the world and we have them all.' Deighton had already had too much: his hands were shaking.

Bill could sense Tanya watching him closely, waiting for his reply. 'No thanks. Water will be fine,' he repeated.

The waiter returned with a cut crystal glass of water. Bill cradled the glass in his hand without taking a sip, then placed it on the leather inset on the table.

'Bill, we know you've befriended the Indigenes,' Tanya said. 'We need your help to ensure they come to us. We want to reach out the hand of friendship to see if we can resolve our differences.'

'Well, I can't say that I've befriended them.'

'It's in our interest that we find a way to occupy this planet without their interference. We are looking for some kind of common ground,' Tanya explained.

'And if you can't find it?' Bill asked.

'If we can't—well, I don't know what will happen to them. It's in all our interests that this trip goes well,' Tanya said.

Deighton leaned forward. His watery blue eyes locked on Bill's and he showed his teeth in what Bill assumed was meant to be a smile. 'Taggart, my boy, the Indigenes have killed key members of our medical staff. The board is worried that the Indigenes will never come to accept us. Unless we're open and honest about our plans for Exilon 5, we will always be looking over our shoulder. I'm sure you can understand that.' Deighton put his glass down and clasped his fingers together tightly. 'For this meeting to go well, we need the Indigenes to trust us. That's where you come in.'

Bill tried not to show his disgust. It made his skin crawl having to sit in the same room as his wife's murderer. He ignored Deighton and turned to Tanya. 'They don't trust you and with good reason. The Indigene you captured—the one you tortured for three months—wouldn't have anything very good to say about you. And that's just for starters.' His tone softened a little. 'But, I'm willing to help if you do one thing for me.'

Deighton's eyes brightened. 'You saw him—Anton?'

Bill heard the excitement in Deighton's voice, which confirmed what Simon Shaw had told him—that Deighton had been behind the bomb that Anton brought to Exilon 5. 'I'm told he's still alive—psychologically damaged, but alive,' Bill said to Tanya.

'When Anton arrived on Earth unannounced, we had to do what was necessary to protect ourselves,' Deighton said to Bill, ignoring the fact that Bill refused to talk to him directly. 'We had no idea why he travelled there and we needed to find out more about his motives. We were merely trying to establish a connection with him, to understand his race better.' Deighton paused and tried to look sincere. 'We don't blame him for killing two of our doctors—it was self-defence, we know that now. Once we were sure he was no longer a threat, we sent him home. No harm done.'

*No harm done?* Bill bit his tongue and addressed Tanya again. 'I need a favour from you. I need to see Laura.'

She shook her head and smiled. 'Laura's resting. We've given her one of Harvey's vials, as you instructed. There's nothing you can do for her.'

'I still want to see her. I'll do what you want if you grant me that request.'

'I really don't see the need. She's being protected. We won't allow any harm to come to her.' Tanya briefly touched her nose.

More like you want to study her, Bill thought, reading her body language. He said nothing and crossed his arms.

Tanya stared at him for a moment. 'Fine, but only for a short time,' she said eventually. 'And only after we're finished here. First, we have business to discuss.'

Bill relaxed slightly, leaned forward in his chair and rested his arms on the table. 'I'm all ears.'

'The board members have tried to maintain peace since—well, since Peter Cantwell's reign as Chair. He gave the order for Exilon 5 to be terraformed all those years ago while the Indigenes were still living there. We, the current board members, have come to realise that killing the Indigenes may not serve our best interests.'

'And you came to that realisation all by yourself?' Bill said, trying but failing to keep the sarcasm out of his voice. 'You've been killing them in other ways—restricting their movements, tracking them, picking them off one by one and experimenting on them.'

'You do want to see Laura, don't you?' said Tanya.

'Of course.'

'Then we'd all appreciate your cooperation, not your hostility,' Tanya said firmly. 'This is not the place to air your grievances. Do you understand me?'

Bill gritted his teeth. 'Aye. My apologies.'

Deighton leaned forward. 'We just need your help to get us a meeting with the Indigenes. We want to talk, that's all. I assume you have a way to contact them?'

Bill thought about the communication stone that he had brought with him. 'They're a pretty intuitive race,' he said to Tanya. 'They'll figure it out.'

'Yes, that's what we thought too,' Deighton said. 'But just in case, we'd like you to take us to their home underground.'

The thought of bringing Deighton to the Indigenes' districts sickened Bill. 'I have no way to do that. Besides, they won't allow it,' he said to Tanya.

Deighton nodded agreeably. 'Chair, Bill's probably right—we wouldn't be safe in their territory, in their world. It would be better if they came to us, on *our* terms, above ground. Only then do we stand a fighting chance.'

'Are you planning some kind of war, Charles?' Tanya said smoothly, staring at Deighton.

'No, of course not,' he said trying to placate her with a smile. 'But if they try to retaliate, which we know they are more than capable of, if we're above ground at least we won't be trapped inside their network of tunnels. That would be suicide.'

'I might be able to convince them to come to you,' Bill added, addressing the Chair, 'but I'm not their keeper and it's up to them.'

'They will trust us if you're on our side,' Tanya said. 'We only want to talk to their leaders. We have an opportunity to work together, to make this union beneficial to all. We can assimilate them into our own culture.'

Bill turned to look at her, frowning harder. 'Can they trust you?' It was a question meant for all four board members but Bill was curious to see where Tanya stood.

'Of course they can,' she replied haughtily. 'This isn't an attack. We know that the Indigenes have rights. We want to give them back those rights, but they need to promise to work with us, not against us.'

'Why did the World Government set out to destroy the Indigenes in the first place, all those years ago?' Bill asked. 'They were your creation, after all.'

Tanya blinked slowly. 'The Indigenes were meant to be Plan B if humans couldn't live on Exilon 5.' She pushed back her chair and crossed her legs. 'But they've continued to evolve and already are too strong for us. Anton is proof of that. Why do you think we surround ourselves with these genetically modified bodyguards?'

'And now?'

'Now we just want the chance to understand their plans for the future—will they continue to plot against us or can we co-exist, find a common ground?' Tanya touched her nose again.

Bill sat forward. 'I want to see Laura now.'

'We're not done here, Mr Taggart.'

'I understand what you want me to do. There's nothing more to discuss.'

'How will you contact them?'

'As I said, they're pretty intuitive.' Bill stood up.

Tanya nodded to one of the bodyguards near the door. 'Okay. But keep it brief,' she said.

The bodyguard spoke into a device on his wrist. A minute later, a burly military man appeared at the door.

Bill's breathing was ragged, his hands clammy as they neared the stasis room. Two modified bodyguards protected the door. The military man indicated for them to step aside. As the man pushed on the door, a tingle crept up Bill's spine. Would Laura look the same or worse? He hoped the solution Harvey had given him would be enough to at least slow the alteration process.

'You have ten minutes,' the burly military man said before mumbling into the wire of his communication device. He closed the door and Bill walked past several long, oval-shaped pods made from toughened glass. Most of them were empty, but some had people inside who looked as if they were soldiers awaiting activation. Bill studied their faces, their closed eyes, and shivered at the thought of giving up that much control to a computer. He read the names on the small display screen embedded in the front of the pods: Robbie O'Shea, twenty-two;

Joel Taylor, forty-eight. Taylor drew his attention; they were of a similar age. He looked quite normal until Bill noticed his upper arms, both of them heavily pockmarked. Voluntary inoculations or forced experimentation? Bill wondered. It brought to mind something Isla had once said about the government-employed lab technicians and medical staff—that they routinely received inoculations each year to combat the live diseases that were stored in the labs. Were these government employees then? His eyes widened at the thought. He recalled the doe-eyed druggies in the recreation room and suddenly wanted to hear each of their stories and know where they came from.

He sought out Laura—blonde-haired, green-eyed Laura, who was also a government employee. Had her eye colour saved her from this one-way trip to Exilon 5? How long before they caught up with her and others with similar genetics?

He found her at the end of the room, isolated from the others. She was breathing unevenly, even in stasis. But her appearance hadn't changed much since he'd last seen her and he was grateful for small mercies. With a hand on the glass he studied her face, her closed eyes, her eyebrows that were now thin and patchy too. And he noticed something else that made him shudder—the smile on her face.

He blinked and looked again. No, it wasn't a smile, but a grimace.

The glass was cool when he rested his head against it. 'I'm here, love,' he whispered. 'I promise I'll fix whatever was done to you, if it's the last thing I do.'

The board members didn't try to stop Bill from going back to his sleeping quarters after seeing Laura. There was nothing more to discuss. He punched in the code to open his sleeping pod and rooted inside his carry-on bag. He breathed a sigh of relief when he put his hand on the communication stone. It was less cold than before and it was emitting a faint blue glow that highlighted the concentric rings on the front. He cocked his head when he thought he heard a noise, a voice. It was faint. It could have been the air conditioning. He waited for a moment but heard nothing more.

Still wearing his green military coat, he climbed in the pod and pulled the hatch closed. He clutched the stone to his chest, holding it right beside the vial in his breast pocket. If they came for either item, they'd have to rip them from his cold, dead hands first.

*Come on, Bill. Think, for fuck's sake. What are you going to do?* He stared into the darkness of the pod. All he could see was Laura's face—her grimace. A lingering pain in his chest made it hard for him to breathe.

He had agreed to the board members' plan to act as a go-between. How was he going to warn the Indigenes that they could be walking into a trap? He didn't trust Deighton, and Tanya wasn't filling him with confidence either. The communication stone felt warmer in his hand. He gripped it more tightly. He thought he heard a faint voice speak to him.

'Laura needs help,' he said aloud. Perhaps Stephen could hear him—it was a long shot, but worth trying. Then it dawned on him what was happening. Stephen had said it could become anything he wanted it to be. It had acted as a compass when he'd needed one, and now it was behaving like a communication device.

'Can you hear me?' he whispered.

The stone continued to emit its faint blue glow. He heard a voice reaching through the darkness. Bill held the stone up to his ear.

'I can see you,' someone said.

*Stephen.*

Bill eagerly listened to the rest of the message.

# 29

*Exilon 5*

The passenger ship arrived in the last week in October. A convoy of land vehicles was waiting for them when they emerged from the New London docking station.

Tanya was reluctant to let Laura out of her sight. 'My personal bodyguard can take her,' she said. But Bill insisted on carrying her, his bag with the communication stone in it slung across his body. So Tanya arranged for two military men to walk either side of him and for her bodyguard to trail close behind.

The board members and security detail climbed into the various black vehicles; Bill and Laura rode with Tanya and her private goon. The windows were tinted, but he could see outside. The road beyond New London was bumpy and he could feel Laura shaking violently beneath the blanket. He pulled out the last vial that Harvey had given him, drew the contents into a syringe and plunged it in her arm. She didn't flinch.

The road surface became smoother as the vehicle travelled along one of the newly constructed roads, its surface barely dry. The half-built construction several miles from New London's city limits came into view. It was the beginning of a new build that would become the seventh city on Exilon 5. A large wooden billboard was staked into the ground, on top of which was a digital sign announcing the name of the city: New Melbourne. The labourers that had once been there were gone. The surrounding area was now occupied by a strong military presence and roving cameras. The unfinished city made Bill think of the abandoned cities that had fallen during World War II. He'd seen the photographs in one of Isla's old history books.

The convoy of vehicles left the immaculate road and bumped along a dirt track leading to the entrance of the new city: a large double gate, fifteen feet tall. The city was surrounded by an equally tall wall. One way in and one way out, Bill noted.

The convoy came to a halt while the military pulled a gate open; then they were waved through. Bill looked behind him to see them closing the gates again. It was a fortress.

New Melbourne didn't seem to be a large city. The main road into its heart was framed by a single row of buildings on either side. Behind it was the raw land of Exilon 5 trapped in the enclosure and yet to be developed. The city was in its infancy. Military men and women in riot gear lined the main road, their backs turned to the unfinished constructions. Bill wondered what size battle the board members were expecting. He got the feeling that talking and negotiation weren't the only things on their minds.

The half-built red-bricked constructions were mostly just two storeys high, although some reached higher than that. Most of them were without roofs, except for the buildings at the end of the road. The heart of New Melbourne appeared to end in a cul-de-sac where a large yellow-stone building spanning several hundred feet stood. It seemed to be the only building that had been completed. Two smaller roads branched off round it, one to the left and one to the right, leading to more cul-de-sacs that were only accessible by foot.

The vehicles pulled up in front of the yellow-stone building. It had two open doors, a couple of hundred feet apart. Bill climbed out of the back and scooped Laura up in his arms. He needed to get her inside out of the daylight. She may have been human, but her body was also half Indigene and sensitive to sunlight.

'Use the door on the left,' Tanya instructed him when she saw the rush he was in.

The room on the left looked like a supply room. Stacked up against one wall were green boxes filled with food, blankets and medical supplies. In front of the boxes, three chairs were lined up and there was a table along the back wall. Laura was getting heavy in his arms, so Bill set her down gently on one of the chairs as several of the military men who had gathered at the door looked on. He heard commotion behind him, then Tanya and her bodyguard appeared at his side. Soon, the other board members and their bodyguards joined them. With all of them inside, the room felt cramped.

Bill's immediate concern was for Laura as she struggled to sit still on the chair. It was clear the war inside her raged on. Her human side was unwilling to give up the fight, but the Indigene side was slowly breaking down her defences.

'Tell the experienced ones to stay with her,' Tanya ordered her bodyguard, nodding at the older military outside the door. 'Everyone that doesn't need to be here, please go next door,' she said loudly. Her bodyguard arrived back with several military in tow. Some stayed in the supply room, the rest lined up outside, creating an unbreakable line. Only then did Tanya leave.

Under the watchful eye of several armed guards, Bill spent the next twenty minutes trying to calm Laura down. Then as it grew dark outside, Bill heard murmurs and military feet shuffling in the dirt. Suddenly, the military inside the room raised their buzz guns to waist level. Bill went to the door, trying to see past the heads of those who blocked the entrance.

Five hooded figures all dressed in black were walking along the road towards the building. The gate to the city was wide open. Bill couldn't see the leader's face. The military watched anxiously, their postures stiff, fingers poised over the discharge buttons of their deadly buzz guns. Bill heard the occasional word—*shit, fuck*—from the military men. But there was no command to fire.

Bill pushed his way outside. Tanya, Deighton and the other two board members were standing at the other door of the yellow-stone building. So too were their personal bodyguards.

Bill heard Tanya reply to someone, 'Not yet. I want to hear what they have to say.'

'I don't recognise these ones at all,' Deighton said.

Bill looked for a familiar face among the approaching figures. Stephen wasn't there although he'd promised he would come. So who were these Indigenes? Just as Bill turned to check on Laura he heard their leader speak.

'We're here for the girl.' It was a female's voice.

Bill, suddenly torn about handing Laura over to a bunch of strangers, wanted confirmation that Stephen had sent them. *This had better be the plan.*

'Where are your leaders?' Tanya asked her. 'We were promised they would be here. We can't let you take her, not until we talk to them.'

Bill snarled at this suggestion of a trade. Laura wasn't some sort of bargaining chip. She wouldn't last long if they had to wait for the rest to arrive. He tried to talk telepathically to the Indigenes.

*If you can hear me, Laura has to go, now! Just tell them your leaders are coming, even if they're not.* His eyes remained fixed on the face of female who had spoken.

'They will be here soon,' she said without looking at Bill, 'but first we want the girl.'

Bill studied the Indigene's eyes, the only part of her that was visible. They were an unusual shade of blue—not quite human but not Indigene either. He continued to stare at the Indigene group who stood stiffly among the military men. He touched his bag that was still slung across his body, tempted to pull out the communication stone. The bag was warm, most likely because the communication stone was hot. *This had better be a fucking sign, Stephen.*

He angrily watched Tanya discuss the request with the others while the bodyguards stood between the Indigenes and the board members, affording enough of a gap for them to communicate with each other. All the while, Bill was conscious that Laura was running out of precious time.

'Okay,' Tanya said eventually, 'take the girl.'

Bill tensed up as the female Indigene walked towards him. The military were now angling their weapons towards the ground. Tanya's bodyguard nodded and the men guarding the supply room moved aside. The female went into the room in a blur, Bill following her. When she was in front of Laura, he grabbed her arm.

She glared at him. 'Don't touch me, human.'

'You're not taking her until you tell me who you are,' Bill said sharply.

'I don't need your permission,' the Indigene said, her voice cold and harsh.

Laura's breathing had become erratic, almost as if she was excited. Bill wondered if it was the presence of the Indigene that was affecting her.

Suddenly, the female Indigene's attitude changed. In an instant, she became alluring and her tone of voice softened as she said, 'Give her to me.'

Bill felt light-headed and felt a sudden urge to give in to the female's demand. But he snapped out of it and with the greatest of difficulty, he stood in front of Laura. 'Not until you tell me where you're from,' he said.

She glanced behind her at the military and curled her finger at one. 'You,' she said. Her voice was gentle, attractive. 'I want you to come to me.'

As if he had no choice, the soldier did as she asked.

'Now, make him give her to me,' she said.

The military man raised his weapon and pointed it at Bill's head.

She cupped the back of the man's neck tightly. 'Don't fire yet—not until I say so.'

The soldier's hand was shaking, as if he was trying to resist.

Bill could hear Laura grunting and panting like a wild animal behind him, and he could feel the crackle of energy building up inside the soldier's buzz gun.

'Move out of my way,' the female commanded Bill.

Just then, another Indigene—a male—appeared at the door and came inside. The military didn't seem to notice or react to him. They were too busy staring at her.

Bill took a step to the right as if someone else was controlling his actions. He wanted to yell at the female, but for some reason he couldn't. Then he saw it, the fleeting smile meant only for him.

The male Indigene swept Laura up in his arms. Bill felt a stab of jealousy as she wrapped her arms around his neck and buried her face in his chest. Before he could tell her that everything would be okay, the Indigene pair had left the room in a blur. Bill strode to the door, pushing the dazed military men out of the way. He caught sight of the Indigenes running towards the open gate, then they disappeared into the night like black, wispy ghosts.

Tanya came over to him, an unconvincing look of pity on her face. 'I'm sorry, Bill. I did everything I could.'

Bill nodded curtly. She had sacrificed Laura for an audience with the Indigenes. The right ones would come soon enough. He pretended to be angry, but he was mostly relieved that Laura was now in safe hands; he had used Harvey's last vial and was out of options. He stared into the distance after the Indigene group.

What had that female just done to him—to all of them? He couldn't even hold on to the memory. He looked at the soldier who had put the gun to his head. All the military were groggy as if they had just woken from a deep sleep. Stephen had told him that an influencer would come for Laura, but he hadn't quite understood what that meant in reality—until now.

Night time settled in and the temperatures dropped steadily. Bill removed his bag and grabbed one of the blankets from the table in the supply room, wrapping it around him. He sat on the chair Laura had been sitting in and shivered as the chill of the night air seeped through the uninsulated walls of the supply room.

Three hours had passed since the Indigenes had taken Laura and there was no sign of any other Indigenes arriving as had been promised. Three military men hovered inside the room and Bill wondered if he was under arrest. He licked his lips, realising he hadn't had anything to drink since they'd left the passenger ship.

'Can I have some water?' he asked one of the military men.

The man disappeared and returned with a bottle. He handed it to Bill.

'Thanks.' Bill unscrewed the cap and took a large gulp. He screwed the cap on again and stood up, shoving the water in the pocket of his military coat. He picked up his bag and slung it across his body. Nobody stopped him when he walked outside, but he noticed one of the military men—a man in his twenties—shadowing him.

'I'm just going for a piss,' he said to the man. 'I'd rather you didn't watch.'

'Don't take a leak outside,' the young soldier said. 'There are dedicated toilets in the building over there.' He pointed to a red-brick building that had the words 'Site for Restaurant' emblazoned across the top. 'We don't want the biodome animals tracking us by our scents.'

Bill went inside the unfinished red-brick building, the young soldier following him. He stepped over stacked bricks and bags of bonding materials. The soldier pointed to a door at the back. There were several toilet stalls on the other side of the door. Bill locked himself inside one, his military escort waiting outside.

Bill sat down on the seat and removed the stone from his bag. The concentric circles were glowing bright blue. He held it up to his ear. Nothing. With someone so close, he couldn't risk talking into it.

Judging by the strength of colour emitted by the stone, they must be right above District Three. Bill knew the Indigenes exited from their tunnels at various points across the land, but with more city walls being built, the less safe it became for them to surface without the risk of being caught inside. It was as if the constructions were deliberately hemming them in like rats in a maze and forcing them to surface at specific places.

Bill sat there for a moment longer while his escort continued to wait for him. The silence in the room was deafening. Bill removed the bottle of water from his pocket and poured some of it down the hole. The bowl sanitised itself and he emerged soon after.

'So what's this city going to be called then?' Bill asked as he washed his hands in the sink.

The young soldier frowned. 'New Melbourne. You did see the giant sign on the way in, didn't you? It's hard to miss.'

'It's a hell of a turnout for such a small meeting, don't you think? How long do you plan to be stationed here?'

'As long as it takes,' the soldier said and shrugged.

Bill turned and leaned against the sink, drying his hands on his black combats. 'There's an odd feel to this city, don't you think?'

The military man frowned. 'What do you mean?'

'There's only one way in and out. Then there are the two small tracks that branch off behind the yellow building. It almost feels like you're in a trap.'

'Excuse me?'

Bill turned to face the mirror, studied his reflection, then laughed. 'I mean, it feels claustrophobic—you get that trapped feeling. Don't you sense that?'

'Er, I hadn't really thought too much about it.'

Bill smiled as genuinely as he could. 'No, I guess not. You move around a lot, see plenty of open spaces. It's probably been a few years since you've been back on Earth.' The young soldier nodded. Bill went on. 'The closed-in feeling you experience on Earth gets under your skin after a while. The last thing you want in a new city is small, confined spaces to get stuck in.'

Bill left the bathroom with his escort in tow. Was it really a new city or had it been deliberately built with the Indigenes in mind? When he emerged outside, he noticed one of the enormous bodyguards leave the yellow building and come towards him.

'Come with me. The Chair wants to see you,' he said with an abnormally deep voice.

Bill followed him through the other door to where the board members had settled and into a large room at the back. There had been a lot of work done in this room and Bill was sure some of it was security-type detail. The walls had been painted sky blue and a stone floor had been newly laid. A large desk was positioned near the back wall. Tanya Li sat behind it surrounded by what looked like maps, or schematics, and a large monitor. She looked up from the desk.

'Leave us,' she said to her bodyguard.

She waited for him to close the door before addressing Bill. 'Where the hell are they? The Indigenes should have been here by now.'

'I'd like to know the same thing too,' Bill said honestly.

'They've taken Laura, but for what purpose I dread to think.' Tanya scrutinised his face.

Bill stayed silent. She was testing him to find out if he had told the Indigenes not to come. The thought had crossed his mind, but in the end they would do what they felt was necessary, not what he told them to.

Tanya stood up and leaned her hands on the table. 'Their actions today do not bode well for them. They've forced us to hand over one of our own, the weakest and most vulnerable among us. It's possible you were wrong about them and that they used you to gain this advantage over us. Now we're the ones on the back foot. Charles Deighton thinks we should dispose of the Indigene race entirely and proceed with plans to change humans into a new generation of super humans, ones that are more agreeable and easier to control. What do you think we should do?'

'My only priority is getting Laura back safely.'

Tanya pursed her lips. 'I would still like to hear your opinion though.'

Bill smiled ruefully. 'It doesn't matter what I think. You'll do whatever you want. But I will tell you this—I'd think long and hard before consulting Deighton if I were you. He's a dangerous fucker.'

Tanya's brows knotted. 'That's funny. Daphne Gilchrist said something similar to me the day before she died.'

# 30

For two days and nights after the Indigenes took Laura nothing happened. There were many false alarms during that time; every stone kicked and every howl in the distance was checked by both the bodyguards and military. But after a while, enthusiasm waned and the checks became an annoyance. On the second night there was a noise in the distance: a struggle, then a whimper, then silence. Somewhere beyond the gate, an animal had run out of luck. The military men and women roaming the streets didn't react to the noise. Buzz guns and impulse tasers remained holstered.

Bill had stopped checking the communication stone for signs of Stephen by that time. He knew the Indigenes would come; he just didn't know when. He was worried for them when they did arrive, for they'd have to walk down the only street in New Melbourne, trapped between a mile-long stretch of unfinished buildings and no easy way out. The last time Bill had been in Tanya Li's makeshift office he had noticed that she was looking at maps or blueprints of the city. Just what were they planning?

But on the third night, when the military were no longer on high alert, Bill heard a new sound. Tanya emerged from the entrance to her office.

'Is it them?' she asked anxiously.

'I'm not sure,' Bill replied.

He heard a click of fingers and suddenly the board members were outside, their bodyguards out in front, towering over everyone else. The military created a tight circle around the bodyguards. So much for talking, Bill thought.

He stared at the entrance to the city, the road leading up to it brightly lit by large solar lamps but the wasteland beyond remaining in total darkness. He could hear movement outside the high walls and the sound of feet hitting the dirt.

One by one, the Indigenes came through the gate and rushed past the military, lining the street. The artificial lights picked up seven Indigenes, who slowed to a walking pace when they were about a hundred feet away. They were dressed in the same hooded black outfits as the group who had come to take Laura. Two females led the group, one of them the one with the blue eyes, the influencer. She was staring at the military that surrounded the bodyguards and the board members.

Bill rubbed his skin vigorously; static filled the air and nipped at his skin. He wasn't equipped with an energy-absorbing suit like the board members and military were. He looked beyond the two females and breathed a sigh of relief when he recognised Pierre and Stephen. His eyes widened and he tried to speak to them telepathically—anything you'd like to share?—but neither of them acknowledged him. Behind them were three other males, Leon, Anton's father, a second around Pierre's age and a younger male whom he couldn't see properly. They appeared to be a welcoming party of sorts. A large group of Indigenes had gathered at the gate and were waiting.

Bill searched Stephen's face for anything that would give him a clue about how Laura was doing.

But Stephen continued to ignore him, keeping his yellow-flecked eyes fixed on the tight group of board members. Their military protectors allowed a small gap to open in their cordon just big enough for Tanya and her genetically modified bodyguard to squeeze through. Bill estimated the modified men were probably as strong as the Indigenes. It would be a fair fight, if that's what it came to.

The female Indigene with the blue eyes continued to concentrate on the military. Then she nodded, almost imperceptibly, in a certain direction and Bill saw how far the military had drifted apart and away from the board members without anyone noticing. She was good.

Pierre stepped forward and Bill tried to catch his eye, but the elder didn't look at him. The hairs on Bill's neck bristled. *Laura! Something's happened. That's why they're ignoring me.* He swallowed hard and stared at the ground. He tried to steady his breathing and reminded himself that Pierre had not confirmed anything.

Movement nearby snapped him out of his thoughts. Tanya and her bodyguard were walking towards Pierre and had stopped about ten feet away from him.

'I need you over here,' Tanya said to Bill.

Bill caught the surprise on Stephen's face; the Indigenes were clearly wondering which side Bill was on. Without any news about Laura, he was unsure himself. If Laura didn't make it, then the Indigenes would be to blame for her death. They had unleashed their genetic code inside her without knowing how their specific mutations might affect a human. It wasn't their fault exactly, but it still didn't change the fact that he was on the brink of losing another person he cared deeply for. Bill took a few steps forward but remained in the middle between the two groups. He'd play it by ear.

Pierre pulled back his hood revealing his smooth, translucent skin. He looked almost ethereal, standing before them. But his calm and peaceful appearance did not match the look in his eyes.

The military men gasped; it was probably the first time they had seen an Indigene up close. Propaganda photos showing the Indigenes as wild, aggressive animals were commonplace, so seeing them in real life, and seeing that they looked quite human, probably came as a bit of a shock. Several of the military let their buzz guns drop; others were more resolved than ever to keep these strange beings in their sights.

The remaining board members emerged from behind the military, their bodyguards close by. Deighton was first, eager to see who had come to meet them. He was clutching his DPad tightly and smiling, looking first at the screen and then up at the group.

'Who do I have the pleasure of speaking with?' Tanya asked.

'Pierre is my name.' His speech was slow and deliberate. The Indigenes were used to talking at a faster speed, or telepathically.

'Pierre, thank you for agreeing to meet with us. We are here because we want to discuss a way forward.'

Pierre looked around him. 'Are you afraid of us?' he asked.

Tanya frowned.

'The military you have brought,' Pierre went on. 'Is this all for us?'

Tanya smiled. 'I couldn't be sure how many of you there would be. You are strangers to us. They go where we do until we can come to a mutual understanding. Then the security presence will be halved.'

'We debated for days whether we would come at all,' Pierre said. 'I was voted down in the end.'

'We're here because humans want to live in peace on Exilon 5 without feeling threatened by the Indigenes,' Tanya explained. 'Some time ago, we considered living side by side with your race, but it didn't pan out that way. We plan to invest a lot of money in this planet and I feel that we can be of benefit to each other.'

Deighton, who had been staring at his DPad, suddenly looked up at Tanya with a fierce intensity.

'Is this a viable option for us to consider?' Tanya asked. 'There must be things that you require from us. In return we would need some assurances that you will not try to harm us.'

'That was the bullshit we fed to Taggart so he would help,' Deighton hissed at Tanya, clearly furious with her. 'I didn't agree to us taking this course of action.'

'Our demands are simple,' Pierre said. 'We want to live in peace without your military tailing us at night. We want you to build your cities far away from our districts. We want an exclusion zone where we can hunt freely.'

'That's a lot to ask without us knowing if we can trust you,' Tanya said.

'Discuss it with the others,' Pierre suggested. 'We aren't going anywhere.'

Tanya turned around and the board members huddled close to her.

'What do you think?' she asked quietly.

'If I'm to vote for a move here, we need a lot more industry to make it financially viable,' the conservative member said. 'I could think of several uses for the Indigenes, but I'd feel much happier knowing they were far away from humans.'

'No, I won't agree to that,' the more open-minded member said. 'They need to pay their way. Anything we give them should be used as a bargaining chip.'

'Charles? If you have an opinion, now's the time to share it,' Tanya said.

Deighton exploded. 'They can't be trusted! Don't believe their lies.' He grabbed Tanya's shoulder. 'Why are we negotiating with them? They should all be put down,' he went on, then pointed a bony finger at the Indigenes. 'Look! Anton's here—the one we caught on Earth, the one who killed one of our doctors. Look into his eyes and tell me he's not a killer! And the one in the front with the blue eyes, that's Serena—another murderer.' Deighton stared at her, a vicious expression on his face. 'And now she's leading their group. It's despicable!'

Anton pushed through to the front of the group. 'I'll never forget what you did to me,' he said to Deighton. 'And I know why you've come here. You gave me the gift of your memories, remember?'

The expression on Deighton's face hardened as he stepped forward, but the military stopped him from getting any closer.

Tanya turned round and looked at Bill. 'You've been very quiet. What's your opinion on this situation?'

He glanced from one group to the other, frowning. 'I didn't think I was allowed to have one.

You seem to have everything planned out,' he said.

'Well, your girl has been kidnapped, so surely you have something to say about that. You know them better than we do. It's in the girl's best interests that you speak up. Should we kill them or offer them a second chance?'

'A barbaric race should not be saved!' Deighton spat out venomously.

'Well, Laura's situation aside,'—Bill looked at Stephen as he spoke, hoping for a signal but getting none—'my personal opinion is that their race is unique and we have no right to decide their fate, even if there are financial gains to be had. They were designed to be a more advanced version of ourselves, but we can now see that they're no longer human in the traditional sense. We continue to persecute them, hunt them and experiment on them, and why? Because they turned out better than we had hoped. They follow their own rules and are no less barbaric than humans are. Yet they seem more capable of controlling their urges. Why not try a different tack and give them the same rights and freedom that we enjoy? Collaborate with them, don't control them.'

Deighton butted in by shoving his DPad under Tanya's nose. 'Now that the omicron rock isn't blocking the signals from the device in Anton's head, I've managed to download his memories. You can see for yourself how "friendly" this race really is. I urge you to consider all angles before making a decision'—Deighton took a deep breath—'and I think they should all volunteer blood samples.'

Tanya's frowned. 'Blood samples! What for?'

Deighton shifted uncomfortably on the spot. 'They may be carrying the same disease that struck down that poor girl, O'Halloran.'

Tanya rolled her eyes. 'The girl didn't get sick because of a disease. She's experiencing changes as a result of mutated Indigene code. Speaking of which'—Tanya turned to Pierre—'we want all the data you have on her changes, before and after she was treated. That's not negotiable.'

Deighton chuckled and looked at Tanya. 'Is that what they told you was wrong with her? How can you be sure it wasn't a disease? Perhaps they're performing tests on us ... maybe even poisoning us, but masking it as some kind of help. You're naive if you believe that. You're all fucking naive—and gullible! Let the doctors take samples. Only then can we be sure.'

'Is Laura okay?' Bill asked hastily, but the Indigenes said nothing.

'See? They can't even give you a straight answer.' Deighton laughed.

'Charles, you seem intent on ignoring me for some reason, considering the lengths you went to get my attention.' It was Pierre who spoke. 'I can understand why you're interested in Anton and Serena, and I can hazard a guess as to why you want our blood so badly,' he went on. 'I wasn't sure how I would feel about seeing you again after five decades, but you haven't changed one bit.'

Deighton pursed his lips and narrowed his eyes. 'It should have been me, not you, Andrew,' he said. 'You pretended you weren't interested in the programme, but that's all you were interested in—anything to get away from your father.'

'I'll admit I didn't have the best relationship with that man, but as I recall it was you who put my name forward for the internal alteration programme,' Pierre said calmly. 'You didn't seem interested in changing into a new species, but you were happy for me to. So here you are now, fifty years later, taking an interest in my life again and punishing me by killing my wife.'

'What's this about? Have you two met before?' Tanya asked, surprised.

'They served together on the World Government board,' replied Anton. He tapped the side of his head and looked at Deighton. 'Your memories are all up here.'

Deighton addressed Serena. 'Have they told you where you came from, my dear? Grown in a lab. You killed one of our own doctors. Now that they know what you are—a killer and a liar—you won't be welcome anymore.'

Serena switched her focus to Deighton. Within seconds, he was clutching the side of his head and grimacing with pain.

'What are you doing to me, you bitch?' he yelled and turned to look at Tanya. 'She has powers. Can't you feel it? You need to shoot her!'

Stephen walked forward and stood in front of Serena. 'We know where she came from and that it was you, Deighton, who killed the female doctor. Anton remembers the day you had the Medical Facility transfer your memories to him and forced him to kill Elise. Serena does not mean us any harm.' He paused for a moment, then added. 'You will not win here today, Deighton—or any day.'

Deighton growled loudly, hatred dripping from every pore of his body, and everyone turned to look at him. Just then, Bill caught the quick nod that Stephen gave him. What did it mean? Was Laura okay, or was he signalling for him to do something?

Tanya's eyes narrowed. 'Who were you in your

human life, Pierre?'

'I was Andrew Cantwell, son of Peter Cantwell the Third.'

Tanya shot a hand over her mouth. It took a moment for her to compose herself. 'Andrew! I didn't serve with you, but your reputation lives on, as does your father's. I can feel him guiding me every time I sit in his chair. Forgive me for my next question if it's too personal, but were you altered ... voluntarily?'

'Yes. I volunteered. But don't revere my father. Deighton was right about one thing. I changed into an Indigene to escape him. He was a ...' Pierre searched for the right words. 'He thought of nobody but himself.'

Tanya frowned. 'And your wife was killed—how?'

'It seems that Deighton has not forgiven me for having a better life than him, so he transferred his personality to Anton and used Anton to kill Elise—my wife—on his behalf.' Pierre looked at Deighton. 'You have a lot in common with my father, I can see that now. And if you're like my father, I assume you need something from us. Why else would you be here?'

'Charles, can you explain any of this to me?' Tanya asked. 'This is before my time. How did we wind up coming face to face, not only with people from our past, but with people from our own board?'

Deighton tried to soften his expression, but the hatred remained in his eyes. 'These are all lies, Tanya. Don't believe these murderers. We need to eradicate them. I thought the board was going to consider plans for alteration, not try to find ways to co-exist with the enemy. We are wasting time talking to them.'

Tanya exhaled sharply. 'The alteration programme was always going to be a long-term strategy, for use once people had settled on Exilon 5. I thought you understood that.'

Deighton opened his mouth to speak but Tanya cut him off. 'Why do you need to change so badly?' she asked.

He stared at her. 'What are you talking about?'

'Daphne Gilchrist called me the day before she died. She told me about Anton—that you sent him back here with a bomb. You're clearly desperate for something.'

Furious, Deighton made a threatening move towards Tanya but her bodyguards intervened. Tanya waved her hand and the bodyguards backed off.

'Is this really why we're here, so we can become all pally with the freaks?' Deighton sneered. 'This is fucking bullshit, Tanya, and you know it.' He pointed at her. 'The alteration programme is our best plan. If it's all about the money, then we can work out a way to make it profitable. We don't need *them* to do that. We can all put our human heads together and come up with a fucking solution.'

Tanya didn't flinch. 'I specifically asked you who the Indigene leader was and you told me that you didn't know,' she said coolly. 'I'm not happy to find out that you've been lying to me—and not just about that.'

Deighton stepped back, looked down at the ground in frustration and back up at Tanya. 'Peter Cantwell wanted higher status personnel as part of the initial alteration programme to control the race from the inside,' he said through gritted teeth. 'Andrew volunteered.'

'Not you?'

'He wasn't suitable for alteration, were you Charles,' Pierre butted in, smiling grimly.

'See? Nothing but lies coming from his mouth!' Deighton's eyes flitted angrily over the group of Indigenes. 'For God's sake, say something!'

At first, it wasn't clear who he was talking to. Then Anton stepped forward, a grin on his face. '*Benedict* is gone, Deighton,' he said. 'You no longer control me.'

Deighton looked confused. 'But you still have the device in your head.'

'You don't know us as well as you think you do,' Stephen said.

Suddenly, the military cocked their buzz guns towards the Indigene group. Serena took a couple of steps towards them, but it only made them more tense. She had lost her influence over them.

'Stand down,' Tanya ordered, but the military remained on full alert.

Bill looked round and saw what it was the military were pointing their guns at. The large group of Indigenes at the gate had edged closer and were silently picking off the military that challenged them. They made no sound.

The bodyguards turned to usher the board members back inside the yellow-stone building, leaving Deighton alone. Just then, Deighton darted towards Pierre, pulling something shiny from his coat pocket. Before anyone could stop him, he plunged a knife deep into Pierre's chest.

Pierre gasped and fell to the ground. Within seconds, Deighton was towering over him, stomping his foot onto Pierre's chest and snapping off the handle of the blade.

Immediately, multiple buzz guns discharged

their deadly electricity into the air. Bill ducked; Tanya was knocked to the ground as they rushed forward. The Indigenes swarmed among the military as Stephen, Leon and Gabriel tried to protect Pierre. The military discharged their weapons again, the electricity making it seem as if everyone were suddenly wading through water. It wasn't bringing the Indigenes down, but it did make them easy targets. With the board members safely back inside the building, three of the huge bodyguards came back out and finished off the slowest of the Indigenes with their bare hands, snapping their necks.

Without an energy absorption suit Bill was at risk of electrocution. He ran for cover to the building where the toilets were just as the electricity in the air multiplied. His eyes searched for the Indigenes he knew, but he despaired for them—the military were gaining the upper hand.

The firing stopped for a moment and Bill seized his chance.

'Put your guns down!' he yelled, standing at the entrance to the half-finished building, waving his hands at the soldiers. He wondered how Isla had reasoned with the more difficult members of her team. One of the men turned in his direction and fired at him. Bill threw himself back inside the room just as the puff of energy shot through the door opening and hit the wall behind him, leaving a large blackened patch.

Bill crouched down and peered outside. The military continued to advance, pushing the Indigene mob back towards the city's entrance gates. The giants swept aside anyone who got in their way; a few fell and were immediately trampled underfoot by the bodyguards. This was no longer a negotiation but an all-out war, and Bill needed to stop it.

The military advanced on the Indigene group protecting Pierre, switching their buzz guns for the less deadly impulse tasers. Tanya's orders, possibly. She wanted the main group alive. They fired directly at them. Bill noticed that the Indigenes seemed to be able to resist the worst effects of the electricity, but there was so much of it in the air that it still made their movements slow and awkward. There was no sign of the blue-eyed female.

As the military moved closer to where Stephen was protecting Pierre, Bill had an idea. He headed for a pile of discarded building material in the corner of the room and pulled out a length of metal pipe. The energy in the air nipped at it, so he dropped it immediately and fished around for something less dangerous. Eventually, he found a long piece of wood, which he took to the entrance and whacked against the door frame.

'Hey, dickwads! Over here!' he shouted.

The banging noise was enough to attract the attention of the military and the bodyguards. The firing stopped for a few seconds. It was long enough for Bill to talk to Stephen: *You'd better do it fast.*

A shot was fired at the doorway he was standing in. Still holding the wood, Bill ducked back inside. The firing picked up again. Bill risked another look outside. Stephen was tossing tasers and buzz guns—whatever he could find—back to his group. Bill spoke to Stephen again: *Fire at their legs. They're unprotected.*

The sound of electricity hitting electricity forced Bill to cover his ears. The military dropped to their knees, surprised by the attack from the Indigenes that aimed at their legs. Slowly the Indigenes outnumbered the military, taking their weapons to use themselves as each soldier fell. But the shots were not working as well on the genetically modified bodyguards.

*You're going to have to kill them. They won't stop unless Tanya commands it*, Bill told Stephen.

More Indigenes descended on the city, pouring in through the city gates, coming to help their comrades. There were too many of them for what remained of the military to keep at bay. Meanwhile, the bodyguards were tramping over the bodies strewn on the ground, snapping Indigenes in half and tossing them aside.

'Gabriel! Arianna! Use lethal force,' Stephen shouted.

Bill watched as Gabriel and Arianna fired repeatedly at the three giant bodyguards with the buzz guns. But their shots made no difference—the bodyguards swatted the shots off like flies.

*Aim for their necks,* Bill screamed in his head.

Stephen said something to Gabriel and Arianna, who raised their guns and aimed for the bodyguards' necks. Their shots were deadly and precise as the first of the genetically modified men fell at their feet, his eyes bugging and his body spasming.

Bill crawled out from his hiding place, having spotted a buzz gun lying on the ground by a dead soldier's body. He also grabbed the soldier's energy absorption suit and threw it on as quickly as he could before more firing resumed. His boot squelched in the thick blood oozing onto the ground as he made his way towards the group around Pierre.

The Indigenes who had just arrived picked up weapons discarded by the military and soon the fight was evenly matched. They kept the military at bay but the remaining two bodyguards just shook off the attacks and kept coming.

Arianna squeezed one eye shut and aimed high at one of their necks. She was about to fire when Tanya came running from the yellow building. 'Stop! Please!'

The advancing bodyguards stopped dead in their tracks and Arianna lowered her gun. The remaining military men and women stopped to look at Tanya. It was long enough for the Indigenes to completely disarm them.

'No more! I surrender.' Tanya approached with her hands up. 'Please don't kill any more of my bodyguards!'

Gabriel left the Indigenes to manage what remained of the military while he, Stephen and Leon hovered over Pierre. Stephen's hands worked at a blurred pace to try to fix the elder and Gabriel pushed rhythmically on Pierre's chest. Anton and Arianna helped to maintain the circle of Indigenes that protected Pierre.

'The wound has already closed over,' Stephen said, his eyes glassy. 'I can't get at the blade. It's still inside him.'

Bill felt around in the pockets of the energy absorption suit he wore. He found a wallet, a set of dog tags and a laser scalpel. 'Here, use this!' He threw the scalpel to Stephen.

Stephen reopened the wound and dug his fingers into Pierre's chest. A second later, he tore the metal blade from his heart. Bill moved in closer to see the wound knitting closed, but Pierre still remained unconscious.

'The heart will heal,' Stephen said to no one in particular.

Gabriel pushed rapidly on Pierre's chest—one, two, three—and breathed air into his lungs through the air filtration device. They tried for ten minutes while everyone else looked on. Bill wished he could do something to help.

'He should be awake now,' Stephen said in a panic.

Gabriel blew out a breath and sat back on his heels. Bill moved in closer and saw how lifeless Pierre still was. The wound on his chest had only knitted half closed. His chest had risen and fallen with the compressions, but he had not responded.

'Why isn't he waking up?' Stephen asked, distraught.

Bill placed his hand on Stephen's shoulder; the Indigene shrugged it away at first. But Bill persisted and Stephen stopped resisting. The Indigene body may be stronger than a human one, but it had the same limitations: it couldn't live without the mind.

Tanya Li stepped forward, her eyes wet. 'I'm sorry,' she said, still looking at her dead bodyguard. 'I should never have allowed it to get this far.'

Bill stood up and jabbed an angry finger in her direction. 'I warned you about Deighton. You should have kept a leash on him.'

'I didn't think he'd go this far.' She sounded as if she believed her own words.

Bill laughed cynically. 'He's a fucking psychopath. What did you expect?' He had a good look around. 'Where is the bastard anyway?'

Tanya's eyes were wide. 'He's not with us.'

Stephen stood up, shaking and tearful. 'Why didn't I see this? I should have seen this coming!'

Suddenly Leon was by his side. 'There was nothing you could have done. The electricity incapacitated us. The blade was lodged in Pierre's heart for too long.'

'No, I meant why didn't I predict this?' Stephen's head swung around. 'Serena's presence was acting as a booster to my envisioning ability. Where is she?'

Bill looked around him. Serena was nowhere to be seen.

It was Anton who noticed them first, on the road that snaked to the right of the yellow building. Stephen, Gabriel, Bill and Tanya followed Anton's pointing finger and saw Deighton leaning against the wall of an unfinished restaurant. Serena was slumped on the ground beside him. A syringe was sticking out of her neck and Deighton's shaky thumb was on the top of it, ready to push.

'Don't come any closer,' Deighton warned as he saw them coming towards him. He kept his thumb on the syringe.

Serena had clearly been drugged. That was why the battle was so easily fought on the human side, Bill thought. Serena couldn't influence them.

'Charles, what the hell are you doing?' Tanya demanded.

With his free hand, Deighton wagged a finger at her. 'Don't you talk to me! You and that whore Daphne have been plotting against me this whole time.'

'This is madness!' Tanya had her arms outstretched. 'Hand the girl over to me.'

Deighton began to push on the syringe.

'Stop!' Stephen yelled. 'What do you want from her?'

Deighton smiled manically as tears began to fall. 'I thought that might get your attention. I don't just want *her*. I want *you*.' He jabbed a finger at Gabriel.

Everyone turned to look at Gabriel. 'What do you need?' he asked calmly.

'I want to be changed like that Laura girl. You need to inject me with copies of Serena's code, mutations and all. And if that doesn't work, then I want whatever is coursing through Laura's body.'

Tanya spoke. 'The alteration programme is only being delayed. It isn't off the table. We'll revisit it at a later stage.'

'No! I want to be changed now. I need it more than you do.'

'We can arrange that back on Earth.' Tanya inched forward. 'Now give me the girl.'

'No, you fucking Asian cow. Alteration doesn't work on me. I've tried it already. I have Parkinson's. I want them to change me. They've already had success with that Laura one.'

'We can change you in the district,' Gabriel said softly. 'You can have anything you want. Without the right equipment, there's nothing we can do here.'

Tentatively, Deighton stood up, pulling Serena awkwardly to her feet and holding her close to his chest. Her arm was draped around his neck. Deighton, still with his thumb on the syringe, led Serena to the front of the yellow building, each step slow and laboured as Serena leaned on him. Stephen and Gabriel walked backwards, unwilling to take their eyes off Deighton and the syringe.

When the group reached Anton, Arianna and Leon with Pierre, Deighton slowed.

'I had your pure genetic code, then they muddied the samples by combining it with human

DNA,' Deighton said to Anton. 'I had what I needed. If you hadn't made me kill that doctor, I would never have been forced to come here and ...'

Anton stared at him with a new intensity.

'But I suppose one good thing came of it,' Deighton continued. He called Tanya's name, his shaky thumb still on the syringe. 'Check the downloaded footage on my DPad. I've only briefly looked at it, but you'll see Anton causing one hell of an explosion.' Then he turned to Anton: 'How did it feel when you wrapped your fingers around the old woman's neck?' He shuddered as if an unexpected pleasure had just run through him. 'Quite satisfying, I'd think. Now you're just like me.'

Suddenly Anton growled and ran at Deighton, aiming for his chest. Deighton's eyes widened in surprise and he let go of Serena, landing hard on his back on the ground. Serena slumped down, the syringe still in her neck. Bill was closest to her and pulled it out, then hauled her to safety.

Deighton gasped uncontrollably, trying to catch his breath. Anton clutched the side of his head as if something was stabbing at it. Deighton looked up and despite his pain, he laughed.

'They can't remove it, can they?' he said triumphantly. 'I put it somewhere tricky, just in case they tried. Sorry Anton, you're stuck with it and now we can see in your district any time we like.'

Anton bellowed at the top of his lungs. His body shook and the air came alive with energy as he released his pent-up aggression all at once. Deighton's smile faded. The hairs stood up on the back of Bill's neck and he instinctively took a step back.

Anton raised a foot and jammed his heel into

Deighton's exposed throat. Deighton screeched, then squeezed his eyes shut. The sound of a windpipe cracking turned Bill's stomach but he kept watching. The murderous look in Anton's eyes faded as quickly as the life in Deighton's.

Tanya stared down at Deighton and composed herself quickly. 'We're not all the same,' she said quietly to Anton. 'You have nothing to fear from us. We'll find a way to remove the device from your head.'

Suddenly Anton smiled. Bill's skin prickled, the same way it had when he had discovered Elise's body.

'You'll never watch us again,' Anton said. He removed the laser scalpel from his pocket and sliced the base of his own skull open.

'Anton—no!' Leon yelled.

Anton stuck his fingers deep inside the cut he'd made and ripped out a small black device. Then his body spasmed and he slumped to the ground.

The military that was left alive dragged Deighton's body off the street and into one of the nearby buildings. There was no blood, but his throat was severely crushed and his eyes still open. A visibly shaken Leon gently picked up Anton's body and carried him off, while Gabriel slung Pierre over his shoulder. Others helped the rest of the wounded Indigenes, leaving behind those who were beyond saving.

Bill faced a rather subdued Tanya Li; the shock of what had just happened was finally hitting her and she was breathing hard.

'You need to go—all of you,' Bill said to her.

'If you and the other board members stay here, exposed like this, it will only stir up more trouble.'

Tanya collected herself and tried to assume authority once more. 'I agree. We'll convene at HQ in New London. It's the nearest place to here.'

'I'm not going anywhere until I know Laura is okay.' Bill turned away from her, watching the last of the Indigenes disappear through the new city's gates and into the night.

'Mr Taggart, as your superior, I'm ordering you to come with us to HQ in New London,' Tanya said sharply.

Bill looked at her, his eyes wide. 'You don't have any hold over me. And given everything that has happened—to my wife, to the Indigenes—you have no right to assume you do.'

It was the conservative member who came to Bill's defence. 'Tensions are too high here. Let's regroup at HQ and give the situation some further thought. Mr Taggart can follow when he's ready.'

Tanya looked defeated. 'Fine,' she snapped. 'Pack everything up. We need to be gone in the next twenty minutes.' Turning to Bill once more, she said, 'I'll expect to see you for a debriefing, is that understood?'

'I'll do what I can,' Bill said, turning to look into the thick black night beyond it. There was no sign of the Indigenes; he knew he wouldn't be able to track them even by the light from the double moons.

'Looks like your friends weren't that bothered about waiting for you,' Tanya observed cruelly.

Bill ran inside the main building and grabbed his bag where he had left it. Then he began the long walk towards the main gate and out into the flatlands, ignoring the hustle of the military men inside the city walls piling up the bodies—for transport or burial, he wasn't sure. A short walk from New Melbourne, he deemed it safe to remove the communication stone. The blue light was faint; he had no idea which way to go. He was about to walk back to the city to ask for a ride to New London when he heard a noise.

He reached inside his pocket for the buzz gun he had kept and swivelled round. He pointed it all around him but could see nothing. Then a cool hand came out of nowhere and pushed the gun down.

'Follow me,' Stephen said darkly.

# 31

*Exilon 5*

District Three was a hotbed of chaos when they arrived. Bill said nothing as he followed Stephen. Several injured Indigenes were being treated for their wounds in the medical bay. They passed by Gabriel doing his best to calm the agitation in the tunnels.

'They've just found out that Pierre didn't make it,' Stephen explained.

Bill heard Gabriel say to one of the Indigenes, 'It's not my fault. And no, I won't tell her what to do. Why can't you accept her? I thought Indigenes were supposed to be more tolerant than humans.'

Stephen pointed to a skittish female. 'That's Margaux, Gabriel's wife. She's a little eccentric. The others don't understand her.'

Gabriel glanced curiously at Bill before turning to Margaux and asking her to help him in the medical bay. They entered the room, the same one Stephen and Laura had been taken to after the explosion in the tunnel. The room no longer looked like a temporary arrangement, but seemed to have become a permanent feature for the Indigenes. Pierre and Anton had been placed on separate beds. Serena, now conscious after her ordeal, was working hard with Leon to repair the damage to both Indigenes.

Bill frowned. Stephen seemed to understand

what he was thinking. 'Yes, technically Pierre's dead, but we want to make sure we've tried everything.'

Serena injected something into Pierre's heart.

'She's giving him epinephrine,' Stephen explained.

Anton was a different matter, as Bill could see. His heart and lungs were being kept going by machines while electrodes had been attached to the side of his head to try to kick-start his brain once they felt he was ready for it.

Bill stood still in the centre of the room. He wanted to ask about Laura, but wasn't sure if it was the right time. Part of him was scared to ask.

'She makes a good nurse, don't you think?' Stephen said.

Bill watched Serena for a moment, a natural influencer, entirely at ease in this environment. 'Do you think she was a doctor in her human life? It's quite possible she was. She seems to know her way around the facility,' Bill observed.

'Perhaps,' Stephen said, 'but I wasn't talking about her.'

Bill frowned. He scanned the room, his eyes stopping on a second female figure cloaked in white. She was leaning over Anton, readjusting the electrodes to the side of his head. He didn't recognise her.

Then Bill's heart stopped. Could it be? No. He shook his head but kept his eyes trained on her. He took one tentative step forward, not sure whether to believe what he was seeing. Her head was lowered, her eyes focused on what she was doing. When Bill came into her peripheral vision, her head snapped round.

'Laura?' Bill stared at her, not sure what else to

say. Her skin was semi-translucent and no longer sickly looking; her hair had almost gone. But a new light was in her eyes that hadn't existed since he'd found her in her apartment. He wondered if she recognised him.

Serena nodded at Laura and she stepped away from the table. She squinted at Bill, studying his face. Bill's hope melted away and he dropped his gaze to the floor. That was it, it was all over. He had lost her. She no longer recognised him. Could she ever love a human in her current form? Would he ever be enough for her, now that she was stronger, faster than he was?

'Bill?' Laura finally said. 'Is that you?'

His eyes shot up and he beamed at her.

'They tell me I'm suffering from temporary amnesia. The memories come and go,' she explained. 'Shit, I didn't know when I'd see you again.'

Serena backed away from the table and ran a current through the electrodes attached to the side of Anton's head. Anton's body spasmed. Then Margaux placed a hand on Anton's forehead and muttered something to him.

Laura turned her attention back to the table. 'I'm sorry. I'm a little busy here. It's really good to see you.' She smiled. 'Can we talk a little later?'

Bill, who hadn't stopped smiling all the time she'd been talking, snapped out of it. 'Aye, love. Any time you want. I'm not going anywhere.'

Stephen motioned for him to walk outside.

'We had to transform her to Indigene, not all the way, but enough that her body would accept the changes.'

'How?'

'As it turned out, it was Serena's DNA that stabilised her. Her thoughts are still very much human but her mind has regressed a little, which has given her amnesia. When things are a little quieter, we can look at reversing the effects of what I did to her.' Stephen dropped his head a little. 'I'm so sorry. I had no idea that the mutations in the copies of my genetic code would affect her like that.'

Bill slapped the side of Stephen's arm with his hand. 'She's alive now and for that I'll be eternally grateful. Can the effect really be reversed?'

'With a little time, we should be able to come up with a solution. But there's just one thing I haven't been able to figure out yet.'

Bill frowned. 'What?'

'Whether she wants to be changed back.'

Bill's frown deepened. 'What about Anton, will he make it?'

'I don't know.' Stephen shook his head. 'I just don't know.'

## 32

*Mid November, 2163, Earth*

Bill Taggart arrived at the World Government offices. He stopped in the foyer to smell the genetically modified lilies that sat in a glass vase on a central table.

'Yes, it was his favourite flower,' he heard the receptionist say to a possible recruit. She was talking about Deighton, but the sincerity that normally accompanies loss was lacking from her words. She almost sounded relieved. Now that Deighton was gone, it was probably only a matter a time before the lilies disappeared altogether.

Bill stopped in front of the huge mirror that stretched from floor to ceiling. He straightened his grey tie and black suit jacket. He was in mourning over the innocent deaths on both sides and he wanted the World Government board members to understand the consequences of their actions.

He got into the turbo lift and at minus Level Three, he got out. Several security personnel scanned him before he was allowed to knock on the boardroom door. He could hear a pair of heels clicking on the floor inside. After a few seconds, a face appeared.

'Bill, we were wondering if you were coming. We were about to send out a search party for you,'

Tanya Li said.

He entered the room and made eye contact with each person. Two places were empty, the spots where Charles Deighton and Daphne Gilchrist had once sat, he presumed. He imagined that while Deighton's poisonous ways would not be missed, there were others who would have agreed with his methods and were no less dangerous. The faces in the room were unreadable and he suddenly wished he had the power to read thoughts like the Indigenes could. What he was about to propose would not sit well with most of them.

Tanya gestured for Bill to sit in Deighton's old seat. As he did, he wondered what things had looked like from Deighton's point of view—what had he seen? What drove him to kill innocent people?

'What happened with the Indigenes after we left Exilon 5?' Tanya asked.

Bill offered up a brief report of events: the deaths, the commotion in the districts, the talk of an uprising. Then he repeated what the Indigenes had asked for: peace on Exilon 5. 'They've also asked for files on any Indigenes who want to know who they were as humans. What they're requesting is not unreasonable, considering how they have been persecuted for their differences—differences that we gave them.'

'The problem is, Bill, I still don't know whether I can trust them,' Tanya said.

'Well, do you trust me?' Bill asked. Tanya raised one eyebrow so he elaborated. 'I mean, at one point, you must have known I was a loyal employee of the World Government. And now, well, my loyalties lie with the race that needs the most help. My ideals have not changed. I have no interest in destroying the human population, nor do I want to see the Indigenes punished for simply existing.'

'What you're suggesting for the Indigenes will not go down well with the human population on Exilon 5 or those yet to transfer,' Tanya said. 'Most people will want the Indigenes as far away from the cities as possible. Providing them with a specific exclusion zone in which to hunt will only bring them closer to where the biodome animals roam, on the edges of the cities.'

'But what you've been doing up until now is much worse—keeping them hemmed in so they have no freedom at all,' Bill replied. 'By allowing them some rights, you are reaching out to them, making them feel included as citizens of Exilon 5.'

'There are other matters that we still need to consider too, like what to do with the people on Earth. As we've said before, there's a lot of money tied up here,' Tanya said, looking directly at Bill.

'I have a suggestion—and you can thank Laura O'Halloran for it,' he said.

'I'm all ears.' Tanya leaned back in her chair and folded her arms. Bill noticed how the other board members mimicked her.

'Split the population up. Select the people you want to transfer to Exilon 5 and leave the rest to live on Earth, but create breathable environments for them. Leave them with the tools they'll need to outlast the conditions and to rebuild Earth. Give them access to clean, renewable energy, so they don't add to the worsening conditions. Give them a fighting chance. By all means, keep your ties to Earth—hell, make your money if you have to—but don't cut them off.'

Tanya pursed her lips, then leaned forward in

her chair and peered over her imaginary glasses at him. 'What you're suggesting costs money, Bill. I don't know if we have it, nor if we can meet the Indigenes demands.'

Bill smiled ruefully. 'It'll cost you a fraction of what you'd spend transferring the entire population to Exilon 5. I think you'll find a way. You have the ability to be a better leader than Peter Cantwell.'

Tanya seemed to focus on a spot behind Bill's head and nodded. 'Give us time to think about this.'

Bill stood up to leave. 'Oh, and I have one more thing to ask. This is a personal request.'


The meeting wrapped up fast after Bill made his request to the board members. Judging by the looks on their faces, what he had asked for had shocked them. But the most important thing was that they hadn't said no. He made a hasty retreat so they could discuss it in more detail.

Back out in the foyer, he slapped the gel mask on his face and pushed through the force field. He wrapped his coat tightly around him when he hit the frigid air outside and smiled when he saw Laura waiting for him. She was casually leaning against a wall, her arms folded, and wearing a gel mask, a heavy coat and a hat.

Mirroring his smile, she linked arms with him. 'Come on, I'm starving!' she said.

They arrived at Cantaloupe near the old Georgetown University in the heart of Washington D.C. Once inside, Laura removed her mask and hat.

Bill stared at her. It prompted her to touch the top of her head. 'I know, it looks strange,' she said.

Bill smiled and cupped her face with one hand.

He stroked her cheek with his thumb. 'You look beautiful to me.'

Her tightly cut blonde hair was beginning to grow back. Her skin had lost its translucent appearance and she was starting to look like her old self. But there were lingering effects that Stephen said might never go even after he reversed the alteration process—her sexual desire, for one. Bill wasn't too put out when he heard that.

Laura ordered a steak—bloody and rare. Her craving for raw meat was also a side effect of the reversal.

'What did they say when you told them about your proposal for the Indigenes and the people on Earth?' she asked once the waiter had taken their order.

'I don't know. But they're definitely thinking about it. I don't see that they have much choice. I hope they come to that conclusion for themselves.'

'And how did they react when you told them you wanted to take up the vacant role of CEO of the World Government?'

'A few jaws dropped, some people's eyes popped out of their sockets.' Bill smiled.

'And how did Tanya react?'

'She didn't say anything, but she seemed the least shocked by the idea. I think she approves of my suggestion for the Indigenes, and of your suggestion for the people left behind on Earth. Whether she can convince the other board members of that, I don't know.'

'I get the impression she's not a fan of the alteration programme.'

Bill grabbed one of Laura's hands and kissed the back of it. 'You're living proof that it's not all that bad.'

Laura laughed gently, then leaned in and kissed Bill fully on the mouth. She pulled away, her expression turning more serious.

'I never thanked you properly for saving my life when I was, you know, not myself. I hate to think what would have happened if you hadn't found me that day.'

Bill leaned in, his dark eyes studying every inch of her face. 'I lost my wife because I didn't listen to my instincts. I was damned if I was going to lose you too.' He let go of her hand and leaned back in his chair. 'Does your mother forgive you for killing her cat?'

Laura grimaced. 'Not one of my finer moments. I couldn't bring myself to tell her, so I bought her a new kitten. This one seems to like me better than her other cat ever did.'

Bill smiled grimly. 'Just try not to eat this one.'

Laura held up her hands. 'Rare steak for me from now on. I'll never forget the look on the cat's face—pure terror. I wanted to stop, I really tried, but it was as if someone else was making me do it.' She shuddered. 'I'm sick of everything controlling me and my life. It's time to make up for all those years I lost and to write my own destiny. I hope you'll be part of that, Bill.'

'Always.'

Laura took a sip of water. 'You'll never guess who called me today.'

'Who?'

'Jenny Waterson. She's hooked up with an underground movement who are watching the alteration programme closely.'

Bill nodded curtly. 'Good. We need someone

on the inside. Considering what's happened so far, I've no idea what direction the World Government will take.' He raised his coffee cup. 'Here's to a new chapter in our lives—hopefully a better one.'

Laura hit her water glass against Bill's cup. 'Here's hoping the future is better for everyone.'

# 33

*End January 2164, Exilon 5*

In District Three's Gathering Room, Gabriel, Stephen, Serena, Leon and Margaux stood on a raised platform in front of the fifty representatives that had gathered before them. A few new faces were among the representatives; they had come to realise that working together was better than going it alone. Stephen scanned the group, looking for one face in particular. He couldn't find her. Then he took a deep breath and addressed the representatives.

'Bill Taggart has sent news of the World Government's decision. They have agreed to allow us to live as we are, and to give us access to exclusion zones where we can hunt without interference. There will be some conditions attached.'

'How do we know they'll keep their promise?' one representative called out.

'Bill Taggart has evidence detailing how we were created. He has threatened to make it public if they renege on their deal,' Stephen replied.

'Is that enough to keep them in line?' another representative asked.

'I don't know, but I don't think they're too keen for the people on Earth to find out where we came from,' Stephen explained. 'It would cause huge disquiet among the humans. They'd question every termination, every disappearance, and wonder if their loved ones really did die or if they're still living as Indigenes. There's one other thing—they've agreed to give us the files for anyone who requests information on who they were as humans.'

The room fell silent until someone asked, 'Will the files contain the truth or more lies?'

'That I can't be sure of. We have to assume their willingness to cooperate is a sign of peace,' Stephen said. 'Think it over. Tell your groups. Let them decide if they want to know about their past.'

'Is there the option to change back—into humans?' asked another representative.

Stephen hadn't considered that to be an issue. It surprised him and he struggled to keep the emotion out of his voice. 'Discuss it with your factions. If it's what you want, then the new elders will discuss it.'

'There's still the matter of leadership,' Leon said. 'Both elders are dead. Who will govern the Indigenes in District Three?'

'The tradition is to go with the eldest male and female in each district,' Gabriel said. 'That would be Sarah and Germaine. But I think it would be good to break with that tradition. I propose that Stephen and Serena become the new leaders of District Three.' He put his hand up.

Stephen frowned at Gabriel and whispered, 'What are you doing?'

'What, you don't think you're up to it?' Gabriel whispered back. 'You've more experience than the entire room combined. You have a good head on your shoulders. You direct others well. You and Serena seem to work well together. I think it's time for some fresh blood.'

Stephen said nothing more while a low murmur

broke out, the representatives talking among each other. A smile crept on to Margaux's face and her hand shot up. 'I second it,' she said. Several other hands went up in the audience.

Stephen squeezed Serena's hand. 'What do you think? We can still reverse what they did to you—change you back into a human.'

'This is the only life I can remember. I feel like I fit in here,' she said.

'You don't seem too surprised at what's being suggested.' He playfully narrowed his gaze at her.

She smiled at him. 'Gabriel already told me what he was up to. Besides, I thought you would have seen it coming, what with your improving envisioning ability.'

He smiled. 'I wasn't expecting an ambush!' He turned to Gabriel and his smile faded. 'I need a moment to discuss something with Serena. Can we take a short break?'

'Well, you're the new leader, you can do what you want,' Gabriel said shrugging.

Stephen held up a finger. 'Not yet.'

He led Serena out of the Gathering Room and into the Council Chambers, then closed the large door and turned around to face her.

She was surprised. 'Stephen?'

'I wanted to talk to you later about this, but things are moving a little faster than I had expected.' He walked over to the flat screen next to Pierre's bookshelf and pressed a couple of buttons. He pulled up a file and motioned for Serena to join him.

'What is it?'

'Bill Taggart sourced your file for me—on your human life.'

'It won't change anything,' she said, shaking

her head gently and smiling. 'I'm here because I want to be.'

'Well, I'm giving you the chance to read this if you want to. The choice is yours.'

'Have you read it?'

Stephen shook his head. 'Not yet. I will only if you want me to.'

Serena stood over the console, keeping Stephen close to her side. 'Let's read it together.'

Standing side by side they read about Susan Bouchard, that she had worked as a lab technician in Toronto, had one sister and one niece, and was good friends with Joel Taylor, her colleague. She had headed up the genetic trials because of her unique way with people.

Serena frowned. 'I guess we know where my ability to influence comes from now.'

Stephen caught her strained expression. 'What is it?' he asked.

'I remember my imprisonment more clearly now. I remember working with Joel in the lab in Toronto. I also recall being on a space craft with many blonde-haired and blue-eyed people. The government had changed the selection policy to target specific genetic types.' She turned to face him. 'I guess that's how I ended up here.'

He smiled at her and rubbed her back.

'Can someone get a message to my sister and niece that I'm fine?' she asked anxiously. They must have been worried.'

'The government sent messages to them on your behalf,' Stephen explained. 'They believe they've been talking to you ever since you left.'

Serena's eyes glistened. 'I need a moment.'

Back in the now-empty Gathering Room, Stephen rejoined Gabriel on the raised platform.

'Serena needs more time, but I've made a decision,' Stephen said, frowning. 'But before we call the representatives back in, there's something I want to ask you.'

Gabriel folded his arms and sighed.

'Is there something bothering you?' Stephen asked. 'Your aura colours are hesitant and unsure—especially when we discovered where Serena came from.'

Gabriel unfolded his arms and blew out a puff of air. 'I won't lie that it didn't cross my mind—to change back into a human. I never felt like Margaux, like I really belonged here.'

'And now?'

Gabriel smiled. 'I like that we're different. It's worked well for Serena and I think that's what changed my mind—she was able to help because she was unique. Besides, I'm too old to consider becoming a human again. But it doesn't mean others here won't consider it.'

Stephen nodded and put a reassuring hand on Gabriel's shoulder. 'Let's get the representatives back in,' he said gesturing towards the door.

The crowd gathered again and Gabriel announced that Stephen would take up the position of leader. Serena, however, needed more time to consider it.

Stephen's eyes searched the crowd again; there was still no sign of them. They should be here to celebrate. Eventually he saw Arianna walking through the door, with Anton following close behind. He still looked weak, but the colours of his aura were bright and his spirit was strong. Stephen jumped down off the stage and went to them. The representatives parted to let him through.

'I thought you weren't going to make it.' Stephen playfully slapped Anton's arms but he felt sad—it wasn't the same without Serena.

'I wasn't going to miss this. You're creating history here. You'll be the youngest leader this district has ever known,' Anton said. 'The question is, can you handle it with that big ego of yours?' Arianna smiled at his quip and squeezed his hand.

Suddenly Serena appeared at the door. Stephen ran towards her and grabbed her hand. 'I wasn't expecting to see you so soon,' he said, pulling her close.

'I've made up my mind.'

Stephen read her thoughts and smiled. 'Are you sure?'

'My ability is accepted here. I'm accepted here. I didn't seem to be helping anyone on Earth. Quite the opposite—all I did was contribute to this mess.'

'But if you hadn't been changed, we might not have gained the advantage.' Stephen kissed her forehead. 'Glad to have you on board.' He turned to Anton. 'So what do you say, do you think you can behave yourself under my direction?'

Anton smiled cheekily. 'We'll see, old friend. We'll see.'

## Acknowledgements

When I finished an earlier draft of Crimson Dawn, I realised there were unanswered questions. One was what will happen to the people left behind on Earth when the World Government leaves? The next book should answer that question. New and old characters will appear and reappear to help shape this new world.

This series is important to me because it highlights fundamental issues with the planet we live on. It shows us how disposable people are and will continue to be as we run out of resources. I have really enjoyed watching this world unfold and I hope you will continue with me on my journey because it means nothing without readers. I could write and publish a hundred books, but you, the readers, are what drive this industry. You are what make stories come alive through your passion to read and share good books.

And so the thanks must begin, because writing a book is never a lone adventure. Thank you to my editor, Averill, for teaching me the importance of self editing before the real editing begins. Thanks to Mary for proofreading my manuscript. It was an absolute pleasure to work with you.

Thanks to my cousin for teaching me the basics of genetics and DNA. She knows a lot! Her interesting lab stories kept me *very* entertained.

Thanks to my writer peeps for showing me that writer generosity knows no bounds.

Thank you to my beta readers, Kathryn and Jessica for your perfect suggestions! Thanks to my third beta reader who generously offered to read the third book, but life caught up with him and he ran out of time.

Thank you to my newsletter readers for their excellent suggestions for the book cover, in particular Cheri Partain and Debbie Schwitzer. You both helped me to knock the ideas loose from my head!

And finally, cheers to Andrew and Rebecca from Design for Writers for making the most awesome covers for all three books. Yay!

## Purchase other books in the series

*Paperback and Digital from all major online stores*

*Becoming Human* (Book 1 in the Exilon 5 series)
*Altered Reality* (Book 2 in the Exilon 5 series)

## Prequels to the Exilon 5 Series, digital only

Discover what happened before *Becoming Human* with these prequels:

*Echoes of Earth* (Bill and Isla Taggart)
*New Origin* (Stephen and Anton)

Both prequels also available in a digital box set.

## Stand alone series, digital only

*Derailed Conscience* (a dark psychological story)

For a limited time, you can get *Derailed Conscience* for free in digital format. Check out www.elizagreenbooks.com to get started.

Coming soon November 2016: *Feeder,* brand new young adult sci-fi. Check out www.elizagreenbooks.com/books for more details.

Word of mouth is crucial for authors. If you enjoyed this book, please consider leaving a review where you purchased it; make it as long or as short as you like. I know review writing can be a hassle, but it's the most effective way to let others know what you thought.

Plus, it helps me reach new readers instantly.

You can also find me on:

**www.twitter.com/elizagreenbooks**
**www.facebook.com/elizagreenbooks**
**Goodreads – search for Eliza Green**

Printed in Poland
by Amazon Fulfillment
Poland Sp. z o.o., Wrocław